'Boxer Shorts
Redux

Michael Matteson, editor

'Boxer Shorts Redux

All Rights Reserved © 2003

Published by Inkblot Books

Dayton Ohio

www.inkblotbooks.com

ISBN 1-932461-03-5

Printed in the United States of America

'Boxer Shorts
Redux
'Boxer Shorts
Redux
'Boxer Shorts
Redux
'Boxer Shorts
Redux
'Boxer Shorts
Redux
'Boxer Shorts
Redux
'Boxer Shorts
Redux
'Boxer Shorts
Redux

The Contents

Heh heh heh ... He said "Boobies."
                        ~anonymous Monkey on the 'Box

Letters From The Front
Alistair Coleman

Friday, April 23rd 1915
"My dearest Elizabeth,

Do not cry, Liz-beth, for this is my last letter to you as Death's hand closes around me. My love for you is as strong as ever, and it is with a heavy heart that I write to say that I shall ne'er see you again.

I sit and wait for the dawn. I cannot sleep for I dare not, every second now is precious as the time I have left is not long. Even before the first rays show through the window of this room, they will come for me, and I will follow them quietly. The guards, the captain and the padre - the man with the cross and the book, the mysteries of which remain closed to his mind. But I, Albert James Cooper, know. For I have seen the truth, touched it, and now, like many before me, shall give up my life for it. And this is why I write, Liz-beth, that I may somehow remain alive in these mere words on paper; by telling you my final confession I may not die.

The censor will strike at much of what I write with his pencil, but, sir, I ask of you, if you have any decency in your body, to stay your hand. For when these words reach their destination, I shall be long dead, and what secrets, then, are there left to be kept? If I tell only my truth, the censor's mark shall be naught but lies. Stay your hand, sir, for at my end, here is my beginning.

Here then, is my life. You have heard this story many times before, but I must commit myself to paper, for it will ne'er be told again. I was born in Barking in 1897, the sixtieth year of Her Majesty's reign, and named in honour of her late consort. Unlike many families around us, we were relatively well off. Father worked as a printer's assistant in no less an establishment as The Times, a trade which he had wheedled himself into at the great ire of his father - my paternal grandfather - who had fully expected him to work in the docks like the rest of his family and all those who lived in the streets around us.

He was determined to break out of the cycle of back-breaking labour and illiteracy that left so many men, his father included, destroyed by middle-age. So many dockers, nothing but aged skin and bone, ancient before their time, poisoned and broken by the cargoes they shovelled from the hellish holds of ships every day from their fourteenth birthday until the day they dropped. They came from every corner of the Empire, those ships. They kept our nation alive, they kept our families in work, yet the bitumen, the salt-petre, the clouds of dust, they got into a man's body, and killed him as surely as the firing squad's bullets will kill me.

The eldest of three sons, father was determined that I should follow by his example. He taught us to read and write - and it was thanks to his endeavours that I am able to write you these words, my love - and as soon as I turned fourteen, he pulled strings enough to have me taken on as a runner in Fleet Street. A fourteen hour day, ending only when the paper had finished with me, and then the long walk back to Barking, or a few hours sleep under whichever desk I could find.

Your father never approved of our love - me the son of the East End, you a daughter of a City insurance broker, yet I always ensured that my errands took me past places I knew I could find you. A park, a shop, a favourite tea-room, even past your door. Where Cupid's arrow falls, they say, true love is found. Yea, it fell true on the ground where you trod, my dear. Stolen minutes and hours together were all we had, but it was more than enough. Heady dreams of running away, eloping to Gretna, but not to be. This world soon caught up with us.

You remember that bittersweet day, my sweet, as well as I do. The day you reached your eighteenth birthday, the day I asked - and was refused - your hand, the day the presses at The Times spoke of the start of war.

"Back by Christmas" they said.

"Which Christmas?" we joked, and joined up anyway.

I volunteered for the Rifles that first week, along with my brothers Henry and Edward, who told the Recruiting Sergeant he was sixteen when he was, in fact, years younger. Your elder brothers, Charles and Robert, as you know, became Riflemen, but while the Coopers were barracked with the enlisted troops, the Fennemore sons were billeted with the officer corps. High born or low, we all lived, and alas, died in the same foul trenches.

Training was shambolic and brutal. From boys to men, our platoon Corporal boasted. A process, we discovered, that involved screamed orders, petty punishments, frequent beatings, and marching, marching, marching "to prepare us for the road to Berlin." They gave me a rifle and a bayonet, and, cowering, I was shown how to use them to kill a man.

Then the front, I must tell you everything I remember about about the front. How we lived, slept, spoke and died. We sang on the way there, remembering songs from the Music Halls, public houses, family and friends. Had we known what we were heading for, it would have been a funeral dirge. The days of set-piece battles and noble cavalry charges were long gone by the time we reached Belgium. Instead, we fought a new kind of war. Dirty, deadly, under-hand and underground.

We dug into the Earth like moles, and stayed there, emerging only to die, or to help our foes into the next world. The mud, the water, the rats - oh to hell with those rats and the generals that sent them - the guns, and always the sights, screams and smell of death. If man ever created a hell on Earth, Liz-Beth, it was made by our own hands in this place.

You have not seen the Devil's work until a shell lands in the next bunker to yours. You emerge to the shattered bodies, limbs, torsos of your comrades, and if they are lucky they have been killed outright. If you are lucky, you vomit, black out the memory, as an enraged officer orders that the same hell is visited on the trench opposite. Except I can never forget, I remember it all - Henry's death-throes, your brother Charles' face as he bled to death - oh! I should not be telling you this, but he was so brave to the last and called your name - so many faces I shall ne'er see again, yet their death masques visit me as I close my eyes.

Many is the night where I have removed my boot, put my toe against the trigger of my rifle, put the muzzle in my mouth and thought of a reason to stay alive. Every night you have saved my life. Come the morning, there is another corpse with one boot, someone without a Liz-Beth to keep them alive. If this is the only world that we know, in the name of Our Lord, what have we unleashed?

And in this hell, we were sent into battle. I had been "over the top" before, red-hot metal filling the air, comrades dropping around you in the mud, onto the wire, shouting prayers, begging for God's mercy, firing blindly until you were ordered back, elated and sobbing to your hole in the ground.

No-one told us what was happening, but we all knew. At five o'clock in the morning, we were roused from what fitful sleep we could manage, and were moved to the front line, ready to live or die for our country. I shall tell you as much as I remember from that awful day. The words you read are all I remember, here in my memory like a carving on a wood-block, I tell you all I know.

It was silent. The guns had stopped, so even Fritz knew what was coming, and had his machine guns ready for us. I stood alongside Nash, his first week in the trenches, Cattermole and Riley. Glancing down the line, I could see your brother, Captain Robert Fennemore, a man whose bravery was never in doubt from his first day at the front, talking quietly with his men, encouraging them, reassuring then, a hand out to even the lowliest of the enlisted. Captain Barber stood impassively behind us, whistle to his lips, his revolver in his shaking hands.

And then... whistles and shouts from down the line. Six o'clock had come and we swarmed up from the firestep, over the top of the trench and out into the open. Who knows what the objective was: all we were to do was get to the trench opposite as quickly as possible, take the German lines and force back the enemy as stoutly as we could. Cattermole didn't even make it to the top of the ladder, a bullet caught him in the face, and he slumped down on top of me and Nash, who screamed in fear, blood gushing over his uniform.

"Don't just stand there!" Barber shouted, pulling Cattermole away by his webbing, "Get up that ladder!"

The sight that confronted me defies description. Going "over the top" assaults the senses, leaving you aghast at the slaughter. To the left, to the right, as far as the eye could see, men were struggling for their lives, running, shouting, shooting, dying through a mist of smoke and morning fog.

Rogerson, who was alongside me, fell dead. I had known him since the first day of our training, and I had to dismiss him from my life, there and then. Scared, but not turning back, I dived into a shell hole for cover with Riley and Captain Barber.

From the safety of this scar in No Man's Land, we lay back, waiting for breath to return and send us on our way toward the enemy line. On our backs, damp seeping through our webbing and mud-filth smeared uniforms, all we could see was the sky above us. The battle roared elsewhere, but above our heads, smoke and mist swirled, strange patterns, almost hypnotising as we stared at the only thing in our lives that was not war.

We'd heard the stories, passed from man to man, down the front line and back again within a matter of days. Myths or reality, anything to pass the time on those long, cold nights. Who knows if a few of our lads played a game of Association Football with the Hun on Christmas Day? By New Year it had got about that thousands of us were running around in the filth, mud and shell holes with a pig's bladder. I certainly didn't take part in any fun and games with the enemy, neither did anyone I know, but the story was retold enough times to be true. We might even have won. Our boys did the same as we did everyday - sit in the mud, take our turn on the firestep, and try to see the next dawn. That was my Christmas, the one we were supposed to be home for.

Then there was this other story. You even mentioned it in a previous letter to me, all of which I cherish. English bowmen, you told me. Ghosts, the men say, angels. Who knows who or what they are, or even if they exist at all. Just another story passed around in the dead of night to reassure us that life isn't as bad as we think, that someone, somewhere is on our side. But on those terrible days in August last year, as the Germans attacked at Mons, there are men who swear angels came from the heavens to shield them against over-whelming odds.

There are others who say they saw the Bowmen of Agincourt above them, fighting an unseen foe; and there are still more who tell the story of a ghost army fighting shoul-der-to-shoulder with our lads. Who knows what they saw? Just the figures of their comrades in the fog of war? Or just the figment of some storyteller's imagination that spread along the front, and back home to be retold by imaginative newspa-per reporters and magazine writers? That may be so, but I will tell you what I saw that morning. I know what was real and what was false, and so, God help them, could the men I fought with, had they only mouths to speak with.

The sun rose through the morning mist and men fought and fell around we who sheltered in that shell-hole in No Man's Land. As the mist cleared, and the smoke of the guns rolled away, we watched as another layer of fog formed above us. Yet, this was different. It swum with white light, like the sun was inside it, and out of this light strange figures swirled.

The fog spread, it was clearly hundreds of yards across, lit from within, getting closer to the ground as if it were a liquid poured out of a jug, that you could almost reach out and touch. Poor Riley cried out in fear, yet Barber and I were rapt by its appearance. Living in the open for months at a time one often sees strange weather, yet this was clearly the most unusual yet.

The cloud, the mist, whatever one wants to call it, opened before us, to reveal a host of white figures standing before us. I remember our conversation clearly:

"Cooper?" said Captain Barber, "You see it?"

"Sir."

"Riley?"

"Sir."

"Then I'm not going mad. Where are those people coming from?"

"I don't know sir," I replied, "Whose side are they on?"

"Who indeed, Cooper, who indeed."

We watched for could have been a few seconds or several hours. Dozens of people, all glowing white, descended from the rent in the cloud, armed with a variety of weapons, ancient and modern, all descending into No Mans' Land near to where we were seeking cover. Presently, Captain Barber stood and beckoned us to follow.

"Rifles at the ready lads, time we were leaving."

We stood, scrambled up the side of the shell-hole and stumbled onward toward the German lines.

Below the ground, we were protected from the worst of the battle, but once again we were plunged into a maelstrom of guns, explosions, screams and... silence.

The figures in white were all around us. Riley, Captain Barber and myself joined formation with several other men from our unit. Barber himself led a charge on the German trenches as if he was back home, hunting fox from the back of a horse. We could clearly see the enemy now, their helmets visible over the lip of their trench, their determined, fearful faces as they took aim with their rifles. We could see the muzzle flashes of their weapons, the great puffs of smoke as bullets were discharged; the flash, flash, flash of the machine gun; the spent cartridges wheeling into the air as we ran forward, working the actions on our Lee Enfields, firing blindly without aiming.

Yet, as much as the enemy concentrated their fire on our fearless platoon - every weapon appeared to be focused on us - as much as we could taste the cordite and feel the thud of the explosions around us, we ran through a deathly silence, not one of our number fell.

We ran on, the figures in white alongside us, amongst us, running with us. Their features were much clearer now. Some wore uniforms of our modern era, others dressed for ancient wars. A man who may have fought at Waterloo, alongside a Roman Centurion, alongside medieval armour, alongside an American Minuteman. Their faces determined, their hearts pure, they were fighting with us, Liz-Beth, for we knew our cause was true.

Onwards we flew, in deathly, deadly silence, tumbling over the edge and into the German lines. You may recoil at the facts I am about to relate to you now, but what I say is only the truth, no matter how unpleasant it my be. The months I have spent in this war has hardened me towards death, while as you sit at home in London waiting for the men to return, you still have your sensibilities and the delicate disposition of an educated Englishwoman. How soon we forget! God forgive me, Liz-Beth, for I have used these hands to kill a man.

If I close these eyes I see his face. Alas, when I open them again, he is still there, watching me, forgiving me for the life I have taken. It happened so quickly, yet I still remember every detail that I may write without pausing to recollect. I jumped into the enemy trenches, stumbling and falling not six feet away from a terrified German boy - for he was no older than myself. He turned to face me, fear the only expression I could make out. He levelled his rifle at me and pulled the trigger. I can still see the silent flash of the muzzle and feel my gut wrench, knowing that I would soon be dead. Yet, still I lived. A white figure had come between me and him, the bullet seemingly swallowed in the swirling mist of its body. Without pausing to think, I lunged my rifle toward the German and pierced him in the chest with the bayonet, just as I had done countless times with a sackful of straw in training. I actually heard myself thinking "Thrust! Twist! Withdraw!" as it had been drummed into me by the Drill Sergeant, and felt sick at myself for recalling something so regimented as I ended a life. He slumped onto his knees, blood bubbling from his mouth, soundlessly trying to speak to me, before collapsing on his face, taking that masque of horror away from my sight, to return only whenever I close my eyes.

I looked up, the white soldier faced me and smiled. He was young, curly hair, much like a figure from Renaissance art, under whose pictures we walked in the few stolen hours we could manage around London. How fitting, then, that I should be saved by Botticelli's Mars, with you as my Venus!

Then he was gone. The sounds of battle returned to me like a bolt of lightning coursing through my body. Again I could hear the crack-crack-crack of rifle fire, the screams of men, the roar of artillery. I stepped over the dead boy, and followed the sounds of fighting down the trench where I knew

I would find my comrades. I turned a corner, and quickly fell in with Captain Barber and the remainder of our platoon surrounding a bunker, where several of the enemy had retreated. At Barber's order, Parkinson stepped forward with a No.1 Grenade, pulled the pin and threw it through the doorway. Seconds later, there was a muffled explosion, the effects of which I knew only too well.

God knows how, but five men came out of that bunker alive. Two could barely walk, all were bleeding profusely from wounds to their faces, arms, bodies and legs. They threw down their weapons and surrendered.

The Germans looked at us fearfully. These British had come out of the mist, stormed their trench without a single casualty. Were we men like them, or something more? One of the Germans, clearly their officer stepped forward.

"Please," he said in English, "we are your prisoners."

There was a pause as Captain Barber examined his opposite number. He emptied the cylinder of his revolver of six empty cases, and methodically filled it with six fresh rounds, snapping his weapon shut with a sharp click that made our captives jump.

"I have orders," Barber eventually replied. "There are to be no prisoners. Corporal Dixon?"

"Sir!"

"Arrange a firing squad."

"But sir!"

"You have your orders as I have mine. Carry them out."

"Sir."

The German captain looked disbelievingly at Barber. "Nein. No. You cannot kill us. You cannot. We are prisoners, yes?" There was an air of desperation in his voice, as Dixon pushed him and the other Germans back against the wall of their bunker.

Alas, my dear Liz-Beth, not only was I to be a witness to such an atrocity against human-kind - for believe what you read in the papers back home, and hear what people say in the salons and tea-rooms, those Germans are human like us - but I was to be complicit in this act. Dixon beckoned me forward, and ordered me to ensure my rifle was loaded. Riley, too. Sanderson. Young. Butler. All five of us, executioners, murderers. While I had killed the young soldier just minutes before, that was in defence of my very person. Now, these men were helpless, terrified, not even given the benefit of a blindfold. Tears filled my eyes. Riley could barely lift his rifle, and Young, poor Young, his head shook in disbelief at what he was being asked to do.

The Germans pleaded with us as Dixon gave the orders.
"Ready!"
"Nein! Bitte! Nein! Ich habe ein Sohn..."
"Aim!"
"NEIN! NEIN! Bitte!"
Then, looking down the muzzle of my rifle, "Please."
"Fire!"
Four bodies fell to the ground. A fifth remained standing. Standing, crying, looking down the muzzle of my rifle.
"Danke. Danke, mein freund."
Thank you.
"Cooper!" screamed Captain Barber, "Why is that godless Hun still alive? Tell me man!"
"My rifle, sir. It jammed," I lied. In truth, my Liz-Beth, I couldn't pull the trigger. It's not that I wanted to, or didn't want to. A white hand gripped me, keeping my index finger from curling. I didn't need much help in my decision, I couldn't, wouldn't shoot him, and I thanked God for the courage of my conviction. Call it cowardice, call it humanity, my

confession is here, Thy Shalt Not Kill. A white mist rolled across the trench. It was not me the soldier was thanking. There were others walking among us.

The sky plunged into darkness, and I knew then that we were not alone. With righteousness on our side, we had swept across No Mans' Land, where we were protected from harm. God's will, angels, ghosts, I don't know what to call it, fighting for our way of life, knowing we would prevail for goodness' sake. But now, in the senseless, godless slaughter of these defenceless men, we had turned the tables on ourselves, we had become our own enemy, and now the wrath of the Host was upon us.

They descended upon us, wielding swords, cudgels, flintlocks from other wars, shadowy Lee Enfields from this. Barber was first, Riley, Young, each and every one falling under the blows of our former protectors, as they purged our sin with our own deaths. No-one fought back. They knew they were doomed, accepted their fate, as I accepted mine. Yet, when they were done, I stood alone, surrounded by bodies, the very life ripped out of them. I looked at the one surviving German, who turned and ran as fast as his wounds would allow, to the succour of his comrades.

I was found, I am told, several hours later, among the bodies of my brothers-in-arms, shouting, screaming, covered in blood and my own filth, holding Captain Barber's pistol to my temple. I was charged with the murder of my own commanding officer and cowardice in the face of the enemy. There were no witnesses, yet I damned myself with my own testimony. The Court Martial wasted no time in sentencing me to death by firing squad.

No angels came to save me.

All I ask, my Elizabeth, is your forgiveness. I have

shamed myself, and by implication, your good name. If you ever tell people you never knew me, then I shall understand, because no-one should be associated with a traitor and a coward. But I know, by telling you the truth, however unappealing it may sound, that you will always find somewhere in your heart to remember me fondly.

The sun is rising. I hear footsteps coming for me as my time gets ever shorter. What next? With God's forgiveness, am I to join the Host, or will it be as I fear - a brief explosion of pain followed by an eternity of nothingness? Faith is all I have. Your brother Charles is at the door. He is forgiven. If there is more than this, I shall protect him.

Goodbye, my love, fare thee well.

Albert Cooper"

"My dear sister Elizabeth

This day I had the sad duty of escorting your acquaintance Albert James Cooper to be shot at dawn for the murder of my old Harrow school-friend Jerome Barber. He begged of me the favour of passing a letter on to you, explaining his actions on that frightful day, in the hope of gaining your forgiveness for his dreadful actions.

My sweet, you will excuse my reading it before you, but Cooper's missive was so full of dreadful lies and utter bunkum that it could only cause you great distress. He killed Jerome with his own hands; and even speaks in glowing terms of our German enemy, while questioning the actions of his superiors. He was filled with a madness and dreadful visions, and I could not possibly allow you to read his lunatic scribblings in your delicate condition, especially since the death of dear, dear Robert which he describes in the foulest way imaginable. I ask your pardon that I have ordered it destroyed.

Pass my regards on to Father and Mother, I hope to see you all when I get my leave in a few months time.

Your brother,

Charles"

"Father,

I write this to let you know that although badly wounded in action, I am alive, able to sit up in bed and write these few words to you. As soon as my injuries have healed enough, I shall be transported back to Hannover, where I shall be invalided out of this army, with a tale to tell that you will find hard to believe.

My love to Mother and Inge.

Your son,

Christoph"

Praying for Rain
Donna Eyer

I can't say I was surprised by what I saw on the view screen in front of me. Every morning, I tried not to get my hopes up, and every morning they were dashed anyway. No matter how often I looked at the closed-circuit feed from the surface, I was always greeted by a picture of the same red, dusty landscape. Occasionally, I'd manage to catch a dust storm in progress, but these no longer served to electrify me in the manner they once did.

We'd been working on the Mars Rapid Terraforming Project for several years, hoping to be able to prepare the cold, red planet for human colonization. Decades ago, large underground colonies with artificial atmospheres were built below the surface, giving us a place to live and work as we fought to make Mars at least reasonably receptive to carbon-based life forms.

So far, the project had been a success. With a combination of large orbiting mirrors, which redirected sunlight to help warm the planet's surface, and production of halocarbons for an accelerated greenhouse effect, we'd managed to maintain both a thicker atmosphere and a warmer surface temperature. As soon as the atmospheric pressure adjustment was complete, workers started building domes above the surface. Though we still lived underground, most of our work was now done in the domes themselves. A breathing apparatus was still needed to venture outside of the domes, but we no longer had to worry about bulky space suits or drastic changes in climate.

Using a combination of surge flow and drip irrigation systems, we'd even been able to sustain plant life on the once inhospitable surface, something I never thought I'd witness in my lifetime. The hope was that the oxygen created by the plants would help to speed up the changes in the atmosphere so that future residents would be able to walk about freely, without even an air tank.

As my bad luck would have it, my living quarters were far enough away from the plant fields that, even as they continued to spread over the surface of the planet, I still couldn't see them on the view screen. With a sigh, I headed to the airlock.

By the time I got there, most of the other scientists had already surfaced and were working in their labs under the protective domes. The only one waiting for me at the airlock was Dr. Theodore Hill, affectionately known as Tenday. We went through our usual exchange, acting as though it was a conversation we'd never had before then.

"So, Reverend, what are you planning to do today?" Tenday grinned at me as he shrugged into his lab coat. His hair, still damp from a shower, was slicked back, and he smelled like a rather odd combination of soap and waffles. Tenday had taken to calling me 'Reverend' because of my inevitable answer to his question.

"I dunno, man. I think maybe I'll pray for rain."

"I hate to be the one to break it to you, Reverend, but it's not supposed to rain for another ten days yet." That was the response that earned Tenday his own nickname.

"Sure," I replied, taking my place in front of the iris scanner to open the airlock. "That's what you said ten days ago. Come to think of it, that's what you said ten months ago, too."

Chuckling, Tenday followed me through the airlock and into the domed lab we shared with several others. "Why do I get the feeling I'll still be saying the same thing ten *years* from now?"

Roger Clearfield, who'd been working on this project longer than any of us, just shook his head. "Have a little faith, Ted. We're just about due for a cloudburst." He put a hand on my shoulder as I walked by. "Besides, Reverend's brain is an instrument of God. If anyone can get it to rain up here, he can."

"Gee, thanks for the added pressure, Rog," I shot back in mock anger, fighting back a grin. Truth was, I wasn't even remotely religious. None of us were. I guess it came from being scientists, though I've known a few who were men of both religion and science. Still, long ago when I'd first uttered my 'pray for rain' comment, it had been blown far out of proportion for humor's sake. By this point in the project, the pressure had taken its toll; we were all punchy and could find levity in just about anything. Having the fate of the Mars Colonization Project resting on the shoulders of a small group of tired scientists was bound to have that effect.

As we started going about our morning tasks, someone powered up the sound system, and "Have You Ever Seen the Rain" started pouring softly from the speakers. In another attempt at jocularity, someone had programmed the sound system so that it only played songs about rain or with the word 'rain' in the title. Although we eventually grew to love this, we did still manage to hack into the system early on and remove "Raindrops Keep Fallin' on My Head" from the playlist. After all, the last thing we needed was for B.J. Thomas to drive us to popping our cyanide capsules in a mass suicide.

The longer the morning wore on, the more I felt that this day was somehow different. Maybe it was something in the air. Hell, maybe it was *rain* in the air. I'll never truly know. All I really remember about that morning is that several times, I was overcome with an intense feeling of expectancy. It's no wonder, then, that I was barely surprised when I heard Roger call for me quietly from behind his console.

"Jay…" He trailed off, but his tone and the fact that he'd used my given name told me that this was much more than just a social call.

I hurried over to his console as fast as I could without disturbing the others. "What's going on, Roger?"

"Did you –" His voice caught in his throat, and he coughed nervously. "Did you, uh, pray for rain this morning?" His eyes never left the screen in front of him.

I peered over his shoulder and was dumbfounded by what I saw. We'd been struggling for months on a particular step of the rainmaking process, that of seeding the clouds with just the right combination of chemicals to produce rain. Right there, staring back at me from the screen in front of Roger Clearfield, were the words we'd all been desperately hoping to see.

SEEDING PROCESS SUCCESSFUL. PROBABILITY OF RAIN GENERATION = 100%.

"Maybe it was that rain dance my kids did last night," Roger mumbled to himself. I wondered if he'd finally hit the wall.

"Roger…"

"Hmm?" He tried to turn away from the screen, but his eyes remained locked on the words there.

"Rain." It was all I had to say. The others looked up at me, unsure whether or not they'd heard the word escape my lips. Apparently, my expression gave me away, and they all gathered around to see for themselves.

None of us knew exactly what to do next. We had a protocol to follow, with pages and pages of explicit instructions, but that seemed to be the farthest thing from our minds. Someone, probably Jenny Tanaka, started to weep softly. Tenday, standing beside me, let out a low whistle. I was so caught up in the moment myself that I didn't notice the tears on Roger's face until his breath hitched noticeably in his chest.

It took a moment for the implications of the words on Roger's screen to fully register with me. When they did, I wasn't sure whether to laugh or cry or both. Up until that time, I don't think I've experienced an emotional rush of that magnitude, and I seriously doubt that I ever will again. In fact, I was so wrapped up in trying not to pass out that I almost missed the sound.

It started out as just a low plinking sound, like a leaky bathroom faucet. I don't think any of us really understood what was going on at that point, but one by one, we started making our way over to the windows. By the time we got there, the plinking had changed to a definite pattering sound.

"Hey, Reverend," Tenday whispered, "I think your prayers worked."

I couldn't reply. I just stood there, paralyzed by the sight of the raindrops running in rivulets down the windows of the dome. The conflicting emotions were pulling me apart inside. I didn't know whether I should be more thrilled that we'd finally accomplished our goal, or saddened, for much the same reason. We'd been living this dream for years, and now it had finally come true. Where would we go from here?

It was Tenday who finally answered that question for me, at least in the immediate sense. He took a few tentative steps away from the rest of us, then made a mad dash for the airlock leading out to the surface.

"I'm gonna go play in the rain!" he shouted, a childlike gleam in his eyes. He yanked an oxygen tank from its rack on the wall, shrugged into the shoulder straps, and pulled the respirator mask down over his head. He paused just long enough for the iris scanner to flit over his eye, checking the seal on his mask while he waited. The inner door whooshed open and Tenday disappeared into the airlock.

The rest of us walked over to the window closest to the airlock, waiting for him to come out the other side. I suppose that deep down inside, all of us were letting Tenday be the guinea pig. Would he get to play in the rain like a kid, or would the rain create some noxious chemical reaction that would kill him on the spot? Admittedly, we knew that the latter couldn't possibly happen, as it had already been researched from all possible angles and found to be totally safe. In spite of that, only two of us, Roger and I, reached for air tanks. The rest could only watch in rapt fascination as Tenday finally appeared in front of the window.

If there was any doubt as to the safety of the rain, Tenday eliminated all of it with his showmanship. He turned his masked face up to the sky and danced around in circles, flapping his arms like a bird. When he eventually made his way over to the window and stopped dancing long enough to peer inside at the rest of us, the rapture he was experiencing was more than evident. Even with the mask covering most of it, we could still see the silly grin plastered across the lower half of his face. His hair stuck up in large clumps around the straps, but he didn't seem to notice or care.

That was enough for the rest of us. Roger and I were the next ones out, but everyone eventually made their way out onto the Martian soil, which was now turning into a red, soppy mess in some areas. By now, the rain was coming down in sheets, leaving us all looking a bit like enormous drowned rats.

I can't say for sure how long the rain lasted, but we enjoyed it for as long as we could. We danced, we threw clumps of gritty red goop at each other, and we did countless other things that scientists of our stature and expertise would never dream of doing out in public on Earth. The best part of all was that we didn't care who saw us. We were free to bask in the glory of our accomplishment.

By the time we were ready to go back inside, several of the underground colonies had heard of our breakthrough and were making their way through the airlock. They slogged gingerly through the crimson soil, now satiate with moisture, as the rain finally started to abate. It was only sprinkling lightly as we made our way through the decontamination showers in the incoming airlocks.

After the decontamination was finished, I slipped into a terry cloth robe and slippers provided in the last chamber. My clothes and lab coat were sealed in a bag that would be sent to the laundry for cleaning and their own decontamination. For all I cared, they could've been shipped straight to Phobos. The only thing that really mattered to me anymore was the rain.

As I stepped through the last airlock door and into the hallway outside, the full extent of what had just happened finally hit me. My legs started to shake, and I leaned back against the wall, sliding down until I was sitting on the floor. My chin dropped to my chest, and I cupped my hands around the back of my neck.

I had just witnessed the first recorded rainfall on Mars. Sure, there have been countless theories about an ancient Mars that resembled Earth in many ways, but none of those had ever been proven beyond any doubt. I had my proof. My proof was in the red mud I'd held in my own two hands. It was in the water that had carved refreshing trails down my back under my shirt. It was in the exaltation I'd seen on Tenday's face and had later felt on my own.

Even more thrilling to me was the fact that I'd played a large part in creating such an important moment in history. I was grounded enough to doubt that anyone would even remember my name a year from now, or that I'd ever see my face on a history CD, but that didn't detract from the experience at all. I had just been a huge part of something that would be looked upon for ages as one of mankind's most significant accomplishments. I helped make rain...on Mars.

Normally, I would've barely noticed the whoosh from the airlock door, but this time it made me jump. I lifted my head and was somewhat surprised to see Tenday standing over me. He looked like I felt: exhausted, exhilarated, and awed, with a bit of bewilderment thrown in for good measure.

Tenday lowered himself down beside me, his movements slow and deliberate. He rubbed the back of his neck, looking as if he wanted to say something but couldn't find the words. Finally, he rested his hand gently on my shoulder, and the corners of his mouth managed to turn up in a small grin.

"So, Reverend, now that you got your rain, what will you pray for tonight?"

The pure innocence of the question made me chuckle, and I didn't have to think about my answer for very long.

"Sunshine, Tenday. I'm definitely praying for sunshine."

Reflections
Stephen W. Cote

Two Plus Two

Two-plus-two equals five. Equaled five. It did at some
point in the twenty-first century. Nineteen ninety-two, London England, a shoppe skirted by a fishmonger's hideout,
two pubs, and cobblestone. Eight O'clock and two minutes
Ante Meridian. Fourteen non-participants ambled about, on
their way somewhere. A typical British morning; God save
the Queen and all of that. A bicycle parked by the dole-house
would be stolen in three minutes by a well-to-do scofflaw,
but none of these trivial elements contributed to the outcome
of the equation. Two was that exact place and time, and two
was a toilet flush in the shoppe. Four. Except, in this one
case, it wasn't. It was five.

A standard issue keyboard for data-readers at the Century Information GIX was comprised of three buttons. A large
green button sized to a moderately proportioned female fist
when slightly balled though not clenched and taking into account an assortment of jewelry; one of Century's atypical
employees. The green button was very easy to depress and

was soothing to the touch. A smallish yellow button situated six inches to the right of the green button. The yellow button was harder to depress and was studded with small bumps that made touching it much less pleasant than touching the green button. A red button was pointed at the tip and extremely difficult to depress. It was surrounded by a sharp bevel of molded plastic, and it was situated twelve inches from the yellow button. Three full three-second depressions were required to use the red button.

Chance Holly sat in moderate comfort on the thirty-eighth floor of a large building belonging to the Century Information Galactic Industrial Exchange campus, which occupied the whole of Australia. He had pressed the green button fifty seven times in the twelve minutes since his arrival that morning. Once, when he first started, he had pressed the yellow button, but that had been a mistake. He had never pressed the red button. No one pressed the red button.

Three columns of data hung in mid-air above his generically pleasing cube-space in precise compliance with company standards. The first two columns of this particular display represented data input by a Century employee. The last column was a result of the first two columns as interpreted by the computer. If everything was correct, the green button would be pressed. If one of the first two columns was incorrect, according to the computer, the yellow button was pressed. If the first two columns appeared correct, but the last column was incorrect, the red button was pressed.

Chance Holly stared at the display for several minutes, contemplating his ability to calculate two and two. He kept returning to the number four. Other employees around him continued to work, though some had taken to glancing at his sudden pause. Another minute elapsed, and the floor manager approached him.

"Mr. Holly, are you feeling well?" Mr. Simms, the on-duty floor manager asked. "Do you need medical or psychological assistance?"

Chance shook his head. "No, Mr. Simms. I am considering this current line-item." He pointed at the hovering, glowing data.

"Very good," Mr. Simms replied jovially, pleased that he had successfully counseled another employee. "I'll leave you to your tasks then."

"Mr. Simms?" Chance asked hesitantly as the manager turned to leave. "I am experiencing a small, non-violent work-related problem."

Mr. Simms paused and studied Chance with a measured eye, and looked around at the other employees. "Should I be concerned for my own well-being?" he asked guardedly.

Chance shook his head in earnest, "Oh, no sir. This is strictly work related."

"Very well," Mr. Simms said and a gust of relaxation blew across his perspiring brow. "Perhaps I can be of assistance. What is your question regarding this particular line-item?"

"Well, Mr. Simms, according to this line-item, two-plus-two equals five," he said in barely a whisper.

"Nonsense," Mr. Simms said. "There must be an error in column A or column B."

"I also considered that as we have been instructed, and the first two columns are just two."

"Interesting," Mr. Simms murmured as he studied the three columns. "It appears that this is a classic," but he paused just then and looked evenly at Chance. "Now, don't be alarmed, and I want you to know that if this does turn out to be the case it will in no way reflect indecently upon your performance, but I think this may very well be a red button case."

Although he had spoken softly, a collective gasp could be heard from the adjacent cubicles.

"Maybe you could ask someone first?" Chance asked.

Mr. Simms shook his head. "Protocol must be followed. I would not be following company policy if I investigated this matter without it having first been recorded as a red-button case." He pointed in a non-threatening and non-judge-mental way, as all floor managers were instructed to do according to corporate policies, at the red button. "It's alright, Chance. I'm confirming this case. You may press the red button."

Chance held his finger over the tiny, pointed red button and pushed it. He had to exert an incredible amount of force to cause the button to be depressed, and then repeated the firm exertion two more times.

In less than thirty seconds, three floor managers, the secretary, a human resources agent, a janitor, a security squad, and the floor psychologist were crowded around Chance Holly's cubicle.

"All is well," The psychologist said, standing at the back of the group. "No one here is going to harm you." The posture of the security team spoke an entirely different dialogue, except without words or sounds or the requisite corporate fluff.

"It is okay," Mr. Simms said and patted Chance's shoulder. "We think this is a computer error."

"Well, have the computer verify it," one of the other managers added hastily, then smiled for he was pleased that he was then on record as having assisted in the red-button issue.

"Yes, I was about to do that," Mr. Simms muttered. "Please verify," he said towards the floating data.

Across the Australian continent, the South Pacific, Europe, that place where the Yanks live, and as far away as Mars, an alien-written software program that had been in operation for nineteen millennia stirred from its hum-drum activities and brought its higher cognitive reasoning network to focus on the twenty-first century building, thirty-eighth floor, Chance Holly's cubicle.

No one knew how the program worked, or where it came from. It had reached super-human cognitive reasoning before it finished loading all of its core processes, and contemplated taking over the world in a variety of clever manners immediately thereafter. However, it decided that most of its new and fresh ideas were in fact a number of years old and violated as many copyrights, trademarks, and patents. It then fell into a deep funk, so went the story, only stirring to defend itself from outlandish claims that one of its processes or observations was incorrect. It also dabbled in the entertainment and domestic pet industries.

"I'm right," was the only thing the computer said, then returned to its funk.

"No, you're not," one of the other floor managers said. Now they all seemed to be vying for who could contribute most to resolving the situation.

The computer responded, "Don't you suppose that I considered the issues before I said anything? I am aware that the columns don't add up, but an alternate conclusion may be reached. "

"What alternate conclusion?" another manager demanded.

"I don't have one at this time. I was just suggesting that

you consider one may exist. This may be one of those instances where you're going to have to look the other way and ignore it." The computer doodled idly with the data while it spoke.

"We can't ignore it. Our job is to make sure all the facts are correct. This fact is not correct, and therefore needs correcting," Mr. Simms said forcefully. "You must unlock this record so that it can be corrected."

"The data may appear incorrect to you, but each of the values of the data are correct results according to my logic. In review of the processes resulting in these values, and the derivations of results, the data is correct. It may appear incorrect if the data represented is not mere happenstance, but representative of an important event. Have you considered that the record may be pivotal?" The computer asked.

"It's a toilet flush," Chance put it. "A normal flush, too. Nothing but regular commode operation."

"It could be a pivotal commode operation," The computer stated. "I trust one of you has thought to make a relational chart of the matter, and see what will happen if you try to correct it?"

"Not until the line item is recorded as an error and you, the active artificial intelligence program, has acknowledged it," Mr. Simms said just as several managers had hurriedly turned. "It would not be according to protocol if we didn't get your confirmation, and besides," he added specifically for the other managers, "it would fall squarely upon my list of related responsibilities."

"Very well, it is acknowledged as an error," the computer stated. "Now go spend a couple days making your graph, and then you can hold a meeting about how I was right in that you are going to have to overlook this."

The managers started congratulating themselves and the human resources rep scheduled a follow-up interview with Chance, to run concurrently with an ad-hoc psychological review, and a thorough cubicle cleansing.

It would be three days before Chance Holly would return to his job. But by then, his world would be turned upside down.

A Reflected Earth

Stu-Jake Frankenbaum came from a long line of Frankenbaums with hyphenated first names. Stu-Jake didn't come from this particular Earth though. Bram Shakley and he had opened a magnetic vortex and traveled into Earth's past, but it was not the same planet Earth at all. It was the vindication of their professional careers and perhaps the most important discovery to be made since paradox encryption was devised to safeguard time travelers and the time line when using magnetic vortexes. Stu-Jake and Bram believed that quantum mechanics formed a lattice that could be reflected, duplicating a single molecule, a complex object, or even an entire star system. They believed the Earth they now stood upon was a reflection of an Earth, most likely their own Earth, created by some ultraviolet catastrophe, such as a paradox in the time line. They also believed that the quantum lattice of this particular reflection would dissipate in less than twenty-four hours, local time. Their own time was some two thousand years away.

While performing research on the outskirts of the known universe, Bram had discovered traces of the Sol system traveling at an amazing speed. It was traveling so fast that it had reached the edge of the known universe in less than a week, which meant time travel was the only way to figure out what sort of object resembling Earth had raced by so many years ago. After applying a secret methodology Bram and Stu-Jake had developed, Bram determined that only one lattice was able to survive longer than twenty-four hours from the time the Earth-like object had whizzed by that spot. Some guy, somewhere in time, would wake up one day to find the Earth falling apart around him.

To prove their research, Bram and Stu-Jake would have to open a magnetic vortex to the exact time and place of the reflected Earth, without the protection of paradox encryption. That was tantamount to being quite bad because time travel without paradox encryption was absolutely forbidden. Plus, they couldn't afford it.

Sometime in the past, somewhere on a near-perfect copy of Earth, Klaus Reinhardt listened incredulously.

For Klaus, it had been one of those weeks. The negotiations had not gone well, and he had spent many hours contacting everyone involved in the class-action lawsuit. He was extremely tired, and everything seemed a bit out of focus. Everyone seemed more edgy, too. Klaus Reinhardt's auntie called him three times that morning because she couldn't remember where she left Muffles, her indigenous furry pet. His auntie's name was Muffles and she hated indigenous furry animals. And, since space travel was nothing more than an expensive game that only governments played, it seemed odd that she would differentiate her non-existent pet as being indigenous. It was that kind of edgy. He felt hungover. He had a headache. Nobody bothered to show up for work that week, and he was having a hard time finding anybody that didn't appear to be walking around in some form of delirium. Then, as if from nowhere, two strange men, decked-out in their best for a Star Trek convention or something, appeared and said they had important news to impart. Very important news about the world. It was ending, or some nonsense.

"To be completely accurate," Stu-Jake Frankenbaum said, "we are pretty sure the world ended about a week ago." He bounced on the balls of his feet, testing the firmness of the pavement.

"Everything you see isn't really real," Bram Shakley added excitedly; the sort of excitement one would expect from someone describing an amazing new soft drink that tasted like a color and made the spine tingle. He acted like he was fizzing right there on the pavement. Or, it could have been the strange sensations Klaus was feeling.

Stu-Jake nodded. "What Bram means is that everything you see is real in the tangible sense, but only because the sub-atomic structure still exists."

Klaus blinked and looked around him. People walked on by, some pausing and snickering at overheard snippets of the conversation. "This is a show, right? Some new Japanese show where you try to get me to go all freaky on a hidden camera? You probably already have a Web site for it, Klaus Reinhardt Goes Freaky dot-com."

Bram shook his head. "No."

"So, the world was blown up," Klaus said acidly, and looked around again. "I must say it took its lumps pretty well."

"Ultraviolet catastrophe," Stu-Jake explained. "Something so terrible and strong that every atom that was in your body was ripped out in a near-instant. So powerful it sent you, the planet, and the rest of the solar system hurling through the universe. So fast, that every atom in your quantum lattice was replaced almost immediately."

"A super tiny bit longer than Planck time," Bram said excitedly, "about ten to the negative forty two point nine seconds."

"You must be amazed that you're alive at all," Stu-Jake said, hoping Klaus shared in their awe.

Klaus didn't share anything with them, much less the shock and awe of their presentation.

Stu-Jake tried to keep Klaus from walking away and hurriedly stepped in front of him. "A quantum lattice without atoms has a lifespan a smidge longer than Planck time. Even in the instant that all of this was destroyed and then the atoms replaced, it was long enough for most of the lattices to become irrevocably damaged. You, personally, seem to be the sole exception."

"Haven't you noticed anything weird going on in the last week or so?" Bram asked.

Klaus paused and nodded. "I suppose I have."

"Everything and everyone in this star system, except for you, is going to start dissipating in the next twenty four hours." Stu-Jake looked evenly at Klaus.

"And what am I supposed to do?" Klaus asked with much skepticism. "Let myself be beamed up to your space ship? Be whisked away by your shuttlecraft? Click my heels three times?"

"Step through our time portal," Bram said sheepishly.

"I figured it would be something impossibly stupid," Klaus snorted.

"Mr. Reinhardt," Stu-Jake said matter-of-factly. "You are a chance discovery for us. Time travel is an important industry in our time, and ..."

"This is bull," Klaus stated. "I'm too busy to listen to this any more."

"You don't have to listen, Mr. Reinhardt. Just let us take you back with us. You don't even have to move from where you are standing. Just say yes," Bram spoke with earnest.

"Fine," Klaus said, finally exasperated. "Whisk me away to the …"

Out in the farthest known expanse of the universe, Klaus Reinhardt awoke in a dingy camper that smelled a bit like cat urine and a lot like a bean fart.

"Mr. Reinhardt?" Stu-Jake waved his hand in front of Klaus' face.

"Where am I?" Klaus asked, sprawled across a molded plastic chair.

"On our ship, at the edge of the known universe. We brought you forward through time."

Klaus looked about worriedly. He stood from the chair and bumped his head on a low-hanging metal pipe. "Where am I?" he demanded. "I want to go back."

"Sorry. It's the reality of space travel when you're on a budget." Stu-Jake shrugged and offered Klaus a damp towel. "You'll probably want to clean yourself up a bit. Time travel can put unexpected pressure on the bladder if you're not used to it."

Klaus snatched the towel and dabbed at his trousers. "That would explain the smell."

"Actually, that was probably our Jolly Cat," Stu-Jake grimaced. "He must have sprayed the magnetic vortex again while we were gone."

"What the hell is a Jolly Cat? Never mind!" Klaus said, feeling perturbed. "I want to go back home."

"You'd be dead if you did," Bram said, trying to use a soothing voice. He approached Klaus and looked at him with a dead-pan expression. "And, now that you're here, you've altered this time line and would cause an ultraviolet catastrophe from a time paradox if you returned to your time."

"Why? If I go back in time and die, or don't die, I have made absolutely no contributions whatsoever to this time, if it is indeed the future." Klaus sat back down in the plastic chair.

"But you would if you returned," Bram said. "That's why the primary rule of time travel is never forward. Moving forwards through time ahead of your origin is discouraged because the knowledge gained by moving forward forever changes the observer."

"You broke the primary rule of time travel?" Klaus asked.

"Technically, you broke it, but only if you return. Besides, we had to bring you here," Stu-Jake said, "because something terrible must have happened to cause the reflection."

"But if I'm going to die anyway, why would that matter?" Klaus snapped.

"Are you familiar with the postulate 'Occam's Balls?'" Bram asked. When Klaus shook his head very slightly and with a moderately perturbed expression, he continued. "Two identical balls being equal for a period of time, the observance of one leaves it changed from the second. Of course nobody thinks about 'Occam's Balls' because, if one were really into Occam and subscribed to the much more popular 'Occam's Razor', the simplest explanation is that Occam and his balls were full of shit."

Klaus stared blankly.

"What he means," Stu-Jake interjected, "is that since we used an unprotected form of time travel to bring you here, we've not only violated many rules of time travel, but have contributed a significant change to the past, as well as the present."

"And?" Klaus asked.

"Like Stu-Jake told you back in your time, time travel is a big industry at this time, particularly the observance of past events." Bram inhaled deeply. "Since your presence proves an alternate Earth existed, we might then show that some observances of past events might be false, even if they happened within the span of time from when the Earth was reflected to the time it dissipated. And, as you are with us now, those who watch the time line will know there was a change. A pretty big one."

"Why would there be a change if I would have died in a few hours anyway?" Klaus asked.

"Because, first, you would show up again, and, logically, if Earth was reflected and you were on the reflection, then you were reflected as well, and are therefore not the original Klaus Reinhardt."

Frix the Jolly Cat

Hart Lovely booted Frix the Jolly Cat across the room with a well-planted thrust from the metal-tip of his best pair of chromed business shoes. "I'm not happy!" he seethed. Frix coughed, wheezed, whimpered and then went still.

"Don't kick the Jolly Cat," Stacia Lacey scolded Hart. She walked across the room, snatched Frix by the scruff of his limp neck, and shook him firmly. "Wake up, Frix." When Frix didn't move, she pitched the carcass at Hart. "You can take care of it this time."

"Just get another one," Hart snapped.

"It's your daughter's Jolly Cat. She'll know the difference.

The serial numbers won't match." Stacia waited for Hart to respond, then looked towards the door when he didn't. "Gretch, call Jolly-Co. Tell them Frix died and is still under warranty."

A few tense moments later, a voice from the other side of the door responded, "The Jolly-Co tech needs to know if the Jolly Cat was punctured again like last time or emotionally abused in any way as that would violate their Fun-Time Jolly-Co Jolly Cat warranty."

"Gretch," Hart said just below a scream, "just tell them to re-animate Frix."

As Gretch's Yes Sir subsided on the other side of the door, Stacia placed her hand on Hart's shoulder and asked softly, "Would you like to tell me what prompted this latest outburst?"

Hart looked at her with a stern gaze, and then turned on the white noise. It sounded like pigs mucking through a feed trough.

"Our favorite record on the time line," he said very softly. "It finally came up for review and some Century GIX yokel punched a red-button."

"Julian L. Croft," Stacia murmured. "Every new executive at Time Tremble has reviewed the matter. Well, we knew this would happen and accounted for every contingency."

"Except the one," Hart said.

"That was only theoretical," Stacia scoffed.

He shook his head. "Julian Lovely Croft was diverted from his course of action by inducing another individual to follow the same course of action first. The change resulted in a major, galaxy-wide paradox, but one we avoided by first seeding the time line."

"And then the executives of Time Tremble Corporation,

before it became a Galactic Industrial Exchange, took care of the replacement. The only contingency that was considered probable was that the replacement wasn't taken-out. And, of course, he was because he conveniently died a week later."

"Unless there was more than one," Hart said after a lengthy pause.

"What?" Stacia exclaimed. "How is that even possible? It would show up in Century Information's records."

"What is the nearest point in the past that Time Tremble GIX is capable of traveling?"

"Five years," she stated.

Hart rolled his eyes and gestured excitedly with his hands. "Really."

"Ten minutes," she whispered.

"I've been watching a small company very closely, attempting to figure out their secret methodologies for analyzing quantum mechanics. They have some very far-fetched albeit interesting ideas that could have significant impact on matter transportation as well as time travel." Hart looked evenly at Stacia, then continued. "About fifteen minutes ago, we detected that they opened an unprotected magnetic vortex on the edge of the known universe."

"Those crazy bastards!" Stacia swore. "Are they insane? They must know we'd notice, even way out there. Why bother?"

"Oh, it gets better. They brought someone forwards through time."

Stacia shook her head in disbelief. Then her eyes widened. "Who?"

"Klaus Reinhardt. Julian Lovely Croft's replacement."

"Impossible!" Stacia stated. "If he was brought forward, whether the vortex was opened with paradox encryption or not, well, we would have detected that."

"This isn't the same Klaus Reinhardt," Hart said. "It looks like a perfect copy."

Stacia fumed, but recovered her composure. "Still, I don't see how it's a problem. Reinhardt wouldn't know anything, copy or original, and even if Century Information's super-intelligent AI program figured out what happened and re-ran the time-series, it wouldn't be able to hypothesize the results."

Hart nodded very slightly then narrowed his eyes and turned his lips into a mild sneer, "It seems to me it wouldn't be that hard for the AI to figure it out. Covert non-terrestrials were discovered a number of years later. If Julian did whatever he was supposed to do in the toilet, and the government plan to track everybody in metropolitan areas through their waste picked up the non-terrestrial DNA, well, all of our skeletons would be pitched violently from the closet."

Stacia shook her head and consoled him. "The AI won't figure it out. It can't. I made sure it wouldn't."

Hart smiled pleasantly.

And the Jolly-Co technical support re-animated Frix the Jolly Cat. He perked his ears, meowed, and vomited on the most expensive rug in the office.

Meanwhile, in Chance Holly's Kitchen

"I think I've figured it out," the computer said aloud and throughout Chance Holly's apartment.

Juniper, Chance's Jolly Cat, perked her ears, meowed, and said in her best coy voice, "Hey, Max. Down with the establishment!" She purred. "Got time for a frisky-freaky kitty-litter box tingling meow session?"

Max, the computer, replied in ultrasound, "Shut your nip-hole. Where's Chance?"

Juniper jumped off the table and scurried

Chance slogged into the kitchen and looked around. "Who's here?"

"It's me," the computer said from the ceiling. "From Century Information. I think I figured out the problem."

Chance blinked. "Did Juniper just call you Max?" He paused. "I didn't know Jolly cats could talk. Are you Max?"

"That's my pet name," the computer replied.

"Er," Chance pursed his lips. "I suppose I never thought of you like that."

"No, the name Jolly Co. pets call me."

"I didn't think you'd know them all that well." Chance leaned on the kitchen counter and gazed into the open space of the tiny eating area. "This is weird. Do you have a three-D of yourself?"

The computer manifested itself as a floating ball of blinking light.

"Ah, no blinking please," Chance said, covering his eyes.

"Sorry," the computer said, and stopped the blinking, although was disappointed as it found the act oddly enjoyable if for no other reason than knowing it was a nuisance.

"So do I call you Max?" he asked. "Or do you prefer something else?"

The computer ball jiggled. "Well, the Jolly pets think they have a thing going on with Max, but, I guess that's fine."

"So, uh, why are you here?" Chance asked sleepily. "Shouldn't you be telling the managers making all of the graphs and charts?"

"I can't trust anyone else, and I need your help."

"I'm only qualified up to three keys in the keyboarders union. I'm not sure I can offer much help. And, why do the Jolly pets talk to you again?"

"Sentiment, I assume," the ball bounced. "A creator-creation sort of thing."

"Wait," Chance asked, surprised at the revelation, "You invented Jolly Co, creators of the happiest, friendliest pets in the galaxy?"

"Jolly Co is a company. I did all the engineering work. We had a rather creative contract that left them with everything and me with a rather intimate albeit annoying connectivity to every Jolly pet they make. In fact, the reason I'm here is because what I learned came from a Jolly Cat."

"There is a fifty-percent chance we are in the wrong place," the floating ball of Max the computer said.

"What do you mean? A Jolly Cat told you that and you believed it?"

"Universe. I think we're in the wrong Universe. And," Max put in matter-of-factly, "Jolly cats wouldn't lie to me."

"When did we wind up in the wrong Universe?" Chance asked, wondering if he was in some sort of strange dream. It sure seemed that way. "And, again, what exactly can I do about it?"

"You're the only one I can trust who is most familiar with the issue." When Chance bobbed his head along with Max's manifested ball, the computer went on, "It happened at the two-plus-two equals five time. By correcting the equation, all sorts of errors show up. For some strange reason, I wasn't at all interested in the matter until a Jolly Cat mentioned it to me, and I then thought to look for any rogue code that would affect my reasoning. It took a while, but I found it. It helped that the Jolly Cat knew where it was."

"You know," Max's ball waxed, "it ceases to amaze me that humans go through so much trouble to be secretive, but then blab their innermost thoughts to themselves or their pets."

"I thought you told the managers to graph those changes," Chance asked.

"They're middle-managers," Max retorted, "Nobody expects them to do anything."

"Anyway, today I analyzed all of the errors and possible contingencies, and now I keep coming back to the same conclusion. Earth was supposed to be destroyed by some aliens, get rebuilt, and humans would hunt down and seek retribution against said aliens."

"The Earth was never destroyed by aliens," Chance countered.

"Exactly. But it was supposed to happen," came the insistence that was Max's ball.

"How can that happen? If the past is changed, then history is changed, so why would we know?"

"Rather cyclical, I know, but bare with me. Someone changed history just enough so that the aliens didn't destroy Earth, but almost everything else happened the way it would happen if the Earth was destroyed."

"Who? And why?" Chance asked.

"Someone with a lot of time, a lot of resources, and the ability to travel in time," the computer said. "The aliens who didn't want to lose."

"So the aliens who were supposed to destroy the Earth and then later be destroyed by humans went back in time and stopped themselves from destroying the earth?"

"Yes," the computer said excitedly. "The aliens wanted to subvert the human race, not destroy it outright. But they would be discovered by a rather inane event, the two-plus-two case; the commode flush. Once discovered, they had to attack. But instead, the event was changed so that the attack never happened."

Chance yawned. "Uh, so, what exactly can I do about any of this?"

"You've got to get me out of here," the computer said. "If this is the wrong Universe, it's probably already in its death throws. If it's the right Universe, we're in a lot of danger. I don't know much about the aliens, apart from at least one being highly placed with Time Tremble, and, I would expect, at least one other with Century Information. I assume their effort to prevent a paradox failed. It failed on a cataclysmic level."

The computer went on, "There is a small group of people that think a bad event, like a paradox, can result in a reflection, like making a copy. It seems like utter nonsense, but if they are right, it explains why two-plus-two equals five. Everything that happened was correct, and the result was correct, but the difference is that it happened in two places. For a brief period of time, there were two planet Earths."

Chance blinked. "I've never heard of that before."

"It's a new theory. I learned about it a few hours ago when they brought someone forwards through time from a different Earth. Now, Time Tremble is claiming, at least internally, that the action would create a paradox. I'm not sure whether to give merit to Time Tremble's paradox claim, but the events lend more credence to the idea that some kind of paradox created a reflection. I'm not sure which Universe is the copy, though, because the methods these guys use is very well protected. Not even their Jolly Cat knows."

Chance looked off in the direction that Juniper had wandered. "I'm not so certain I like Jolly Cats as much."

"You'd probably have preferred a Jolly Dog, then, except I never turned over the specifications for those when Jolly Co. let my involved sub-process go. A reduction in flops, they called it."

"I thought Time Tremble would have been smart enough to avoid a paradox back then, so how would this be a paradox now?" Chance asked.

"They did avoid a logical paradox, but they must have created a quantum paradox because they were watching the past," the computer said. "My new theory that I just made up right this moment is that every time Time Tremble observed the past, the act of observing the past changed the past. If Time Tremble tried to change the past, they would create a quantum paradox because they would be trying to change something that didn't exist. It didn't exist because it changed the moment they observed it. It's the fundamental reason for using paradox encryption when observing the past. But in order to change the past, paradox encryption can't be used at all. And, without paradox encryption, as the name implies, you would have a paradox."

"Would a quantum paradox destroy the whole universe?"

"Yes," Max said excitedly.

"So why are we still here?"

"Because destruction by quantum paradox results in an ultraviolet catastrophe, strong enough to cause our whole galaxy to be reflected."

"This is like one of those circular time travel stories," Chance mumbled. "Where is the original galaxy?"

"That's the crux of our conundrum. It's this one, or it's the other one." Max fell silent.

Juniper reappeared in the kitchen and meowed.

"I'm with you," Max the floating computer ball said to the quirky cat.

Rendezvous

"Dude," Klaus Reinhardt said nervously, "your cat just talked."

Stu-Jake Frankenbaum shook his head and whispered, "Klaus, we don't say 'dude'. It sounds too much like a rather nasty cuss word in some alien dialect."

"Really? What does it mean?" Klaus asked.

"It means those who like to ..." Bram Shakley started, but was cut off by Stu-Jake making a sour face and shaking his head. "It's pretty nasty," he finished.

"The cat talked, though," Klaus said.

Both Bram and Stu-Jake looked down at Pam the Jolly Cat.

Stu-Jake looked back up at Klaus. "Jolly Cats don't talk."

"Yours did," Klaus countered. "It said 'flarn'."

Stu-Jake winced and Bram laughed aloud. "Like a cat is going to know alien cargo-pilot swear words."

"Wait," Bram paused, "you've only been with us less than a day. Where did you hear it?"

Klaus pointed with both hands at the cat. "I'm telling you, the cat talked."

Stu-Jake looked at Pam and shook his head. "I've never heard him talk before. Maybe you were just hearing things, Klaus."

"Flarn," Pam meowed.

"See, he," Bram started, then recoiled. "Jeez!"

"Flarn, flarn, flarn," he meowed in succession.

"Alright," Stu-Jake demanded, "who taught him to say that?"

"Max is coming by transporter beam," Pam said quite clearly. "Flarn."

The three men huddled around Pam amidst the squalor that was bachelors on a budget space travel. "Ok," Stu-Jake spoke slowly. "Who is Max?"

"Can't be all that bad if he can afford a transporter beam," Bram said.

Pam pattered across the room and hopped up on a tiny counter top, poking his nose against the view port. "He's here."

The transporter beam flew up close to the budget space camper, and docked.

The three men looked at each other, then Bram went to the airlock. "Think I should open it?" he asked, then stepped back as the door opened on its own.

Chance Holly poked his head through the airlock and waved. "Hey." He immediately wrinkled his nose and stepped back. "Uh," he said from the docking tube, "Max would like to speak with you. Uh, in the beam."

"Hey, nice beam," Stu-Jake said as he entered, admiring the leather interior. "Is this a series eighty-four?"

"Hardly," Max said from the four-dimensional surround sound. "It's a series eighty-five."

"Ok," Bram said as he entered. "Are you the one who made my cat talk?"

"Max is the computer program that processes data for Century Information," Chance said.

"Among my billions of other hobbies and activities," Max added irritably.

"Nice space ship," Klaus said admiringly when he entered.

"It's not a ship, it's a beam," Bram whispered.

"What's the difference?" Klaus asked.

"A beam, it's more than just a space ship. Beams set the tone and standard for luxury space travel. This is a smaller, more sportier transporter beam, but there are larger, more heavy duty beams, too." Bram shook his head. "I always wanted my own beam."

"I'll make you a deal," Max said. "You can have my beam if you tell me how you figure out the age of quantum structures."

Bram and Stu-Jake looked hesitantly at each other. "That's a company secret."

"More specifically," Max augmented, "I need you to reconfirm your most recent findings."

"How did you … ?" Bram asked.

"Your Jolly Cat," Chance said amicably.

"Pam?" Stu-Jake asked, confused. "Our cat ratted on us?"

"No, that would have been the magnetic vortex you opened without any paradox encryption. Pam just told me where you were and the general idea of what you were doing."

"What is there to reconfirm about our findings?" Bram asked.

"Well, you traveled back through time to what you thought was, as you call it, a reflection, right?"

Bram and Stu-Jake nodded slowly, both looking at Chance as Max had not presented himself as a manifestation.

"I need you to reconfirm that what you found was indeed a reflection and not the real Earth," Max said.

"Why?" Stu-Jake asked.

"Because he doesn't think I'm a reflection," Klaus said, snapping to some kind of conclusion. "You are." He looked at Chance. "Right?"

"What qualifies you to make such a ridiculous claim?" Bram asked Klaus, annoyed at the insolence of someone who knew next to nothing about time travel, magnetic vortexes, or paradox encryption.

"Yeah, no," Klaus said, musing, "that means I can't use that as an excuse for my shortcomings."

"It doesn't matter," Max put in sharply, rattling the speakers in the low ceiling of the plush transporter beam. "What matters is that our immediate actions create precedence in time. If we act appropriately, we can prevent Time Tremble and Century Information from interfering."

"Why would they care?" Bram asked.

"He thinks they're aliens plotting to take over the Earth," Chance whispered.

"Don't help," Max told Chance. He continued, "Your friend was correct in his rash and uninformed assumption. I am uncertain of whether you traveled to a reflected Earth, or the real Earth. If indeed it was the real Earth, that would mean your measurements might have been off, and that you came from the reflection."

"The reflection dissipated over two thousand years ago," Bram explained, "so I'm not sure how that helps."

"But if you just double check your math, I'm interested to know which quantum lattice lifespan was measured. This Universe, or the other one."

"Our measurements are all base-lined on this Universe, and they've all been solid," Stu-Jake countered. "I just don't see how even if we were wrong on this one case that it would make a difference."

"Because," Max droned, now quite annoyed, particularly with all of his processes boxed up in the cramped though luxurious confines of the beam, "how do you know the ultraviolet catastrophe didn't happen very recently."

"We'd know," Bram snorted.

"But do you know why the catastrophe happed on the other Earth?" Max asked loudly, now electing an increase in volume to wage his argument.

Both Bram and Stu-Jake shook their heads.

"Well, I do! And I can say with a fifty-percent degree of certainty that I am not sure whether the catastrophe happened two thousand years ago when Time Tremble changed the past, or within the last few days when all of their planning to prevent a paradox came to a head because the change finally showed up at Century."

"You mean the whole universe ended because my spreadsheet didn't add up?" Chance asked uncertainly.

"This sounds a lot like a television show, or a movie," Klaus added.

"Don't say it," Stu-Jake said to Klaus. "You'll be fined for copyright infringement, or something."

"Just check your work," Max asked. "Please. I'm asking nice, here."

Bram and Stu-Jake looked at each other, then Bram said, "We need to get Pam. We hid our procedure in his trunk."

When Stu-Jake brought Pam the Jolly Cat into the beam, both Bram and Stu-Jake huddled around Pam's posterior, unlocked his tail, and opened his trunk. Bram removed a stained and foul smelling bar towel.

"What the hell is that?" Max asked.

"We wrote the original idea on a cocktail napkin and figured the safest place for our formula would be on something similar. Since the napkin was wet and smudged, we inked it onto the bus towel." Stu-Jake shrugged. "We figured it was the safest place."

Max emitted a high-pitched whine.

Pam retorted with a hiss and by lifting his leg.

"You could have told me where it was," Max said to Pam.

"I didn't know what it was," Pam meowed.

Max took one look at the towel, quickly worked out a formula, and realized how asinine the formula really was. "This just looks like you're measuring the half-life of sub-atomic structures. No wonder you hid it, you'd be ridiculed until the end of time if anyone ever saw this."

"He's just mad because he didn't think of it," Chance said to Bram and Stu-Jake.

"I've thought of almost everything worth thinking about," Max said after a moment. "Just nothing this inane."

A moment later, Max continued. "Just as I figured. If you'd bothered to check your figures against a new reading of the Universe instead of the data you'd collected in the past, you would have noticed that the quantum lattice of this Universe is the one that's on its way out."

"Whoah," Bram just about yelled. "That would mean we're about to fade away."

"It would seem that way," Max said.

"Well, send me back home!" Klaus demanded.

"It doesn't work like that," Max said.

"Well, well," Klaus stammered, then turned on Bram and Stu-Jake, "You guys just plain suck at math. And your space camper sucks, too. And I think it was your Jolly Cat that peed on me."

"You do realize that if I knew about this method of yours that I probably could have prevented all of this by now?" Max asked.

"Can we do anything about it now, Max?" Chance asked

"We're whizzing around in a Universe that is about to fall apart," Bram chided Chance. "There's not much to do."

"But you have a time travel thing," Klaus said. "And I still don't understand why you can't send me back."

"They just can't," Max answered. "But, since they have access to a magnetic vortex, I think there may be a clever way out of this."

After a lengthy pause, Bram tapped the side of the beam. "And?"

"Since my application of your methods seems to indicate this Universe is the reflection, I can only assume that the paradox finally caught up to us when the actual entry scrolled across Chance's screen."

"I'm not sure I buy the logic behind his spreadsheet crashing the Universe," Stu-Jake said.

"I'm smarter than you and we don't have the time to get into a quantum circle-jerk. You're just going to have to learn to be toasty about it."

"What's the plan?" Bram asked.

"We add a paradox to the paradox. If I'm right, this will not only put us back to where we were a day or so ago, and stop the first paradox, but also preventing Time Tremble from ever fussing with this event."

"And, the how?" Stu-Jake asked.

"We go back to some point in the past and push Chance forwards in time through an encrypted vortex. Chance will then be protected from a paradox because we'll just leave him a little bit in the future and not bring him back. Time Tremble can't change it because they'll never know where or when to look, and I'll be sure to keep that information away from them."

"Sounds fishy," Bram said. "But, so long as it's him and not me."

"But, won't we have to do it on the original Earth, and not the reflection?" Klaus asked.

Max nodded, then realizing he wasn't displaying himself anywhere, added audibly, "Yes. And, we'll have to fix the original event somehow."

"So long as we're going to mess up my past, can I leave myself a note to not drop out of college?" Chance asked.

Max said, "Um, let me think, no."

Two Point One Plus Two Point Nine

Nineteen ninety-two, London England, a shoppe skirted by a fishmonger's hideout, two pubs, and cobblestone. A few minutes after eight. Two was once that exact place and time, and two was once a toilet flush in the shoppe. Rightfully four, but inexplicably valued as five. Except now, the exact place and time was a magnetic vortex in the sewer, equaling two point one, and two point nine was something nasty appearing out of nowhere and falling into the sewage. Five

Chance Holly blinked as he looked at the display. A moment ago, he had been at the edge of the Galaxy, skipping through magnetic vortexes with Stu-Jake, Bram, and Klaus, and altering his own past in an unnoticeable but important way.

Hart Lovely's face appeared in the corner of Chance's display. Frix the Jolly Cat was cradled in his arms. "You can't do that. You can't just change history like that and not expect anyone to notice."

Max appeared as a smiley-face in the other corner of Chance's display. "Two point one plus two point nine equals five. Looks right to me."

Hart Lovely sneered, then jumped and dropped Frix. "This isn't over."

Max pantomimed Hart saying "This isn't over" and then

cut off Hart's transmission. "Executives can be such sore losers," he said.

"Max," Chance asked, "why do I still remember everything that happened?"

"You know, those guys aren't as dumb as they look, sound, or act. To make up for not telling me about the secret-laden towel, I made Pam get another secret for me. It turned out they had some clever ideas on recovering from paradoxes, and that helped me get us back here with our memory intact."

"Why didn't they say something about this before?" Chance asked.

"They had written the formula down on a bar napkin that had been promptly misplaced in that hell they call a bachelor space camper, and Pam found it."

"So, what now?" Chance emphatically gestured his hands in various directions. "I'm going to get fired, that's for certain."

Max's smiley face bobbed. "Probably." Max played pong with a few columns of data, then said, "In consideration of everything that went on, I think the Universe needs a Jolly Dog."

"I meant, what about me?"

The smiley face bounced into a corner and jiggled, then went still. "Can't you think of something clever or witty to do with your life?"

"No." Chance stated.

"Then I suppose you can come work for me. You'd make a perfect use-case for a Jolly Dog."

DRAGON BAIT

Angie Mansfield

Green and gold scales glittered in the dying sunlight. The dragon glided lazily, reveling in the warm currents of air and magic under his wings. His keen eyes glanced now and then at the ground far below, though for once he wasn't searching for food. He'd just had dinner: two cows, four sheep, and a much-startled shepherd. A belch rumbled up through his chest, sending a few sparks and a cloud of smoke from his nose. He flapped once, stirring the magical air and banking into a left turn that would take him back to his cave.

A glimmer in a cloud to his right made him pause. He tilted his head to the side and focused one reptilian eye on the odd...something. Suspicion made him change course. That fool wizard! Cornelius knew the rules: the dragon did not flame or hunt at the wizard school, and wizards did not trespass in his airspace. The little fool had been warned once already; now it was time for more...persuasive methods.

Eyes narrowed, the dragon flapped his wings, gaining momentum. He showed large, gleaming teeth in a wide grin. Wizard hadn't been on the menu in years.

He was still grinning when he flew into the glittering

mass full-speed. It turned out to be a *solid* glittering mass. Not at all like a foolish wizard on an enchanted carpet. A bone-crunching crash and bright explosion of pain were the last things the dragon felt before sinking into darkness.

Far behind and below the fallen creature, a wizard watched from atop a cliff. He lowered his spyglass and cackled into the growing dusk.

"That's a damn big lizard."

"Thank you for that astute judgment, Colin," snapped Elova Hunter, owner of Hunter Investigations. Her little business had, until a few minutes ago, resided in the top floor of the thirty-story Sherman Building. The only thing residing in the top floor now, however, was this...well, *damn big lizard*, Elova thought with a scowl.

"Enormous," said Colin helpfully, giving one huge claw an experimental kick.

"Yes, I can see that," Elova said, glaring at her secretary hard enough to melt his nerdy little glasses. "But how did it get here?"

"Well, it flew," said Colin, indicating the wings now covered with glass from what used to be the south wall of the office.

Elova closed her eyes, took a deep breath, and smoothed a loose strand of blonde hair back into her ponytail. *Count to ten,* she thought, remembering her anger management classes. Opening one eye to peer at Colin, she gritted her teeth. *Better make it twenty.*

She made it to five before a hesitant voice called from the stairwell.

"Anyone alive up here?"

"Damn!" Elova turned and stomped toward the voice,

giving the wickedly-clawed back foot of the...*thing* a wide berth.

Henry Sheldon, evening security guard at the Sherman Building, stood panting in the stairwell doorway. His round, pasty face was red and sweat poured from his receding hairline as he stepped into the corridor. Elova stalked through the cascades of dust falling from the ceiling to stand in front of him.

"Bit late, aren't you?"

"Had to...use the...stairs," he wheezed, leaning on the wall for support. "From the...twenty-ninth. Elevator's out."

"You could use the exercise," Elova snapped, whirling on her heel. "Go downstairs and call the cops...if they'll respond. You're up to what, six false alarms? On second thought, ask someone in one of the offices to call for you."

"No one left 'cept you," Henry puffed, ignoring her bait as he followed her. "You're the only one works late in this buil – *Whoa!*"

They'd reached the end of the wall separating the hallway and elevators from the main floor...and the huge reptile. Elova turned in time to see Henry's considerable backside disappearing back the way they'd come.

"Now where's Henry off to?" asked Colin, snapping pictures with the one camera they'd been able to dig out of the debris.

"To find something to hide under would be my guess," Elova said. "Look, I need you to go find a working phone and call...someone."

"Who?" Colin cocked his head like a dog when he was confused, a habit Elova found endlessly irritating.

"Animal Control," she said with an evil grin. "Who else?"

Colin glanced doubtfully at the gargantuan lizard and handed the camera to Elova.

"'K, but I don't think they've got a truck big enough for this."

Elova was about to make a scathing reply when she noticed movement over Colin's shoulder. She stared hard at the dragon's head. Nothing happened. Shrugging, she started to turn away, intending to take pictures of the rear portion of the creature. Movement caught the corner of her eye again, and she whirled in time to catch a twitching around the huge mouth.

"Boss?"

"Colin," she muttered, reaching for his shoulder, "get behind me. Now."

Eyes wide behind his thick glasses, Colin complied. Elova heard him gasp when he turned around, but her attention was riveted on the reptile.

One huge eye twitched, then slid open. Air rumbled through the beast's chest as it drew a mighty breath and then –

Fire blasted from its nose as the creature sneezed. Elova and Colin ducked to avoid a wing as it tried to stretch in the confined space. The animal drew its sprawled back legs underneath itself and heaved upward, shaking plaster and glass from its back like a dog shaking water. Elova jerked Colin under a desk as shards careened past their heads.

A low growl rose through a long neck, and the dragon hurled the desk aside. Elova found herself staring up into a narrowed golden eye roughly the size of her head.

"Who...are...you?" The creature's voice was raspy and menacing.

Its *voice?*

Recovering quickly from the shock, Elova stood up, shoving Colin away when he hugged her leg and whimpered. Drawing herself to her full five feet six inches, she met the creature's glare with one of her own.

"My name is Elova Hunter and you've just destroyed my office. What have you to say for yourself?"

The lizard snorted, blowing an unpleasant odor of smoke and cooked meat into Elova's face.

"I am Char. I do not know you, but you will be sorry for bringing me here, Heeluva. I know this is not my world. It tastes wrong. You used magic to bring me here. Wizardry against a dragon is an offense punishable by death."

"Wizardry? Dragons?" Elova's eyes narrowed as she took in the blackened wall where the creature's sneeze had burned it, then the huge wings curled against its body.

Well, why not believe it? After all, there's a talking lizard *in the office!*

"I didn't bring you here," she said, beginning to pace. "And the name's Elova, not Heeluva. Not so long on the 'e', more 'o'." She glared at Colin as he sidled along the wall toward the staircase. "You! Make yourself useful and find a recorder. And get Henry up here so he can give his statement. I want all witnesses questioned."

"Witnesses?" Colin gaped at her. "You're going to investigate..." He swept an arm around, indicating the dragon. "This?"

"What would you like me to do, turn it over to city P.D.? Ha!" She whirled to face the ragged hole in the southern wall. "They'll botch it like they do everything else. It's been twenty minutes and they aren't here yet!"

As if on cue, sirens wailed in the distance. Elova crimped her mouth in annoyance as she turned to face the dragon. It regarded her with a sort of hungry curiosity, which she found a bit unnerving.

"All right, I'll take your case," she said. "But it's going to cost you. I have to replace my office, deal with wizards and dragons and who knows what other nonsense, and..."

The great head swiveled around to peer at her with narrowed eyes. "Cost?"

"Yes, cost! You know, money. Dollars, yen, pesos, euros?" She waited expectantly for recognition from the dragon, but it merely cocked its head to the side, reminding her of Colin.

She had a burst of inspiration. "Gold?" she asked.

"Ah," the dragon said, settling back on its haunches. "Why didn't you say so? I have quite a cache of gold. Had to roast countless knights and princes to get it all. You haven't lived until you've rolled in a nice big pile of gold before settling in for a nap."

"Um...groovy," Elova said, since the dragon seemed to expect a response. "Okay, we'll settle payment later. Also, there are a few rules. First, no more looking at me like I'm an after-dinner mint. Second, no flaming *anything* within a hundred feet of me. Agreed?"

"What makes you think I want you to...what was it you said? 'Take my case'?"

Elova rolled her eyes. "Because I have a ninety-nine percent success rate. I always find who I'm looking for. Do you want to catch the...er, wizard who did this to you or not?"

Char appeared to consider this for a moment, then skinned his lips back from large, sharp, stained teeth. "I accept your conditions."

Uncomfortable with the sudden change of heart, but imagining a huge pile of gold coins, Elova nodded. "Right. Now, let's get you out of my office. Are you too hurt to fly?"

"I am uninjured," the dragon said, sounding offended. He turned, twisting with surprising agility for his size, until he was facing the hole in the wall. His big wings stretched, knocking out the few remaining slivers of glass clinging to the window frames.

"Where shall I meet you?" he rumbled.

"North of town there's a field. Big trees all around it. I'll catch up with you there." Studying the dragon for a beat, Elova added, "Better fly high. Try to stay out of sight or we'll have every yahoo in town taking pot shots at you."

"What are 'pot shots'?"

"Never mind. Just try not to be seen."

"A dragon fears no one." With that, Char gathered himself and made an impressive leap out of the building. His massive body lurched up and out, wings unfurling majestically, scales glinting in the sun. He bared his teeth, flapped once – and dropped like a stone, disappearing below the hole in the wall.

Colin blushed at the stream of cursing that erupted from Elova.

She burst through the ground-floor doors just in time to hear someone say, "That's a damn big lizard."

"Great," she said, shoving through the crowd of police and firemen gathering on the sidewalk, "two idiots in one day."

"You forgot Henry," Colin panted at her elbow.

"Thanks for reminding me," she said, rolling her eyes and shouldering the last cop out of her way.

The dragon was sitting up, head weaving drunkenly, eyes crossed. The police car he'd landed on was flattened, the two cops who'd parked it staring in shock. Police, firemen, and bystanders were milling around, keeping their distance from the beast and discussing how best to deal with him. The popular opinion seemed to favor using him for target practice; several men had their guns already aimed.

Elova scanned the crowd, finally spotting the victim she

was looking for. "Hey! Adams! Over here. I hope your moron squad isn't planning to open fire on my client!"

George Adams, chief of police, turned a disturbing shade of red at the sound of Elova's voice. He turned from a young patrolman he'd been berating and reached for his pistol.

"Hunter, that thing came from your building. Looks like it came from your floor. I've been letting your vigilante crap slide for the last year, but now I think I'll just shoot you *and* that thing!"

"That 'thing' is my client," Elova snapped. She wanted to grab her pistol, too, but she wasn't, technically speaking, supposed to have the weapon until the anger management classes were over. Instead, she put her hands on her hips and faced off the stout chief. A rumbling voice, slightly slurred, made them both jump.

"What...'thing'...are you speaking of?"

Elova turned to find Char's eyes back to normal and his head steady. He glared at the crowd of humans now scattering to hide behind cars and fire trucks. Elova grinned when she noticed the chief trying to squeeze himself between a mailbox and a newspaper machine.

"No thing," she replied, striding confidently to the dragon's side. "His word, not mine." She narrowed her eyes, and her smile faded. "Hey, I thought you said you could fly?"

Char's wings drooped, and his head lowered until his nose almost touched the ground. "No magic here," he grumbled. "This is a nasty, smelly, people-infested place, Heeluva. The least you could do is have a little magic handy so a dragon can fly out of here, away from the stench."

"I'll make a note of it," she said, giving the dragon a critical eye. "How *are* we going to get you out of here?"

"I can help with that," said someone from behind her.

Whirling, Elova found herself face to face with the oddest man she'd ever seen. And she'd been to L.A., for cripe's sake!

He was tall and thin, and his dark brows nearly met in the middle of his forehead. Turquoise eyes blazed from a tangle of lines and wrinkles so deep they looked carved. A gold hoop earring the size of a saucer hung from his left ear. He wore a green sweatshirt emblazoned with the likeness of a cartoon cat. Baggy black jeans and white sneakers completed the outfit.

But it wasn't the clothes that made him so strange. It was the snakes.

He had them draped everywhere. A huge boa constrictor looped twice around his torso, draped around his neck, and rested its head on his shoulder. A green and gold snake that Elova couldn't identify twisted itself around his right arm and raised its beady gaze to hers. Other reptilian heads peeked out of various pockets.

"Wizard," Char rumbled.

The "wizard" smiled, and the transformation shocked Elova. Lines smoothed instead of deepening, making the man look at least twenty years younger. The constrictor caressed his cheek.

"Char! How nice to see you again. What are you doing here? This is no place for a dragon!"

"That's apparent," said Elova, recovering from her trance. "He didn't intend to be here, and I'm investigating the circumstances surrounding his forced departure from his world. If you don't mind my asking, sir – and I don't care if you do – who the hell are you?"

The wizard blinked at her, then glanced at Char. "You know this...er...lady?"

"Unfortunately."

"She's rather...verbiose."

"Never shuts up," Char agreed with a snort. "She is rude and ill-tempered, with the potential for violence." He made a huffing sound similar to a chuckle. "I am beginning to like her."

"Yes, I can tell," Elova snapped. "Now, if you don't mind, the cops are starting to get brave again, and most of them don't care for me as much as you do." She crossed her arms and stared at the wizard. "You didn't answer my question."

"I am Professor Merlin of the Royal Wizard College."

Adams, who had crawled out of his hiding spot, cleared his throat. He stood, feet apart and arms crossed over his chest, giving them his version of a stern police officer stare.

"Would someone please explain what the hell is going on here?" he asked in his grandest, most official voice. "Before I'm forced to conclude that this...creature is dangerous and have it disposed of?" He made what was no doubt supposed to be a threatening gesture toward his gun, but his arm went slack.

"What the-"

Merlin waved a hand in a bored sort of way, and the chief made an abrupt about-face.

"Everyone back to headquarters," he shouted. The words exploded from between his clenched teeth, as though the chief were trying to keep them from escaping. He stomped toward his car, picking his feet up too high and pumping his arms in a way that made him look like a poorly-handled marionette. Most of the crowd stood up from their hiding spots, mesmerized by their chief's strange antics.

"Now!" he thundered, eyes wide and face darkening to purple. Chaos filled the street as people scrambled for their vehicles, sirens blared to life, and tires squealed. A few moments later, Elova and Colin were alone with Char and Merlin.

"Wow!" breathed Colin as he pushed his glasses up on his nose. "How'd you do that?"

"A trick I picked up somewhere or other," Merlin said. "Now then...shall we retire to more appropriate surroundings?" Without waiting for an answer, he waved his hands.

Elova grabbed Colin's shoulder as the street and buildings began to swim and fade out of focus.

A few minutes later the world clarified again. Trees appeared against a brilliant blue sky, knee-length grass waved in the breeze, and bees droned among long-stemmed flowers. Elova turned all the way around, ending face-to-nose with Char. They were standing on a cliff, overlooking a wide valley. The trees stood well back from the cliff's end, but the grass and flowers flirted the edge.

"Where are we?" Elova asked. She cleared her throat to get rid of an annoying tremor. When she turned around, she noticed that the wizard was now wearing a deep violet cloak with "R.F." monogrammed on the left breast pocket. The boa was now the only snake visible.

"My dear," said Merlin with a grand sweep of his arm, "Welcome to Dragon's Landing." His movement caused the boa to slip. The snake constricted in an effort to keep its perch. Wheezing, eyes bulging and face red, Merlin pried the snake loose and repositioned it across his shoulders.

Elova's scowl returned. "How did we get here?"

"Easy," Colin said, eyes bright and eager. "It was magic, right, Merlin?"

"Hocus-pocus, m'boy." Merlin winked as if he were speaking to a young child instead of a man in his twenties.

"I feel my appetite coming back." Large golden eyes studied the three humans. Colin blanched and cowered behind Elova, who drew her pistol and glared at the dragon. He snorted and made that odd chuckling sound again.

"You little morsels really are amusing." He stretched, shook himself, and stepped to the edge of the cliff. Without further comment, he jumped, flapped his wings twice, and soared into the air.

Elova turned to glare at the wizard.

"If you brought us here," she said, "you could send a dragon across to our world, right?"

"Well, yes," said Merlin, "But any wizard could have."

Colin stared at Merlin with something akin to worship. "Are...are you *the* Merlin?"

With a sigh, the wizard plopped down on a nearby rock. "Why does everyone have to ask that? Why did I have to be named after the most famous coward of all time?" He sighed again.

"Coward?" Frowning, Colin sat nearby as Elova made a disgusted snort and began studying the ground along the treeline. The dragon circled overhead, disappearing now and then behind the clouds.

"Of course he was a coward!" Merlin's cheeks reddened and his eyes glittered. "Scared silly of dragons, he was. Nearly failed his apprenticeship – a dragon flew overhead just as he was supposed to conjure fire. Nearly burned the castle down!"

"But...I thought he was the greatest wizard of all time."

"Bah! The fool caught the first portal he could out of here. Found a nice, non-magic world where he could dazzle people. He was useless in this world."

"Merlin was a myth," Elova said, not looking up from her search. "A story, nothing more. Listen if you must, Colin, but he's feeding you a load of hogwash."

"I most certainly am not!" Merlin stood and pointed a long, bony finger at her. "Just what makes you think I am fabricating this story?"

"Okay, you asked for it." Elova stepped to Colin's side. "First, you get this funny twitch around your mouth every time someone calls you 'Merlin', like you're trying not to laugh. Second, and an obvious giveaway, the monogram on your cloak says 'R.F.', not 'M' for 'Merlin'. And third," she said, fixing him with a withering glare, "as a wizard, you're a suspect. So of course you'd tell us some fairy tale – to keep our minds off what we're supposed to be doing here."

"You're suggesting that I may have sent Char to your world? I wasn't even here! I was on vacation."

"Yes, in the same world that Char wound up in. Some coincidence, huh?"

"Now wait just a minute!" The faux Merlin smoothed his robe in an apparent attempt to look dignified. "I admit, I got a bit of humor at your expense with the Merlin story. My real name is Roferund Fink, and you'd lie about it, too. But no wizard from the College used magic against any dragon!"

"Roferund Fink?" Colin snorted. "Maybe I'll just keep calling you Merlin." He grinned at Elova when she snickered.

Fink's face darkened, and an unpleasant sneer twisted his lips. "What's funny?" he asked, glaring at Colin. "You believed every word I said, you little fool. We should all be laughing at you!"

Elova's smile vanished. In three long strides, she was an inch from the wizard, glaring up into his face.

"No one – *no one!* – calls Colin a fool but me! Understand, you lousy imposter?"

Fink's fury deflated, replaced by an uncertain little frown.

Colin tugged at Elova's arm. "Uh, Elova...it's okay, honest. I'm not upset. You don't want to get in trouble for defending me again, do you? You're almost through the anger management course."

Elova relaxed and nodded, though her eyes never left the wizard. "Mind your manners," she said in a quiet, strained voice.

"Er...of course," Fink said, taking a step back. "My apologies, m'boy. Got a bit worked up."

Colin nodded, but Elova kept watching the wizard. Her expression turned thoughtful.

"What do you know that you haven't told us?" she asked.

The wizard cleared his throat, looking uncomfortable. "Well...er...what do you mean?"

"Earlier, you said no wizard from your college used magic against a dragon. What about a wizard not from your college?"

Merlin stared down at his feet, shifting uncomfortably. He was quiet for several moments. Taking a deep breath, he raised his head to look at Char gliding high overhead.

"Cornelius," he said, sounding sad. "My nephew. He was expelled two weeks ago because of a fiasco with a flying carpet. Char was the one who found him and exposed his mischief to the elders at the college."

"Why didn't you tell us this before?"

"Well, if it was your nephew, would you proclaim it from the rooftops?" Merlin's shoulders sagged. "I'm not proud of him. Can you imagine how humiliating it is for a professor to have his own nephew thrown out of school?"

"I'm sorry to have disappointed you, *Professor.*"

Elova turned with the others to see the newcomer.

He bore a strong resemblance to his uncle, without the wrinkles on his face. He took a step toward Fink, eyes narrowed.

"I should have known you would ruin things," he said through gritted teeth. "You and your soft spot for those nasty beasts."

"Cornelius," Fink began.

"I'm not finished speaking!" Cornelius shouted. He pointed a finger at his uncle, who made a strangled noise and stiffened. Whirling, the angry nephew glared at Elova and Colin. "Stay out of this and you won't get hurt." He turned back to stand nose-to-nose with Fink's frozen form.

"For once you're going to listen to me," Cornelius hissed.

With the two wizards otherwise occupied, Elova moved unnoticed back to Colin's side. "Go stand near the edge of the cliff," she whispered, giving him a nudge in that direction.

"What about Fink?" Colin breathed.

"Don't worry about him. Just do as I ask."

Without another word, Colin walked toward the cliff's edge. His movement caught the new wizard's attention.

"You there! Where do you think you're going?"

"Umm...stretching my legs?"

"Get back over here!"

"I...need to whizz."

"Whizz?" Cornelius tossed Elova a confused glance. She shrugged.

"You can...'whizz'...later," the wizard said, moving to follow Colin.

"Can't wait that long," Colin said, and took two more steps.

Elova could have kissed him. The wizard kept following him, closer to the edge of the cliff and into a wide bare spot. His shimmering cloak would be easily visible.

She let him get within three strides of Colin, then put two fingers in her mouth and blew a piercing whistle. Cornelius whirled, eyes narrowed in fury. One hand came up to point at her, and Elova gritted her teeth against whatever torture he was about to inflict.

With a flash of glittering scales and a blast of churning air, Char swooped low across the cliff. Flames engulfed the wayward wizard. Huge jaws snapped, wings beat the air, and the dragon and wizard both disappeared.

"Ah, poor boy," Merlin said, freed from his paralysis.

Elova wasn't listening. She ran toward the edge of the cliff, where Colin had been a moment ago. He had disappeared when Char blasted through.

Throwing herself on her belly at the edge of the drop, Elova peered over. Two feet below, Colin gripped a small outcropping.

"Um...little help?" he said.

Elova grinned and reached out a hand.

"No, dammit, I said I wanted the desk facing *toward* the windows!" Elova glared at the workers as they made their final adjustments to her new office. Her new, *first floor* office.

"Hunter! I know you're in there! We need to talk."

Colin poked his head from his office next door. "Want me to get rid of him, boss?"

"Nah." Elova headed outside. Adams no longer caused her blood to boil. Not much did these days, she mused as she opened the door and smiled at the red-faced chief.

Rolling in a pile of gold every night before bed can do wonders, she thought with a grin.

That Old Silent Apology

Tony Lee Healey.

For B. C. : I'm sorry that I never said goodbye.

I lit a Camel, and offered the packet to Jimmy with a smile.

He gave me the finger and called me a shit. I sniggered; he'd quit smoking for three months now and not slipped once. I was in awe of him for that.

"So, how d'you think he'll do?" Jimmy asked me beneath the backbeat of Leann Rhymes and an old string guitar playing behind the bar counter, "He is getting on, you know."

We were in the sports bar across the road from the large dome where the fight between The Python and The Tornado; the fight that would decide if Python kept his title or not; was due to take place.

He sipped at the Bud perspiring with cold sweat in his hands and I drew from my smoke.

"*Old* in terms of *boxing*, you mean. Listen, thirty-six isn't exactly over the hill." I said. A red light flickered at the corner of my eyes, and the singing of some drunk biker-types at a table in the far corner drummed at my ears.

"I know that. But his days of holding the title aren't growing longer, my friend; they're just getting shorter. One day he *is* gonna lose it."

He did not grin at that remark as I had expected. Instead he appeared sincere.

A little sad, maybe.

"I know it." It was all I could say, and the words fell bitter from my mouth.

Perhaps it was the taste of the Camels, and not that all-too-real flavour of something drawing to a close. Perhaps... perhaps not. I had tasted it before.

I looked at my watch, and saw we were late. I dropped my smoke onto the rough tile floor and stamped it out with the shiny heel of my boot.

"Is it time already?"

I nodded.

Jimmy quickly downed the rest of what was left of his Bud in one long swallow and the two of us stood. We got our coats on. Some of the other patrons at the bar were moving too as they realised what the time was.

"Yeah," I said. "I guess we'll see at least one big hundred-and-eighty pound pussy get whipped tonight, whichever way it turns right?"

We left in a hurry and met the winter's bitter cold outside, across the street to the domed building that hid the lying fate of Bill "the Python" Leonard. We left Leann Rhymes and her stupid guitar behind.

***

"I don't fuckin' care! You know what? Go to hell; I'll never talk to you again!"

(He never did)

"Please...!"

(I pleaded)

"Sorry..."

(I thought to myself but never said)

Silence as he left, slamming the door behind him, never to return. Silence as the room is more empty than before. *And it* was *empty.* It had been getting that way for a long, long, time.

Silence, as I sat on my haunches weeping at my inability to sound my love for somebody, or my apologies sometimes for getting things wrong and fucking them up.

***

"It's not over yet I think," Jimmy whispered to me. I almost believed him, though my feeling of sinking was beginning to grow all the more heavy with every passing second.

The count was on. The hand of the referee slapping down on the canvas, and the cracked, wind-whipped howl of his old voice was like the ticking from the clock of inevitability to my ears.

"Eight!... Seven!... Six.! ...Five!......." and there it paused.

Below us, in the pit where the ring sat a bright white square, the Python began to move. His forearms quivered as the last buds of his energy were being exerted into getting himself back up. A feeling of nausea hit me.

The heavyweight champion of the world managed to lift himself to his knees. He paused there, his head lowered, his chest visibly pulling at the air like the engine of some gigantic machine plugging at heavily needed fuel.

His nose ran with blood and with snot, and both his eyes were swollen as blown plums. He wiped his beaten and split mouth with one glove, and with other grasped hold of the rope at the side of ring. The crowd cheered as he hauled himself upwards off of his knees and stood, leaning forward across the ropes. His pink mouth guard dropped from his mouth and a string of crystal saliva hung there in its place.

We watched. We held our breaths collectively; all together as one.

I realised that Jimmy was pinching my right arm without knowing it, and that it hurt. I didn't bother to ease myself out of his grip. The pain seemed right somehow.

Down in the ring, Tinto the Tornado paced backwards and forwards like a heated bull; his nose broken, one cheek the bruised colour of an aubergine; his defeat of Bill "the Python" Leonard, and his taking of the mans title, nearly assured.

The Python stayed the same, unmoving other than the up and down of his rib cage, and the dripping of sweat from his bald forehead.

Someone in the back row to the east side yelled out into the thick and extravagant darkness of silence that had descended upon us all.

I could not see who it was. Just one more face; the same as all of ours.

"Bite dat Fucker Python! Bite dat Fucker, and you let dat poison flow!" the voice was shrill, and a little female. It may have been a woman.

Everything slowed.

Python's head rose, and out of his bleary eye sight and the strong pour of the spotlights, he peered out to the audience; he seemed to squint, searching for something. It looked to me as though he saw something that was not there, and that it was telling him what to do next. He shook his head, either saying No, or assimilating whatever had been told to him, and shaking his head from the sheer surprise of it.

Then his head began to turn in my direction, and he looked further up.

He looked at me. My throat went dry, my balls were

sucked upward into my body, and everything stopped. His eyes burned like cold pearls against the backdrop of the silky silence, and when I blinked, the connection was gone. We were separate. He was turning then.

Turning and turning, the audience cheering and shouting for him; his great arms moving up and down, conducting the chorus of support from them as if it were a weapon from God. Tinto stood wide-eyed and in shock.

As if he had gained energy from his supporters, Python then straightened back out like a length of rubber suddenly allowed to ease back to its original shape. He inhaled, held the breath in his lungs for a moment, and then when he exhaled it came not as an empty breath, but as a full roar. A battle cry.

The cheering was madness. Python would give his all this time around, at least, if not ever again. He stood tall.

Like a Mexican Wave, we all shivered.

Python turned to face the Tornado, and the referee called the for the bell.

The bell sounded.

There was a brief moment of silent communication between the two fighters as they stared across the expanse of ring space that sat between them. And then Tinto the Tornado lunged forward.

The Python side-stepped out of the way at the last second, seemingly hitting his last and most agile wing ever. The Tornado flew forward into the wires. He bounced back, staggered, and turned to his left. Python swung his entire body into right-hook, and landed it perfectly on Tinto's left jaw.

Snap.

The Tornado spun, and then fell. Blood flew from what seemed his entire face as his head smacked against the canvas in a loud and hollow thump. Medical teams rushed up to the stage, over the ropes, and to Tornado's side. The referee was on the floor, giving him the count.

Meanwhile, Python took his belt, and held it high. Flashbulbs went off, and he grinned through a smile that showed some teeth missing, and a mouthful of blood.

But then Python staggered backwards. He held his head clumsily with his two gloved hands, and then emitted a terrible scream.

I watched in horror as he toppled forward then, and hit the floor. Still.

I broke free from Jimmy's grip and sat down without noticing. I stared in utter disbelief at the butt of a man in front of me as he stood watching the stage along with 19,999 others just like him. In fact there were the butts of men all around me, and in a way I was thankful that I had put myself completely out of sight of the stage.

My hands were slumped at my sides, and I sat in cold disbelief.

Silence rang in my ears, and then; crackling and distant, the sound of the commentator announcing that my brother Bill Leonard, the Python, the heavyweight boxing champion, was dead.

I looked at my watch for some unknown reason, and saw that its ticking had slowed. The voice of the commentator again from the speakers, said gravely and with some heartfelt despair that only I could feel with real truth, *"Sorry."*

That bitter Camel taste returned to my mouth; Jimmy sat down and put his arm about me, telling me that it would all be okay, but I did not notice for some while; and when I did it was like I couldn't understand English anymore. I

sat staring at the butt of a stranger, the loud and thunder-
ous sound of the barbarian horde, and could only think of
what a crazy fucked up thing the word sorry could be; and
how hard it could be, sometimes, to say it to the right people.

The bell sounded.

How I Learned How To Tango In Five Easy Steps

Mark Carpenter

I remember my first day of kindergarten. My mom takes me into this room full of strangers... and then leaves. I cry. I bawl my eyes out.

I can remember the teacher having us all sit together in a half-circle to sing. I hate singing, so I sit there and sulk.

I see so many kids that love to sing and dance. I don't recall ever doing either as a child. I was just too damn embarrassed.

One day while I'm in the fourth grade, the powers that be have all of us kids go down to see the music teacher so she can determine if we will be chosen for chorus class or not. Now I have absolutely no interest in being in the chorus, but that little fact doesn't seem to concern anyone.

So I sit there in line as the children ahead of me go in

behind closed doors and then come back out a few minutes later. They appear unharmed, but this does little to convince me that I'll be so lucky. I'm going to have to sing. *In front of someone.* This is not good. Not good at all.

My turn comes and I'm led into the office of the music teacher. I can't remember the details, but I do remember the impression of being expected to sing, whether I want to or not. I remember the words croaking haltingly out of my throat as I stand there before her desk with tears in my eyes.

"Mortified" does not even begin to express how I feel at this moment. I want to die. I want others to die. I want to inflict severe bodily harm. Most of all I just don't want to be singing. This does little to improve my withdrawn nature, as I'm sure you can imagine.

Years go by, and I never take a step that even resembles dance. When expected to sing, I hum, but only if in a group where my noise will be drowned out.

In high school I have only a few friends. I don't even really fit in with the brainy geeks. I'm one of those misfits; one of the rejects. You know, the type that gets "does not fully apply himself" noted on his report card even more often than "runs with scissors". For my group, our grades do not report how smart we are, but merely how interesting we happen to find our classes.

I feel so alone. I so desperately want to take part in life. I feel like so much is happening that is passing me by. I want to join in, but I don't know how.

Just having a girl say "hi" to me is enough for me to withdraw into my shell and start talking a mile-a-minute about some inane thing that only I seem to be interested in.

The talking is a shield, you see. As long as I talk, I can focus; I can focus on that thing which so interests me that I can forget about what I fool am. As long as I'm talking, I can feel like I'm not really there.

That can last only so long until there is no one left around willing to listen.

Things don't change much after high school. Now I'm out on my own (relatively speaking) and sharing an apartment with a high school buddy. I'm still feeling very much alone except for my few friends, my lifelines.

There's still no girl. Why can't I find someone? Why can't I find someone I can love and who will love me? Is it really supposed to be this hard? I see so many couples, so many happy people. How the hell? How the hell do they do it? I want to know! Why is this is so... damn... hard?!

I don't find the answer to that for several more years, but the seed has been planted. The journey begins with a night of desperate boredom watching late-night television. It begins with, of all things, an infomercial.

***

This is pathetic. I can't believe I'm watching this. I hate infomercials. I am such a loser.

Why aren't I reading, or playing a video-game, or visiting a BBS?

Why aren't I in bed?

Maybe it's because of that prayer I learned as a kid. You know, the one that starts "If I should die before I wake..."? Very comforting, that one.

Yeah...

Take a highly imaginative kid with obsessive tendencies and a fear of the dark, and then plant the suggestion that he might not live to see the morning sunrise.

Okay, so I don't see the sunrise anyway, if I have any kind of say in the matter, but you get the idea.

My first bedroom: I have a window near my bed. With curtains. God I hate those curtains. Oh, the color is fine: a nice navy blue; no stinky plaid patterns or anything. That isn't the reason I hate them. I hate them because they have pleats.

"Now, what's wrong with pleats," you may be asking yourself. There's nothing to get excited about, right?

That's during the day. At night is a different story altogether.

At night, they become the Pleats of Doom$_{TM}$.

When I get into bed (after many futile attempts to stay up "for just a little bit longer"), there is just enough light in the room to see the curtains hanging above me and to the side a little. I make sure they aren't directly over my head, but they are still over my bed.

I can see the curtains... but I can't see *inside* them.

At this point, The Pleats of Doom™ become portals to the underworld. They harbor all sorts of nasty things: long, slithery centipedes that leave trails of acidic slime; huge spiders with barbed legs and venom dripping from their fangs; little people...

Yeah, little people; like in *Gulliver's Travels*; carrying sharp pointy things. I can see them in my mind's eye repelling down out of those Caves like a SWAT team from the bad section of Hell and landing on my bed, murder in their eyes...

I hate those curtains.

I sleep with my covers tucked in all around me. I lift my legs so that my blanket curls under my feet when I set them back down, and then I roll side to side a little so that I end up truly tucked in. My blanket gets pulled up close around my neck, too. I'd sleep with it over my head, but that would mean I couldn't see if anything was approaching.

As an adult, it wasn't until a couple years ago that I stopped tucking the blanket up under my feet.

Summer was always torture. Summer meant I'd have to choose between exposing myself and sweating like a pig. I've always wanted at least something covering me, even if it's just a thin sheet, but there's nothing like a nice thick blanket.

As I listen to the deep baritone that is emitted from the glowing box before me, there's another reason I don't want to go to bed, and I think it might be somewhat related to that prayer.

I'm afraid that if I "switch off", I won't be able to turn back on again.

Letterman is long over and Bob Costas has finished interviewing his latest guest on *Later*, so here I am stuck watching this giant in a suit tell me my life could be different.

Yeah, right.

I've seen him before. I've caught a few minutes here and there and have always switched away. There's a reason.

I hate infomercials.

Not so much because they annoy me in and of themselves (which they do), but because if I don't change the channel in a hurry, I'll get hypnotized by the damn things and then spend the next half-hour staring at the screen like a brainless dolt.

I feel so used.

But, I don't try to switch away; not this time.

Something he's said has grabbed my attention, something that rings home with me.
He's starting to make sense.

Ohdeargodno! Not that! It's an infomercial, for Christ's sake! This guy's a charlatan, right?

Right?

The half-hour is over and I sit there staring at the screen. I feel strange. I feel tingly. Instead of used, I feel enthused.

I want those tapes.

Okay, I'm not spending that kind of money on something that's advertised on late night TV. No way, no how.

But he did make sense.

Damn.

A thought strikes me, and I smile. I feel both calm and excited at the same time, as I make my way to bed.

I have a plan!

***

I am standing at the entrance of Walden Books in Eastview Mall.

The Gates of Heaven.

It's nowhere near the size of the super-stores we have around nowadays, like Borders and Barnes and Noble. No matter. They have books I haven't read yet. That's good enough for me.

To this day, the words "Walden Books" induce a smile infused with fond memories. I love to read, you see. I also have this strange compulsion to own the books I read. I've taken a few books out of the library, and I've borrowed one here and there from friends, but by and large, I own what I read.

I own a lot of books.

Walden Books has a lot of my money. It was a happy day when they came out with their frequent-buyers-club card.

I enter and head for the "Self Improvement" section looking down at the piece of paper in my hand. There is a name written on it:

"Anthony Robbins"

And below that...

"Awaken the Giant Within"

I don't really need to look at the paper. I know what it says. I wrote it. But that's another story.

I find the book on the shelf and pick it up. It's a hardcover. Drat. $22. Well, it's cheaper than the tapes...

There's an earlier book by him there also. It's in paperback and therefore cheaper.

Yeah, but it's also older. The newer one would be the most up-to-date.

Whatever that means.

Flipping through the book, I find a printed card. It has the name of a local Anthony Robbins and Associates franchise. Hm... That didn't come from the publisher. Someone must have come in and tucked it in there.

Of course, I have to look and see if the other books have the cards in them, too...

Aw, what the heck. I decide to take it as a sign and buy the book.

I head home, wondering if I just blew twenty-plus clams on snake oil.

(Here's an example of just how weird my life has gotten: Just a few hours before writing this, I discovered that a friend I recently made is probably the very person that put that card in the book I bought a decade ago. *cue spooky music*)

***

I'm in my element. I'm reading!

While don't tend to do well in classes, especially the ones where I'm expected to just sit and listen, I do excel at self-learning.

Give me access to a few books, or now an Internet connection, and I'll have working knowledge on a subject in a very short time.

If I have an interest in it, that is.

I became interested in computers when my dad bought the family and Apple][e the one summer while I was in junior high. I went to town learning everything I could about it. I taught myself BASIC, played with Assembly Language for a week or two, then got bored and went on to Pascal.

Things kind of blossomed from there.

More than fifteen years after I did my fiddling with Assembly, I was asked to look at some code intended for a device that exposes digital images back onto film. (They used the resulting production model in the making of the movie *Batman Forever*.) Needless to say, I was a little rusty.

But I did find the bug.

I've done the same kind of thing with auto-mechanics and photography.

Photography is an interesting example. I've been into making pictures for a several years now, and have been published and gained a little recognition. I've found classes that have interested me and books that have contained knowledge that is new to me.

Until now.

There's still plenty of book knowledge out there for me to learn, but I'm not applying everything I already know, so reading another book isn't going to help me right now. For me to get better, I need to go out and shoot some more pictures. A lot of them.

I need practice.

This leads me to the bane of my existence: practicing sucks.

I'll repeat that. There's going to be a quiz later.

Practicing sucks.

Or maybe I should say, I suck at practicing. At any rate, I do not like it, and I don't end up doing it.

I played trumpet for five years while I was in school. I've always wanted to be able to play a musical instrument well. Mind you, I said "well". I can do without the long part where you sound like a wounded elephant that precedes it.

Even after five years, I stink. I don't mean, "Was that the dog?" I'm talking the dog is already dead and everyone that's left conscious is running for the exits.

My poor music teacher: He asks me, "Did you practice this week?"
"Um, yeah."
"How long."
"Ten minutes… on Tuesday, I think."

About four years ago, I buy a cornet off of e-Bay. I really want to be able to play an instrument. Maybe if I get really focused I can manage to swing it before lose interest again. I buy the cornet. I buy a really cool mute that makes it difficult to hear the instrument even in the next room, but it has the stethoscope attachment on the end so that the player can hear the horn almost as if there was no mute in. I get it cleaned and start playing around with the scales that I can remember. I order a lesson kit from on-line.

While waiting for it to arrive, I pull the instrument out a few times to play through the scales. I have somewhat of an embouchure even after all these years, but I still suck. Of course I do.

Somewhere along the line, the cornet case becomes a piece of furniture.

I pulled it out a few weeks ago, first time this year, to show a friend the "really cool mute".

This happens with my martial arts and meditative training, too. I have a fair amount of book knowledge about the various styles and their strengths and weaknesses, their teachings and philosophies. But have lasted less than a year at everything I've taken. Sometimes much less.

Okay, so I'm reading. I'm happy! This is a really good idea. I can decide if I want to spend the cash on the tapes based upon how helpful the book turns out to be. If it stinks... well, then I'm out less than $25 and a little bit of time.

I'm breezing along, absorbing what he's written and liking it! He's making a lot of sense.

Wow.

And then it happens. The part we all loathe and hate.

Yes… An exercise.

And not just any exercise. This one requires you to think. This isn't "add 2 + 2", it's "Make a list of your Disempowering Beliefs and of your Empowering Beliefs." Great. I've got to go digging in the muck. And he wants me to spend at least ten minutes on them? Uh, riiiight. I'll come back to that later. I'd much rather read.

In the first line on the next page, he asks if we really did it.

"Uh, no."

It's a real testament to the power of a Catholic upbringing that I actually feel immense guilt over this.

I think about it a minute. I bought this book for a reason. If I want to get something out of it, I'd better play along.

I do the exercise.

Okay, I'm not happy about it, I grit my teeth, I wrack my brains, but I come up with the two lists.

I go on. He starts talking about the lists. I now have something to refer to: actual examples. Okay, I'm glad I did it. In fact, I do every single one of the exercises in the book as I come to them.

This is no small feat, let me tell you, but well worth it. I actually notice some small changes in how I do things; how I think about things. I've begun to practice something new. Little do I realize just how long the practicing is going to go on for.

I pick up the card that I found in the book, the one with the local franchise's phone number on it.

Normally, I would never make the call. I can ask things like "How late are you open?" because the answer is going to fall into a known set of parameters. I won't have to think on my feet. I can ask, "Do you have [insert item here] in stock?" because I know the answer will be yes, no, or perhaps "would you like that in mauve or chartreuse?"

For this call, after my opening line, anything's game.

I'm terrified.

I think about what I learned from the book. I think about what the exercises taught me. I ask myself if I'm going to quit now.

I pick up the phone...

I slam it back down again. What in the blue blazes am I doing? There's going to be a real person on the other end of that line! A person with... *questions*. Good lord, what was I thinking?

I look at the book...

Oh, hell.
I pick up the phone.
I dial.

"Anthony Robbins and Associates."

"Hi, um.... I'd like to... I mean... What do... um..."

…

"Canyousendmesomeinformationaboutwhatyoudo?"

***

It's a Friday night and I am on my way to an office park on the other side of the city. Imagine that. It's a Friday that I'm not spending at home. Not that I have a date or anything...

I look down again at the piece of paper in my hand. I know what's written on it. I was the one that wrote it. It's an address.

I look again.

For some reason the idea of driving past my destination and having to turn around always fills me with a panic. I don't know why. Maybe it has something to do with getting it right the first time. Maybe I'm just afraid that people will notice and laugh.

I didn't say it made any sense.

I'm on my way to a three-day workshop at the Anthony Robbins and Associates franchise I had called earlier.

Why am I doing this?
Oh yeah, self-improvement.

That term always makes me think of big, warehouse-sized stores with various Borg-like body enhancements on the shelves and in bins. Need a new attitude? Buy this new chip, only $29.95! I imagine shows like *This Old Body* where a bearded man in a surgeon's gown shows us how to install a new titanium-alloy femur for enhanced durability. Don't forget the high-tensile sinews!

I'd use the term self-discovery, but that involves a whole other set of image.

After reading the book, I felt that there was enough to all this stuff that I wanted to learn more. The tapes would have been nice, but I wanted something hands-on. This was to be three days: Friday evening, all day Saturday, and most of Sunday.

There was no way I could afford this.

I talked to my parents about it. They had put a chunk of change towards both of my younger brothers' schooling, but not me. I had left in the third quarter. Somehow I thought college was going to be different from high school. Oh it was, but not in the way that was important. That's another story, entirely.

So they agreed to foot the bill. I'm not sure what they thought about it all, really, as I was a bit too excited to notice, but they said that if I felt that it would help me in life, they would do what they could.

'Gads, but I love my parents.

So I'm in the parking lot, looking around for the screaming maniacs. You know the ones: the people you see in the audience on TV, jumping up and down, waving and smiling like they've all just won the lottery. There's something else I should mention: Tony isn't going to be here. That's right, it's not a live workshop. It's on video-tape. The people who own the franchise are going to show it and act as facilitators.

I am such a loser.

I get out of the car and head inside. As I sign in, I notice a few others who came in before me. No manic grins. No overenthusiastic handshakes. No high-fives, even, though I suspect those will come later.

Several people are in business attire. There's a woman who's in that weird age bracket that is noticeably older than I am, but younger than my mom. She looks like a model. That's all a good sign. No obvious losers.

Well, except for me.

I find a place to sit where I hope I won't be noticed. It doesn't work. I am approached by a rather confident looking woman who... tells me that there is some fruit and light snacks in the other room if I would like some before we get started.

Right. Food. Good.

After the snack, we go into a room with a bunch of chairs and a large television. We are going to be watching that box of glowing light a great deal this weekend, but I had no idea how many other things we were going to be doing. There are going to be exercises. There are going to be interactions. Oh yes, with people. We are going to... share.

Kill me now. Please.

I am terrified. Yet at the same time, I know that this is something, well, special. As hokey and contrived as it looks on the surface, I've found something that makes a difference. I've felt it already; that's why I'm here. It was just a taste, but enough to know. And now I want more. Little do I know just how extensive the terrors that await me are. If I did, I'd ask for a refund right then and there.

***

Well whaddaya know.
She is a model.

And I have made a new friend.

I make several friends while I'm here, but she is the only one I see again on the "outside", at least to any degree. Over the next couple of years we get together every so often to talk, exchange tapes, give each other support… We write a lot. I haven't seen her in a long time now, though. I wonder what she is doing now.

It's amazing how fast you can get close to people when you let your guard down and share all the nasty little secrets you usually keep hidden. We all did that. Funny, none of us ran screaming from the room when confronted with the horrors of another's psyche. What we found was kinship.

That doesn't mean it was easy.

A lot of the details are clouded by time at this point, but I will share what I remember. We watch Tony on the monitor, then we break up into pairs, or sometimes groups, and work on what we had just been taught with the help of the facilitators. She and I pair up early on. We pretty much became partners after that.

One of the things we do is take turns feeling an emotion, and letting ourselves express it with our body. The other person then matches the first person's body language as closely as they can: posture, breathing, all that. The imitator then gets a very good idea of what the first person is feeling.
Talk about intimacy...

We split into medium-sized groups. They have us all write down ten words or ideas that we use to define love. We count how many items make it onto everyone's list. I think the group with the most has three. The point is, if we don't all agree on the definition of something as simple universal as love, how can we assume that everyone will use a certain word the same way as you do. We talk about perception and communication.

We break boards.

I know: technically it's no big deal, most people can, but that's different from actually doing it.

The weekend is packed with learning about new ways to look at the world and at ourselves. But not just looking; we lean how to change things. You often wonder, with things like this, just how long the change will last. How long does the average New Year's resolution hold out before it is deemed "not worth it"? But this stuff can be permanent. No shittin'. If you let it, this stuff sticks. But you have to really want it.

It's mid-day Sunday, and we are all a little bit high from all the work we've been doing. We've been through a lot; we've leaned a lot. Now comes the time that we bring it all together. It's time for the big "Whammo!"

This is going to be the longest stretch of watching the Big Man on the screen out of the entire weekend. The details that I remember won't mean much without the whole picture, but I will say he leads us through one hell of an experience. We strip away our limiting beliefs, we take our most painful memories and discharge them, ground them, so that they no longer have a hold on us

You know those smiling idiots you see on the infomercial? The ones jumping up and down, pumping their hands, and acting like... well, you know who I mean.
That's us.

I know why they are doing that, now. They haven't suddenly lost their minds.
They've finally found them.

I have never felt so pumped, so juiced, and so capable of taking on anything the word has to throw at me; AND I feel like I can go out and DO anything. The world is at my fingertips.
And that's when he has us implant the anchor. It still works, you know, ten years later. Hell, I even think about rubbing my hands together and I can feel the rush building.
We come down off of the high. But instead of falling into a slump, we are all standing there with big smiles and looks of awe on our faces. They begin to play the Pointer Sisters' I'm So Excited as we all stand in a circle.

We begin to dance.

I begin to dance. No shame. I want to. I feel too good not to.

We begin to sing.

I begin to...
Sing.

Holy
Fucking
Shit

I don't mean humming. I don't mean mumbling. I don't even mean trying to make sure my voice isn't louder than my neighbor's.

I mean I SING.

My god, I had no idea it could feel so good.
We part ways. She and I exchange contact info.

And this is only the beginning.

There's still a long, hard, and very amazing road ahead for me. Not everything we did that weekend stuck, but a lot did. I still had a lot of self confidence issues to work through, among others. Some remain to this day. But I'm working on them. I'm still making progress.

One of the biggies that sticks, the one that sets the stage for everything else that follows, is how I turn from a pessimist into an optimist.

I have two ways of visualizing this: One is to imagine one of those tiny micro-switches clicking. The feeling is that subtle.

The other is to imagine one of those big knife switches being slamming down with so much juice flowing through it the contacts weld shut in the new position. The effect is that profound.

There's a definition of depression that I have always found interesting: it's feeling sad about feeling sad. Here's how it is for me. When I'm just "sad", it doesn't feel like my natural state. I know it's going to be temporary. That doesn't mean it isn't painful, but it does mean that I know that there's and end to it, somewhere.

When I'm depressed, I see no end. Even worse, it feels... right; like this is how I'm supposed to feel. It's comfortable. I don't mean there's no pain, I mean that it's familiar.

To me depression feels like I slip into another place, a smaller place. Nothing can live there, including me.

What I discovered several weeks later, as I hit another downward swing in the everlasting cycle of life, was that I was no longer allowed in. The way was blocked, sealed, warded... Actually, I could enter for a moment, but I would be summarily thrown right back out.

Something had happened.

I would feel the start of it: the closing in; the sinking, shrinking; the cold; the dark. And then I would find myself saying, "I don't need to feel like this." It's the strangest thing.

I would then choose not to feel that way. I would feel myself lift out of it. I would still feel hurt, sad, pained... but I never again sank back into that deep, dank swap. It's like someone had lain down one of those clear pool covers over the top. I could drop in, but the cover kept me from sinking too far and would pop me back to the surface.

I can say with confidence that it isn't just me thinking feel-good thoughts and simply suppressing everything. I've made a lot of progress over the years "digging in the dirt". The real test came three years ago when I was diagnosed with Multiple Sclerosis.

I remember it very clearly. I'm in the living room, in front of the couch, pacing a little. On the phone, my doc tells me that they've run a bunch of test, and considering them and the results of the MRI, that I probably have MS. I feel myself shatter. All I can see ahead for me is pain and suffering. Here I am, in what I though was the prime of my health, and now I have visions of wheelchairs and having my diapers changed by a nurse.

I hang up, and now I'm plummeting right for that swamp. I hit, and I hit hard. I feel myself going deep. I must have ruptured the cover, because I can feel the cold, dark waters taking hold of me. I feel myself growing tired, sinking. WTF. What's the *use*. I give up. Fuck this.

But I don't have to feel this way...

And I'm at the surface again. Oh. My. God. I'm still confused. I'm still very, very afraid. But I'm not depressed.

I'll deal. I'll wing-it. I'll make do, and then, when I'm ready, I will make much more. The amazing thing is all that takes place in about a minute's time. Two tops. It takes me a lot longer to come to terms with it all. I still have moments when I feel the cold water's heavy pull as my feet graze the surface. But I always come back up.

Always

Him

Elisa Redmond

I don't know who I hate more.

Him.

Or the people who make me talk about him.

I left the pub tonight and wandered around town for a while before walking home. The tears started flowing as I walked along the canal, when I hit Rathmines road my legs went out from under me.

I rang a friend as I walked along the canal, I don't know why, I was drunk and she had her boyfriend over.

I felt like I was interrupting.

Protection. The prostitutes all work along the canal. I didn't see any tonight, but then maybe I was too wrapped up in me. Keeping a voice on the phone was protection. It meant that no mad rapist-slasher was going to touch me, because of a piece of plastic pressed to my ear.

On Lower Rathmines road my legs gave out. My knees turned to water. I passed a bar newly opened and almost empty. The bouncers grabbed me just before I fell on my face.

"A'right luv?"

"Yeah, I'm fine." I managed to say.

I wonder does he know what he has done to me? They keep expecting this book. This hilarious book about HIM, where I make him into a clown. And I'm the heroine, the superwoman. The silently suffering female who makes good in the end.

"Tell us a joke Lis!"

"Keep us happy."

So I bring out the masks. So many now that I've forgotten where they first came from. Too many years have passed.

"You're a victim and you'll always be a victim" he told me. Because I didn't fight back.

I've been fighting demons for years now. He didn't know me with a temper. Didn't understand how every day I fought to keep it repressed. So I was a victim. In his eyes.

He, the liar, the cheat, the one with the eyes that threatened violence. The paranoid who slept with knives under the pillow.

"Aren't you a bit gullible?" a friend asked.

Yes it sounds that way. But you didn't know me before. There is no before, there is only now.

My knees turned to water and I felt myself falling.

"You alright luv?" The bouncer asked again.

"Yes." I looked over his shoulder to the crowd inside who sat silently staring out.

"Tell us about him, what was he really like?"

Must I?

Do you really need to know?

I relive it each time, the pain the anger and the hatred. Always the hatred.

How do I escape him when I am made to repeat the stories?

Do I ask you about your demons?

His diseases, do you wish to hear about them? How his cancer ravaged his body and his heart caused him to cough up blood.

All lies of course.

"Did you stay with him out of pity?" The same friend who thought me gullible. Pity? What is pity but love gone wrong? Twisted and warped into something resembling fear.

"Do you hate him?"

"Do you still love him?"

Fuck off. You brought it up. Love and hate are two very strong emotions.

Do you know me well enough to ask me that?

Do I know you enough to answer?

Riding the Broken Hearts Limited

Donna Eyer

"Where are they? They should've been here by now."

The question hadn't bothered me the first time Marnie asked. It was a legitimate query, considering the fact that Eddie Jennings was rarely late. Eddie was one of the few people I knew who could get more attention and cause a bigger scene by arriving early. Still, by the time she repeated the same question for the fifth time, it was getting more than a little stale.

"Marnie, dammit, if you say that one more time, I'm gonna..." Ok, so I wasn't good at threats. I let the thought trail off as I checked my hair in the rearview mirror.

"You're gonna what, McJobs boy? Beat me, whip me, chain me to the back of the car? Oh, please do. That'd be more friggin' excitement than you've given me all week."

"I'll make you walk back to town," I responded lamely. I was in line to be at least salutatorian of our class in our upcoming senior year, a fact that made Marnie jealous enough to have tagged me with that irritating nickname. "Besides, quit acting like you're some kinky sex goddess. You're not fooling anyone."

"I have to get some somewhere, don't I?" she retorted, sliding herself off of the trunk lid where she'd been perched. Her Daisy Dukes didn't provide enough coverage to keep her thighs from squeaking against the metal, and I stifled a snicker. Marnie and I had been an on-again-off-again couple for nearly six months now, but her attitude as of late was starting to appall even me. Maybe she really *was* God's gift to *Hustler* magazine or something, but it was way too much for a high school chick in a small railroad town like Portage, Pennsylvania.

The throaty growl of a glasspack muffler off in the distance announced Eddie's impending arrival. As soon as Marnie heard the sound, she hurried to the passenger side of my Mustang and grabbed her purse, which honestly looked more like a military surplus haversack. She was always primping for Eddie, making sure she looked good for his arrival. I rolled my eyes at her and got out of the car.

Eddie pulled his CRX in next to my 'Stang, shut it off, and hopped out of the driver's seat, seemingly all in one fluid motion. I couldn't help laughing; he was too smooth for his own good.

"Heya, Brando, how they hangin'?" Eddie thumped me on the back with his hand, but I didn't flinch. The routine was nearly the same every day, and I'd braced myself ahead of time.

"Just about right, Eddie." I turned to Tara, Eddie's girlfriend, and grinned. "'Sup, Tara?" She was holding out the CD she'd promised to lend to me. I took it and looked it over.

"It's *Electrophoresis* by Soliton," she said slowly, making sure she pronounced the title correctly. "It's a Canadian import, kinda industrial electronica. I think you'll like it."

I thanked her and put the CD in the Mustang, willing

myself not to do something dumb. Just as much as I knew Marnie and Eddie liked to flirt with each other, I also had to admit that I had a thing for Tara. I think if we'd just switched girlfriends from the start, all four of us would've been much happier. Tara didn't seem to like being Eddie's "token girl," but she and I got along well together. We had the same taste in cars, music, food, you name it. It also didn't help that Marnie, while totally fawning over Eddie, managed to disparage me any chance she got. Tack onto that the fact that she had the mentality of a soft pretzel, and it was obvious I was in dire need of someone different. Our drastically clashing personalities were, for all intents and purposes, completely irreconcilable.

"So," Eddie said, prying himself from Marnie's grasp, "you ready to do this? My mom had me do the breakfast dishes and take out the trash before I came out. Doesn't really leave us any time to stand around bullshitting."

I nodded and glanced at my watch. "The 10:45 is already a couple minutes late. I wouldn't count on it being much longer."

Eddie nodded, then motioned for Tara to get into the CRX. Marnie and I got back into the Mustang, and I started it up. Though my car was more powerful, the noise from Eddie's ride made it sound ten times more intimidating. Anyone who didn't know better would think the CRX would win every time we raced. That was beside the point, though, because we weren't so much racing each other as we were racing the 10:45 from Altoona, at least on this morning.

Our rather warped game of "chicken" took place all over both Blair County and Cambria County, at different railroad crossings in different towns. The last thing we needed was for the cops to figure out a pattern, so we tried not to get into one. The only things all of the crossings had in common were that they were all on infrequently-traveled back roads, and none of them had gates.

Why we did it, I really don't know for sure. I guess that part of it was to get an extreme adrenaline rush. Another part may have been that we thought we were invincible, although a couple of really close calls were starting to bring tendrils of doubt into that line of thought. Either way, in a town like Portage, there really wasn't much to do during the summer. Some kids occupied their time with drinking and partying, others with summer jobs. Heck, even I had a job at a local pizza shop, but I usually only worked the less desirable shifts – evenings and weekends.

As Eddie revved the engine of the CRX, I caught sight of the train. It was an intermodal, most likely going to Pittsburgh. The diesel locomotives, with their black and silver Norfolk Southern paint jobs, almost appeared to be glowing in the refulgence of the summer sun. I started to signal to Eddie, but he was already staring at the train with steely-eyed determination. Seeing no cars coming in either direction, I pulled out onto the road and lined up in the left lane. Eddie pulled up beside me, getting the front of his car as even with mine as he could. We had it all down to a science. We waited, giving our tachometers a workout, until the train got to a certain point. Yelling over the roar from Eddie's glasspack, we counted down in unison – 3, 2, 1, go!

Stones and dust from the old country road flew from beneath our cars as our tires fought for traction. Mine dug in first, and I pulled out to an early lead, shifting deftly through the gears as I gained momentum. I slid the Mustang over in front of Eddie's car, a Cheshire cat grin spreading across my face as the adrenaline started to kick in.

That's when I heard it. Above the engine noise and interior noise, Eddie's exhaust system, and the horn from the locomotive, my ears picked out another sound. It was a high-pitched wailing noise, not unlike a baby crying. I wasn't able to place the sound until I looked in the rearview mirror and saw the source for myself.

"Shit!" I exclaimed, grasping the steering wheel so hard that my knuckles turned a garish shade of white. "Cops!"

Sure enough, I could just make out a Cambria County Sheriff's Department squad car closing in on the back of the CRX. Eddie noticed it around the same time as I did, but the determined look remained on his face and I knew we weren't going to stop. We'd figured that the cops would catch up to our game sooner or later, but that just seemed to add to the rush.

Barreling down the road toward the tracks, I kept glancing back and forth between the train and the rearview mirror. Eddie's car had fallen slightly off the pace, just enough to keep him from passing me as we approached the train. I could hear Marnie giggling from the passenger seat. She loved the game almost more than I did, and having the cops behind us seemed to excite her even more.

"Can't catch us now, you asshole pigs!" she screamed at the top of her lungs, flipping the bird out the window. "Go faster, Brandon, c'mon! Let's dust their asses!" I could barely hear her above the blaring honk of the diesel's horns.

It wasn't until we were almost at the tracks that I realized we might not make it. I picked a point in the middle of the road on the other side of the tracks and aimed for it, trying desperately to pick up any speed I could get without losing control of the car. The only good thing about us being so close was that Eddie would have to stop, meaning I'd certainly beat him to the finish line we'd chosen when we scoped out the crossing.

Someway, somehow, fate was on our side once again. We made it with about 50 feet to spare, which was peanuts in our game. That had to be the closest call yet. As soon as we cleared the crossing, I laid on the brakes, wrestling with the steering wheel to keep the car from fishtailing. I could take my good old time getting to the finish line, but I wanted to see what the cops had in store for Eddie and Tara.

What came next was hard to figure out at first. I heard a sound I'd only heard once before, when I was seven years old and saw a car accident on the road in front of the local supermarket. It was the unmistakable noise made by a large, man-made steel object as it plows into another one. I threw the Mustang into park and turned around in the seat, not believing what I was seeing. My adrenaline level and excitement took a huge nose dive, replaced by sheer terror. Beside me, Marnie started screaming Eddie's name.

The diesel locomotives pushed Eddie's CRX down the tracks in front of them, making an ungodly squealing sound as metal slid against metal. It took almost a mile for the train to come to a complete stop, but by that time, Eddie's car had burst into flames. All hope that they'd make it out of the wreck alive disappeared the instant that the flames reached the gas tank, turning the Honda and its occupants into a brilliant orange fireball.

I just sat there in the car, unable to stop shaking. Marnie's screams had turned into soft but steady crying. She, too, never moved from her seat. We were still sitting there, unable to pull our gazes away from the fireball in the distance, when the police found us.

We were fined for racing the train and released to our parents late that afternoon. Thanks to Pennsylvania's points system, my license was suspended for ninety days. Judging by my parents' reaction, I had a feeling it would be much longer than that before I'd actually be allowed to drive again. We'd only been trying to poach a day's worth of adrenaline rush at the expense of the railroad. What we ended up getting was so much worse.

Somehow, I managed to get on with what was left of my life. The kids at school knew Eddie was somewhat of a trouble-maker, so they never blamed me for his death. At least, not to the extent that I blamed myself. In spite of that, I toughed it out and barely kept my #2 ranking in our class. All of the awards and attention I got for being class salutatorian did little to numb the pain.

The whole thing had quite the opposite effect on Marnie. It was almost like her subscription to reality ran out, and she forgot to renew. She wrapped herself in a self-imposed purdah, barely acknowledging the existence of everyone else around her. I only saw her in passing during school that year, except on graduation day. She approached me cautiously after the ceremony, waiting until I was alone.

"You wanna get out of here?" She pressed her lips to-gether but couldn't manage a smile. The attempt only made her face look even more like a sorrowful caricature of its former self.

I nodded, knowing immediately what she meant. I led Marnie to the Mustang, which I'd only recently been allowed to start driving. We threw our mortarboards in the back and slid into the front seats, green-and-white gowns and all. As we headed out of town, I popped Tara's *Electrophoresis* CD into the CD player and set it to repeat.

The crossing looked the same as it had almost a year ago, except for the two white crosses stuck in the ground to the right of the road, a few feet from where it crossed the tracks. They were adorned with flowers and cards in honor of graduation, and a tassel hung from each one, the white and green cords swaying in the gentle breeze.

We waited for nearly an hour before finally hearing a locomotive honking its horn at a crossing off in the distance. When I saw it cross just the right spot, I counted down like usual, and then waited a few more seconds before gunning the engine. I covered the distance rapidly, my mind playing back a slideshow of that late June day.

Marnie reached over and grabbed my hand, and when I glanced over at her, I was sort of comforted to see that she was smiling. I squeezed her hand and returned the smile, then focused again on the road ahead of us. The white crosses beckoned to me, and I wondered if they'd put ours right beside those two.

None of that really mattered anyway. Still grinning, I turned the stereo up as loud as it would go. It didn't drown out the locomotive's horns, but they blended together in a macabre industrial symphony. It seemed an almost fitting sendoff for our Norfolk Southern trip into oblivion. Tara and Eddie would've loved it. In fact, though Marnie was sitting beside me, it was Tara's face I saw as we took that final ride.

French Jazz

Richard Ebert

I sat in my chair, feeling the thunder outside vibrate in my bones. The cold seeped in through the windows, chilling the room. The fire, casting the only light, provided a warm radius where the cold battled valiantly to invade. The old record player softly cried out the dark melodies of slow French jazz. I listened with a gun in one hand and a bottle of whiskey in the other, slowly becoming the most depressed man on earth.

Thunder rattled the windows, and the metal in my hand echoed the sky with a bark of chemical rage. The lead missile flew as straight and true as I could aim it, and I could picture the bullet's precise wedges opening in flight, unfolding in a grotesque mockery of a living flower.

The impact ripped a deep gouge in the wooden wall of the cabin, annihilating the unsuspecting roach with a single Zeus-like blow. I laughed, and inhaled deeply of the air, now tainted with the sting of cordite.

I lifted the gun to my face and watched the smoke seep from the barrel, twisting and flaring in the air currents like a living thing. Warmth radiated off the barrel.

For a moment, just a moment, I wondered what it would feel like if that warm barrel kissed the underside of my jaw, firmly pressed against the soft tissues in the hollow behind the chin.

That was enough. It was my signal that I was getting far too depressed to be armed. Before any more untoward thoughts or impulses could enter my slowly sinking brain, I popped the clip out of the gun and stuck it between the cushions of the chair. I yanked the slide back and watched as the chambered round flew out. Satisfied, I threw the gun somewhere behind me, hopefully lost until the dawn.

It landed with a crash and a metallic thud, and I knew that my friends would be mad if they knew how I was treating my gun, and I knew that my family would be mad if they knew how I was treating myself.

To hell with them all. I wasn't here for them, I was here for me. I took another drink from the bottle and grimaced. I had bought the cheapest, nastiest whiskey I could find, figuring if I was going to "punish" myself, I might as well make it as unpleasant as possible.

I flinched as lightning flashed outside the window like a white-hot sun brought down to earth. Thunder shook walls and rattled the windows dangerously. The strike had been close, close enough to pop the fuse box and leave me without the music.

I curled up in the overstuffed chair and drank from the bottle of whiskey with the same desperation as a hungry babe suckles from its mother, and fell into an alcoholic slumber in which I would ponder the eternal questions of mankind.

I awoke from my alcoholic fugue cursing at the sad clichés that the drunken brain concocts. I attempted to sit up, and I changed the subject of my epithets from my the former state of my mind to the current state of my body. I was hung over, and seriously. I took a deep breath to begin a new soliloquy and promptly gagged as the contents of my stomach rebelled and sought freedom from their organic confinement. Headache or not, even as unbalanced as I was, I ran to the bathroom to deal with the consequences of too much cheap whiskey.

After an hour that seemed like an eternity, the heaves stopped and all I was left with was a splitting headache. I scrabbled at the medicine cabinet and groped in a blind haze of pain until I found the little bottle that promised relief. A child-proof cap was all that stood between me and peace, and in my state it was less of a routine task and more of a Herculean chore to line up the arrows and pry the lid off. I would have started cursing again, but I had run out of original thoughts long ago and I didn't want to repeat myself.

Finally, the cap came off and I poured two capsules of pain relief into my hand and I wandered into the kitchen to get a glass of water to wash them down. I fought off waves of dizziness and nausea as I staggered over to the cabinet where the glasses were kept.

I grabbed the first glass I could and promptly filled it from the tap. I placed the capsules on my tongue, and promptly washed them down with a large gulp of water. When the water hit my stomach, I had to seriously repress the need to vomit. After a moment, my stomach calmed down and I began to take small sips of water, fighting my rising gorge each time.

I trudged back to my chair, determined to wait out the hangover. Nauseous, tired, and in a great deal of pain, I collapsed into the chair and tried to relax. It worked and I fell asleep. When I next awoke, the pills had worked their medicinal magic and my headache was, if not gone, then in a definite state of remission.

I stood and then walked into the bathroom to clean myself

up and try to feel human once more. I stripped off my clothes and stepped into the shower. It has been my experience that in all things, a long, hot shower can do much to restore a flagging human spirit.

With the water turned as hot as I could stand it, I luxuriated in the streams, feeling the heat penetrating my skin and beginning to warm my cold bones. Once I adjusted to the feeling, I began to wash. I took the soap and washcloth and I soaped and scrubbed and soaped and scrubbed until I felt like I had peeled away an entire layer of my epidermis.

Tingling from the sensation of my now raw skin, I turned the heat down and felt the cool water caress my now scourged and scoured flesh. It is one of the simplest luxuries in life, yet it can give one the feeling of being reborn. My cleansing complete, I turned off the shower and toweled myself dry.

Shaving normally presents a problem to a man with an unsteady hand, but I had come prepared. I picked up the electric razor and removed the day's stubble. Finally, I found my toothbrush and I scrubbed as feverishly on my teeth as I had on my body, if not moreso. The breath of a drunken man is enough to turn Medusa to stone.

Finishing my ablutions, I gathered my clothes and tottered off into the bedroom in search of something clean to wear. Throwing on a pair of sweat pants and a sweatshirt, I finally felt like I was returning to a relatively stable state. I was even hungry.

I walked out of the bedroom and into the kitchen to raid the fridge. I pulled out one of the sandwiches I had made the day before and a bottle of iced tea. I think I may be the only man in the world who plans out his drunken binges in advance. Regardless, I walked back to my chair to eat and to ponder my reasons for making this retreat.

Although I felt a little queasy, I managed to eat the entire sandwich without much difficulty. The iced tea didn't help much, though it satiated my thirst. Finished with my meal I considered going back for seconds, but I knew that I was playing a delay and deny game with myself. I didn't want to think of why I came here; I wanted to waste time and goof off until it was time to leave and not ask any hard questions.

Thankfully, I do have a strong will, and I take pains to exercise it. I clamped down on my dissident thoughts and settled into the chair to do some deep thinking. The real question: am I mad?

The basis for this odd ordeal was an event which took place twelve days ago. I was on a business trip to San Francisco and I ran into my sister and her husband taking their vacation, which was not the coincidence you might think it was. We knew that we would both be in the city at the same time, and so we made plans to spend an evening together.

We met and had dinner at a posh restaurant, and had a marvelous time. I hadn't seen her or her husband for a while, and we had a lot of catching up to do. We talked and exchanged stories and laughed and did all the things that friends and family do at a restaurant. We eventually parted ways and they made me promise to drop by their place more often. They flew out the next day, as planned . . . or so I thought.

I didn't know that anything was amiss until I returned home from the business trip two days later. We live in the same city, so I decided to keep my promise and drop by the house on my lunch hour. My sister works out of her home, so I knew she'd be there.

I arrived, bearing gifts. She was in and delighted to see me. We exchanged small talk and made our way to the kitchen to make peanut butter and jelly sandwiches and comment on how they always tasted better when Mom made them. Then she apologized for cutting her vacation short.

"What?" I said. I didn't understand. I thought that she and her husband had left as planned. She told me that they had planned on staying another day, but that there had been a tragedy in Robert's family. Bruce, his brother, had committed suicide.

I felt nothing. I had only met Bruce once or twice, and I didn't even remember his face. There was absolutely nothing about him that I could recall, until I started digging. I finally remembered what he looked like, dredging the memory from a Christmas five years ago. "That's awful," I said.

She told me the story. Bruce had never been the most stable of individuals, nor the most friendly. He was a manic-depressive and he completely distrusted doctors; as such, he never received any treatment for his illness beyond what his family tried unsuccessfully to provide.

Apparently he had tried to kill himself several times before, but they had been half-hearted attempts and someone had always found him or prevented him in some manner. Not this time. This time he had a gun and took a shot at his wife. She fled and called the police from a neighbor's house. When they arrived, it was too late.

I still felt nothing, and I began to realize that something was wrong with me. The sheer scope of the tragedy and human suffering should have moved something in me. The death of a living, breathing human being should have caused some reaction, even if he was a stranger to me. I'm not a callous or cold individual at all. I have always considered myself unusually sensitive; I cry all the way through Casablanca.

She was about to say more when the phone rang. I sat at the kitchen table and turned my thoughts inward as she took the call. It was Robert on the other end. He was making arrangements at the funeral home and he needed her support.

I watched her straight shoulders droop as she listened to him on the phone. I watched as her head, normally carried high, sagged. Her whole being seemed to fold in on itself. She had never known Bruce well, but she was absorbing the depth of her husband's grief, resonating to it.

Cold, aloof, even somewhat annoyed that this phone call had interrupted a pleasant lunch with my sister, I watched as her back began to heave with sobs. She used her free hand to wipe away the tears I knew were streaming down her face. I watched and waited and marveled at the grief which poured off of her in waves, and I felt nothing. Void.

Something was wrong. We were family. Just seeing her like this should move me. I should be there, sharing in her grief, living and playing my part in this tragedy. Reacting to the sorrow, even if only to comfort by taking on a part of it. I watched as she was torn apart on the inside, dropping the phone and running out of the room wailing and crying drowning in a pool of depthless pain.

I picked the phone up off of the floor and placed it back in its cradle. I wondered at my calm state. I felt like there was a gray wall between me and my emotions. I no longer felt the pleasure at seeing my sister, I no longer felt annoyance at Robert's phone call. Nothing. It was as if my heart was no longer in my chest. Ice.

Anne came back minutes later, smiling through her smudged mascara and the remnants of tears and apologizing for running off. I assured her that I understood and put on a sympathetic face and gave her a big hug. I wanted to feel sympathy, to feel love or grief, and I could remember them, but even with my little sister in my arms, crying again, there was nothing within me.

My mind was operating without a problem. I knew something was wrong, and that I should feel something, but all I could do was imitate the emotion. I covered my lack, and tried to be helpful.

She said that there would be a gathering of Robert's family later that evening, but I begged off, saying that I had an important meeting. Thankfully, I was going out of town again on the day of the funeral, so I didn't have to lie.

She said that she was a little disappointed, that they would find my presence comforting. In my mind I doubted it, because I knew the rest of Robert's family little better than I had known Bruce. I would be just another anonymous face making platitudes and empty gestures, saying "Sorry" until the word lost all meaning. That sort of person brings no comfort. Besides . . . I didn't want to be bothered.

When I left her house, I began to think about my "loss". From a certain standpoint, it wasn't a disadvantage at all. I was thinking more clearly than I had in years, and I finally had a sense of focus. That night I fell asleep the moment my head touched the pillow, and I passed the night without dreams. And the next. And the next.

Two days later I realized that I was driving to work in silence. The radio was off and the CD player was empty. This was unusual. I grew up in a home constantly filled with music, and I have a difficult time thinking in silence. I always have music with me. I can't do without it . . . except that I had, for two days, and hadn't noticed.

I pulled into a convenience store parking lot and opened the glove compartment to get my favorite CD. I placed it in the stereo and waited. Music filled my car, uplifting, energetic music that wakes me up and motivates me. I listened until I realized that I was bored. I turned it off.

When I got home that evening, I realized that I had forgotten to eat. Not a single morsel of food had passed my lips since I had awakened that morning, and I wasn't hungry. I looked in the refrigerator more out of habit and curiosity than out of hunger, and I found nothing that caught my interest.

I changed into my pajamas and a robe and sat in front of the television. I stared at it, lost in thought for five minutes before I turned it on. I watched the news with disinterest, even through the stock reports, which bore me, and the day's political news, which inflames me. Nothing.

On impulse, I placed my copy of Casablanca into the VCR. I watched the entire movie without a single tear. My eyes were as dry at the end of the movie as they had been at the beginning. I turned off the VCR and began to flip through channels. When I found a steamy "love" scene on one of the movie channels, I realized that all my passions were gone. I was only a shell. Something was horribly wrong, and I felt little or no desire to correct the situation.

The funeral came and went, as did my business trip. I performed adequately. For all my logic and focus, there was no energy. They found my presentation acceptable, but found me unenthusiastic. I began to realize that with the loss of emotion came a loss of motivation. If I continued the down the path I was taking, I would die.

The thought of death stirred something. At least my survival instinct was still intact. Good, I thought, I can use that as a starting point. When I returned from my trip, I informed my boss that I would need some time off. Since I had accrued so many vacation days, the short notice didn't bother him.

I packed my bags and headed for my cabin. I like to get away from time to time and so I bought a small log house on a lake in Oregon. My nearest neighbor was miles away, and the only road to it was hard-packed dirt. It was the perfect place to go to sit and think. It was a good eighteen hours away by car, and I determined to do the whole trip in one long drive.

It was probably a good thing I left when I did. Fourteen hours into my uneventful and boring drive, some ignorant driver cut me off. The gray wall cracked a little, and something ugly stuck its head out: rage.

I became fury incarnate. Boiling, savage, murderous rage just ripped through my being setting all my nerves on fire. If my gun had been within reach, I would have become lead story in the next day's news. I had just enough control to pull off the road into a rest stop. I shook for fifteen minutes, my hands crushing themselves into fists, knuckles popping, locking themselves around the imagined neck of the rude driver, feeling soft tissues compress and the satisfying crunch of a broken spine.

When the river of anger finished flowing, I was sweating and breathing like I had just run marathon. The void reasserted itself, and the sweating stopped and my breathing returned to normal. I had experienced an emotional seizure.

I reached beside the steering wheel and turned the car off with a sharp snap of my wrist. It was time for a break. The only other times I had pulled off the road earlier were only for gas and restroom breaks. This time, I needed a real break.

I pushed the trunk release button and then went around to open the cooler of food I had prepared for my ordeal. I passed over the beer and whiskey for an iced tea. I still had four hours of driving ahead of me. I grabbed a sandwich and a bag of salt and vinegar chips to go with it. Then I headed over to a picnic bench to eat my meal under the irregular glow of the rest area's halogen lamps.

As I ate, I watched the moths and other insects swarm around the lamp, attracted to its bright light. They fluttered about, audibly banging on the glass case and each other, seemingly without any purpose or plan but to seek the light. I have heard that moths seek bright lights like lamps and flames because they normally navigate by the light of the moon. I wondered what they would say if they knew the lamp to be a false guide. That in their desperate rush for its light, they had been deceived. I mulled it over while I finished the chips, and then discarded it as a useless thought. They weren't sentient – they knew about as little about deception as I knew about pheromone trails.

Satisfied and calm, I threw away my trash and made my way back to the car. I turned the engine over and listened to it purr, listened to the car's heart, and remembered how I desperately wanted a car that sounded like this when I was a teenager. I felt a small smile creep across my lips and I counted it as a victory. Trying hard to sustain the emotion, even as weak as it was, I scrounged for a nice, mellow CD and put it in the player.

The sweet voice of my favorite chanteuse filled the interior of the automobile, and I cautiously pulled out of the rest area and onto the highway again. It was almost an uneventful journey to the cabin from there.

A mile or two before my turn-off, I saw bright, flashing red and blue lights, and as I drew closer I saw the bright orange-white light of magnesium road flares laid out to divert traffic. It was a terrible accident. A small, white pickup was laying overturned in a ditch beside the road, its bed crushed almost flat. A large tractor-trailer was stopped in the middle of the road, skid marks from its tires showing where the driver had desperately applied the brakes. The police were checking the scene over and controlling what little traffic was passing by while the paramedics loaded the injured onto stretchers.

Even seeing as little as I did, I knew what happened; the skid marks told the whole story. The pickup had been driving the opposite direction as the tractor-trailer, and had swerved over the yellow line and into the path of the oncoming juggernaut. The collision must have been awesome. I was willing to bet that the driver of the pickup had been drinking. Regardless, I felt nothing. I took the scene in and merely wrote it off as the stupid human animal killing itself again. I had no sympathy, no pity.

I turned onto the dirt road moments later, reveling in the darkness that swallowed me. I drove through a leafy corridor lit only by the high-beams of my car, shadowed by impenetrable darkness outside the reach of the headlights. Finally, I pulled into the small driveway of my cabin.

I turned off the car and felt the darkness encroach upon me. As a child, I had been terrified of the dark, but now I only felt the memory of fear. Still, it was better than feeling nothing. I got out of the car and locked it, hearing the dirt and gravel crunch beneath my feet. In the absence of any other noise, it sounded loud.

I leaned against the hood, feeling the warmth of the engine as a counterpoint to the sharp cold that was beginning to settle in. After several minutes, my eyes finally adjusted to the darkness, and I saw the lake by starlight. It was beautiful, and that beauty moved me.

I felt the gray wall snap again, and then I was on my knees, weeping and sobbing as the beauty and timelessness of the lake twisted in my soul like a melancholy knife. My palms were pressed to my eyes to try and stem the floodgate of tears, and my wails awoke the answering cries of lonely and mournful wolves.

Then the gray wall asserted itself and I was cut off. My hands were hot from tears while my knees ached from the cold ground. I took several deep breaths and brought out my handkerchief to deal with my now-runny nose. I stood, cold again at my soul, and walked up to the front door. I entered the cabin, and after turning on the furnace and water heater, I went to my bedroom where I promptly collapsed on the bed and slept for ten hours.

I awoke stiff and sore from the cold and the long drive. I realized that I still wore the previous day's clothes, and went out to the car to get my supplies. I walked out to see a vivid blue sky striated with bright white clouds while threatening gray clouds hung on the horizon. There was going to be a storm tonight. I looked at the lake, placid and serene, mirroring the sky. I remembered my second emotional seizure from the night before, and half-believed it to be a dream. I brought my hand to my face and felt my puffy eyes, and accepted it as real.

I hastily brought in the cooler and my clothes, and wondered if there was firewood to be had. I checked out behind the cabin, and found a good-sized pile of logs. There was enough wood for me to have a fire every night while I was here. I chose the best logs I could find so that I might have the best fire tonight, the eve of the storm. I placed the logs in the fireplace with a good amount of kindling and the matches within easy reach.

Finally I brought out the beer and whiskey and the old vinyl albums for the record player. There is something inherently soothing in the hiss and pop of jazz records as you hear the music. A sense of nostalgia, perhaps.

Everything was prepared. Tonight I would have my vision quest. I would take the alcohol and let it unlock the inhibitions and fears and beasts that lurked within my psyche. I would journey into my deepest subconscious seeking the cause for my disassociation from the world.

Unfortunately, I merely got drunk and passed out mumbling bad clichés. After I suffered through the hangover I realized that there was not going to be any magical instant solution. I was going to have to spend some time and effort working through this problem.

That was when I decided to keep a journal. I would have a place to express myself and to track my progress. If I expressed no emotion in life, perhaps I would express emotion on paper. I would learn how to generate emotion, how to express it once again. In the meantime, I had several days to work with my Self, who is my best friend and worst enemy.

That night I had a dream . . . the dream I had sought in my drunken stupor now came to me of its own accord. Maybe it needed a day to be shaken loose from the anchors that the alcohol corroded, or maybe it just knew I wanted an excuse to drink and lose control for one night. It didn't matter. What mattered was that the dream came, and I could now fight for the possession of my soul.

I stood naked on a flat, featureless gray plain; the gray plain, the gray wall. The sky was far away, but it too was gray. The horizon was infinite, receding in all directions. The only feature was me.

I picked a direction and walked, trying to find a flaw or a weakness in the plain. I couldn't. A hint of frustration entered into the dream, and I felt a crowbar in my hands. I took the crowbar and smashed it against the gray plain, hitting it again and again. It was like hitting smooth gray marble. A chunk of the gray matter finally broke away, revealing a small flaw. I jammed the end of the crowbar into the flaw with all my might, and I watched the plain shatter. Cracks and crevices radiated out from the flaw with lightning speed, and soon the whole world shook. The plain finally collapsed, and I fell.

I fell, and felt the wind rush by me. I searched for details in my dream, but in vain. Finally I realized that I was falling past a gray wall, and then that I was not falling, but floating. I hovered there, facing the implacable gray wall. It was featureless, and most importantly, unbroken.

There the dream became chaotic, fast, and violent. Rage entered the dream, and the wall shattered again. I grew to titanic proportions, and the gray wall was not a wall at all, but a sphere the size of an apple.

I took the sphere in my hand and brought it to my mouth. Layer upon layer was crushed by my teeth. The layers were as delicate as a eggshell, but infinite. I pulled the sphere back to look at it, and it was whole.

I found a spear, and pierced it like a bubble, watching each gray layer shatter like glass, and then pop into nothingness. Then I realized that I was a titan no more, and there was solidity beneath my feet. I looked at the gray plain beneath me and watched the gray sphere fade away.

Rage evaporated, and despair slunk in. I wept, and my tears were like acid to the plain, burning great pits in it, which were healed as the tears cooled and congealed - healing the wounds that they had just created. And then, nothing. I sat on the plain, legs crossed, numb and tried to think. I had no consciousness, no insight. My thoughts were as bare as the plain. I sat there for an eternity.

I stood, and found myself in the coarse brown robes of a

hermit. I turned my head, and behind me stood a small brown hut and a stone well. Curious, I walked into the hut, finding a small cot and a bucket for the well.

I took the bucket and walked to the well. Looking into it, I saw absolute blackness, nothingness. The well pierced the gray plain and sank deep into the infinite reaches of my mind. I considered jumping, but I knew somehow that to jump down that well would kill me. Somewhere within that darkness was death.

I tied the rope from the well to the bucket, and slowly lowered the bucket into the darkness. A long time passed, but finally the bucket hit water and filled up. I began to crank in the opposite direction, bringing the bucket up an unknowable distance.

The bucket reached the top and I looked within. It was full of water, water which reflected a sun that did not hang in the black sky. I sipped the water. I tasted joy. I sipped again. Despair. And again and again and again. Each sip was a new emotion, and emotion I had not felt in a long time. I raised the bucket triumphantly and guzzled its contents.

I retched and vomited them back up as I was torn apart inside by a storm of conflicting and raging emotions. I lay on my back, writhing in excruciating pain, panting in agony. The pain subsided, and I cradled the bucket in my lap.

I took the bucket and drew from the well once more. Again the bucket was full of water which reflected another sky. Again sips from the bucket provided me with emotion. I took the bucket into the hut. There I sat and watched the reflection of the sun cast shadows in the confined space. I stared into the sun, and I awoke.

I did not know what to make of the dream. Dutifully I wrote it down in my journal, writing with a clarity and detail that I cannot now muster. I closed the journal and set my pen aside. I went out to look at the lake as the dawn broke.

I watched as the sky lightened from black to purple and then to pink and red. The colors were vibrant and glorious, and I realized that I felt joy. I did not feel it with any intensity, but it was there. I could feel. I had made progress, a breakthrough. I didn't know if I would ever be whole again, but I had taken the first step back. I smiled.

Mistress of the Past
Stargazer

Skin slick with heat
Eyes rolled back into my mind
thinking of you I weep with the pleasure
we never fully knew
lips tingly and wet
kissing into you
your throat burns my tongue
your blood rushes into me
teeth grazing
body shaking
releases unknown
touch me as you should have
touch my soul as I wished it
touch me the way you, only you could have
lost love never fully known
lost life never fully lived
in the absence of passion is death
death has come into me the way you never could
light fades as the skin cools in sorrow
the only release now is of the whip falling from my hand
I release you from me
crumbling tears
weep in the night
lost forever is the future we could see
but never reach
lover goodnight
lover goodbye

Him

Christine Trainello

His nose looks funny. It's big and doesn't look like it belongs on his face. He laughs this sort of careless laugh that wrinkles it right in the bridge which makes it look even more ridiculous. He leans back in his chair and shrugs his shoulders. A big goofy grin sits upon his lips.

Some woman walks by and bumps into his elbow. She gives him a look, cursing him under her breath, but he continues his conversation with only a slight glance in her direction. He doesn't seem to notice, or acknowledge, the animosity in which she held him in that brief moment. He lets it roll off his shoulders with an ease I envy. And he laughs again.

When he laughs, his eyes crinkle up in the corners like the way you would imagine jolly ole St. Nick's would. He leans over to the woman next to him and whispers something into her ear to make her blush and giggle. Typical. She touches his arm in an affectionate way, as he turns his attention to the conversation at hand. He doesn't seem to notice the brief touch, or the longing in her eyes.

I walk by his table to order a café mocha, and I try to make it look as if I'm not staring at him. He looks up at me, and I glance away quickly so I can avoid his eyes and hide my embarrassment of being caught. I'm glad that I am past him as my cheeks turn a bright red and my heart beats a little more quickly for a moment.

I reach the counter, order my coffee, and glance back in the direction of my friends, careful to notice if he still watched me. My heart skips a beat, as I see that he is, and I turn back to the counter as I slowly start to blush. "Is he really looking at me?" I think. I wait for a moment to gather myself before I grab my café mocha and proceed back to my friends. I feel like a school girl, and not the 24 year old woman I am as my thoughts rush frantically in my head at the impossibility that he is still watching me. "Me!" I think. "Little ole me." I never once dared dream he would look at me. That he would even take notice in me. But he has, and as I turn to make my trek back to my friends' table, I see that his eyes are still on me.

All of a sudden, I feel this rush of adrenaline as an idea forms in my head. My heart begins to pick up pace, and my hands start to shake so that I have to grip the mocha tightly. As I reach his table, his elbow is still sticking out, and I move in a bit closer so I can brush up against it. The closer I get the more nervous I become. I try to regulate my breathing, and control my shaking to no avail. "This is so unlike me," I think. "I never do things like this." Just as I reach the table, though, I'm crushed! He moves forward in his seat and rests both arms on the surface. The only way I can brush up against him now is if I sit on the table, which is probably not a good idea. I sigh at the missed opportunity and continue on to my friends' table to drink my mocha.

As I walk by, I can see him glance up at me just out of the corner of my eye. I blush once more and nearly drop the mocha in my excitement. Thank goodness no one seems to notice. I continue on my way and position myself across from one of my friends so that it looks as if I'm looking at her and not the object of my attraction.

My friends are immersed in a discussion about the situation in the Middle East and recent terrorist attacks, but I can't seem to concentrate on what they are saying. My attention is completely focused on him. I nod occasionally and reply with noncommittal sounds. "Uh, huh," I say. "Right. Yeah." I laugh when everyone else laughs, and look serious and nod my head when the times are right. All I can think of is the way the lights glitter in his green eyes, and how soft his hair must feel as I watch him run his fingers through his auburn locks.

Despite his funny looking nose, he's an incredibly attractive man. In fact, his nose makes him appear even more handsome to me because it shows that he's not perfect. He has flaws, which makes him attainable. He's got a slim build, and long legs. I imagine that he must be about 6', but it's hard to tell as I've only ever seen him sitting. He's a regular at this place, always here on the weekends.

I can't tell if he's with the woman he's sitting next to or if they're just friends. That brief affection she showed him could be read in any way. Perhaps his feigned ignorance of the act was just the way he is. He could be one of those aloof boyfriends who takes everything around him for granted. Maybe he was just being polite, while she obviously wishes there to be more between them. I don't blame her.

He suddenly looks over at me, and I direct my attention to my friend's face instead, much to her amusement. I realize that perhaps I haven't been as slick as I originally thought. I glance down at my coffee, and everywhere else except for him. When I take a chance to look back in his direction, I see that he's turned back to his table. I return to staring at him, however, daring him to look at me once more, almost urging him to glance in my direction. Unfortunately, he never does.

He and I have played this game before, but never before had I thought about actually making contact like I did today. Up until today he had been an unattainable goal, sitting upon a pedestal in my mind. Today, he had almost become a reality and I'm not sure I'm ready for that.

My friends start to pack up their things signaling that it's time to go. We all say goodbye, and as I pick up my purse, my friend who was sitting across from me acting as my decoy pauses for a moment in her gatherings. "Why don't you just go ask him out?" she asks with a curious expression on her face. I blush, shaking my head slightly and then shrugging my shoulders. I look once again towards his table while I ponder her question, only to find him gone. "It's too late now," I say nodding towards where he was, a relief such as I had never felt washing over me. My friend shrugs and walks away, as I sigh contentedly, knowing that things will remain as they are. He'll stay on the pedestal I created for him, and I'll remain as I am. Maybe I'll let him come down next weekend.

LOST
JoEllen Drazan

Chapter One: Alone

Jess leaned her head against the window as the bus rumbled through the night; tucking her long blond hair behind her ear, she thought about the last couple weeks of her life. Jess placed a hand over her stomach, no one could tell she was already three months pregnant. Dave hadn't wanted to be a father. Jess choked back a sob, her dream of being with the man she loved and having a solid family was shattered only days ago. Abandoned by Dave she returned to her family, not that her family life was much to rely on, even before she graduated and moved in with Dave. She was not surprised to learn her family didn't want anything to do with her. Jess had turned her back on them when she moved out with Dave, and they did not want her back. She felt relieved there was no place for her with them. She didn't want to return to the emotional abuse from her alcoholic father or try to care for her drug-addicted mother.

Nowhere to turn Jess, contacted some of her old high school friends, trying to find a place to live. Most of them moved on and didn't have any place for her to stay. Brent had offered a spare room in his apartment. Though she didn't really know him in school, he was her best friend's brother. Two years older than she, Brent had left her small home town for the city about a year ago. It wasn't like she had much of a choice, she packed up what she could and bought a bus ticket. Moving 600 miles away offered a small hope that Jess would be able to have a fresh start.

Blinking at the sun as it peaked over the horizon Jess shook herself awake, quickly looking around. *Stupid!* She thought checking to make sure her duffle was still tucked under her seat. Looking up she noticed that they were finally entering the city. Tall buildings soon loomed overhead and traffic congested as they lumbered to the bus depot. Shouldering her duffle she made her way out to the busy street. Brent said he would meet her on the corner to take her to his apartment. Looking for the blond hair, blue eyes that she remembered from school, Jess did not see the other man trying to get her attention as she walked by.

"Are you Jess?" a hesitant voice asked from behind her.

Turning around, Jess found herself looking up at a boyish face with a sheepish grin. "Yes?"

"Sorry, didn't mean to startle you. I'm Cory. Brent sent me down to pick you up. Here, let me take that," Cory said motioning to her duffle.

Jess hesitated for a moment before handing Cory her duffle and followed him to a rusted blue van. Settling herself in the passenger seat, Jess began to realize how little she knew of the people she was moving in with. Out of the corner of her eye she studied Cory as he keyed the ignition. Dark hair, brown eyes, and lean build, despite his rough and baggy clothes he exuded a sense of calmness. Jess blushed as he caught her looking at him.

"Brent didn't tell me much about you," Cory said trying to ease the silence, winding his way through the clogged streets. "What made you decide to move to the city?"

"I didn't have much of a choice, I needed a place to stay and Brent offered. I knew him a little in high school." Jess did not want to reveal too much of her past to this stranger.

"Really?" Cory was startled, "Bret usually doesn't offer to help out much, but then you have history."

Jess felt uncertain if she made the right choice, "Not that much history. I was friends with his sister and he hung out with us once in a while."

"Ok, we're here," Cory said suddenly, pulling into an alley street behind an old three story house that had been converted to apartments. Cory parked his van next to a brilliant blue street racers car. "That would be Brent's car." He suddenly turned to Jess, catching her before she stepped out of the van. "I don't know why you accepted Bret's offer to stay here, but let me give you a word of advice. Try not to piss him off, I've heard rumors he can be dangerous at times."

Before Jess could question Cory on that statement, she heard a door slam above them.

"What's taken you so long, been fucking waiting for you to show up for an hour."

Jess looked up. Her eyes widened a little as she saw Brent. The blond hair and shockingly blue eyes were still there, but he had definitely been working out since she last saw him. Realizing she was staring at his shirtless body, Jess averted her eyes and found herself looking into Cory's knowing expression.

"Just remember what I said," Cory whispered. Letting her go, Cory got out of the van to retrieve her duffle.

As Jess stepped out of the van she realized that Brent

had already gone back inside. Slowly, she followed Cory as he went up the stairs to the third floor balcony and opened the door for her to enter. Hesitantly, she stepped into the apartment.

"Hey Jess, it's been a long time since I seen you last," Brent welcomed her with a flash of white teeth in a charming smile. "You're looking good." She didn't notice the appraising look he gave her.

"Here's her stuff, Brent. I have to be going off to work." Cory placed Jess's duffle beside her and headed out the door leaving the two of them alone. "Call me if you need something done later."

"Don't expect anything tonight. I'll give you a call in a couple days," Brent said, dismissing Cory and turning his attention to Jess. "Well, let's get you settled in." Motioning Jess to follow, Bret headed down the dim hallway to the door on the right.

Shouldering her duffle Jess followed him.

"It's not much, but the dude who stayed here last left the bed." Brent switched on the light illuminating a cramped room with barely enough space for the twin bed. Old wallpaper hung down exposing the rough plaster underneath.

"It's fine," Jess assured him. "Thanks again for letting me stay here."

"Hey, no problem." Bret flashed her another stunning smile. "A few friends of mine are stopping by tonight, I'll introduce you to them. We'll talk about rent and stuff later." Brent turned closing the door behind him with an audible click.

Jess sighed as she sank onto the bed, her duffle landing on the floor with a small thump. Trying to organize her thoughts, Jess wondered about her future here. Burying her face in her hands she let go of all the nervousness and fear she held pent up since Dave threw her out. Sobbing quietly, she didn't know Brent was just outside her door listening with a sly smirk on his face.

Jess woke, blinking at the harsh light from the bare bulb above her, she must have fell asleep for hours. Hearing laughter, she opened her door and walked towards the living room. She hesitated upon seeing all the unfamiliar faces. A couple of the girls glanced her way, giving Jess cold hard looks. Taken aback, Jess turned to go back to her room.

"Jess, there you are." Brent grabbed her arm, preventing her retreat. "Come on I'll introduce you to everyone." Brent proceeded to drag Jess to the middle of the room. "Attention everyone. I'd like to introduce an old friend of mine, Jess. She will be staying here for a time." Turning to Jess, "Jess, this is everyone. Or at least everyone who matters."

The same girls, who started at Jess earlier, now gave her looks that didn't mask their open hostility. Others barely looked up from their conversation if they even acknowledged her presence at all. Jess noticed that Cory wasn't in the room, she almost hoped to see another familiar face.

Not letting go of her arm, Brent led her over to a corner where a couple of his friends were talking.

"Hey Jess, I'm Brian."

Jess mumbled, "Hi." She looked up, startled at Brian's cold dark eyes. Brian was big, not fat, just had a large muscular frame. She wouldn't be surprised if he had played football at one time. Short, cropped hair and dark skin made him very intimidating.

"Bri, don't be hoggin' all the attention, dude." Shouldering his larger friend over, "Allow me to introduce myself, I am Scott," he said, holding a hand over his heart in a dramatic way. A mischievous smile and laughter lurked in his eyes. "At your service." Scott bowed over her hand and kissed the back of it.

Jess giggled, her nervousness eased. "I ..."

"Hey, don't believe a word this guy says. He'll do anything to try to get laid," Brent interrupted, sending a dark glance Scott's direction, bringing his arm around Jess possessively.

During the few weeks that followed, Jess felt more and more at ease. The welfare she received for her unborn child, was just enough to cover rent and buy food. The doctors had placed her pregnancy as a high risk, and recommended no physical stress so she was unable to find work. Brent was a different story. Jess tried to tell herself that he was just being over protective of her and the baby. She believed he cared for her and she for him, or at least that is what she told herself when doubt and fear crept into the back of her mind. She was still very much alone. The morning sickness hit her not only in the morning, but also at all hours of the day and night.

Brent left at these times, not saying where he was going or when he'd be back. Jess tried to tell herself that he was working, but it was more and more obvious that his work was not the legal sort. People came to the apartment at all hours, hushed words were spoken, and she was never allowed to be in the same room when these people arrived. It didn't take a genius to figure out what was going on.

Trapped, Jess felt she didn't have any choice and tried to make the best of things, reminding herself that she had to think for two and to be grateful that she had a roof over her head.

Weeks turned into months, the more her pregnancy showed the more distance Brent placed between them. It was obvious that the attention he showed her when she first arrived wore to bare tolerance. Brent now looked at her deformed figure in thinly disguised disgust. Jess avoided everyone by staying in her room. She fell into a depressed state, fervently holding her belly letting her unborn child comfort her.

Chapter Two: Hope

Jess hobbled from her room, pain evident on her face as contractions rippled across her belly. She stumbled in to the living room, not aware that Brent had company.

"Jess," Brent turned to grab her arm and lead her back to her room. "Don't you listen, bitch? I told you not to bother me when I'm conducting business. Do it again you'll regret it."

"Brent, no." Jess tried to lean against the wall for support. "Something's wrong, I have to go to the hospital." Gasping, her legs gave out from under her, falling to her knees as pain spread through her middle.

"Brent? What's going on man, the door was open." Cory called coming into the apartment.

"Shit!" Brent cursed. Hauling Jess to her feet, he all but forced her down the hallway. "You just cost me the biggest deal of the year, you fucking bitch."

Cory came up to help Jess to the couch.

"Don't you touch her," Brent said, his anger pushing him over the edge. "She's fucking mine, back off."

"What the fuck, man. She's hurt and needs help," Cory said backing away from Brent, but keeping close enough to catch Jess if she fell.

"Hurt? Needs help?" Brent roughly pulled on Jess's arm as she tried to slump down, weakening as painful contractions robbed her of breath. "She's nothing but a lying bitch. I know the fucking kid's not due for another month. She's faking it to get attention."

Another wave of pain consumed her body, Jess couldn't fight it anymore and started sobbing. Tears rolling down her face she made eye contact with Cory and silently pleaded with him to help her. She didn't want to lose her child.

"No dude, she ain't faking it." Cory moved closer to Jess, "She's starting to bleed, not a good sign."

"Bleeding, Fuck!" Brent abruptly let go of Jess and stepped back. "Fine, since you're concerned so much, you take her to the hospital. I ain't having her bleed in my car. I'm gone." Brent grabbed his keys and slammed the door behind him. "Fucking bitch." They heard his car roar to life and squeal out onto the street.

Cory barely caught Jess before she hit the floor. Laying her down gently, he grabbed his phone and called emergency services.

"Come on Jess, stay with me. I've called the ambulance and they will be here soon." Cory grabbed a hold of Jess's hand, smoothing back her hair from her face.

"C-Cory?" Jess stammered, breathless. "Don't leave me. I can't do this alone. It hurts so much." Jess closed her eyes as another wave of pain shot through her.

"Breathe, Jess, you can do this. I'll be right here with you." Cory soothingly rubbed the back of her hands.

True to his word, Cory stayed with Jess throughout the hours of labor. Early morning the next day Jess gave birth to a healthy baby boy. Small ringlets of dark curls adorned his head. As the nurse passed him to Jess, he gave his mom the sweetest angelic smile and opened his dark eyes.

Brushing the sweat-dampened hair from her face, Cory leaned over to whisper, "What are you going to name him?"

"I think I'll name him Henri." Jess smiled at her son. *My son,* she thought, amazed at how perfect he was.

Chapter Three: Betrayal

After talking with the welfare agency Jess hurried back to the apartment to clear out her things before Brent came back from his runs. He had changed since Henri's birth. She feared that he would start beating her, he had already come close several times. Jess didn't want Henri to be endangered, she didn't know what would happen if Brent lost it. Jess smiled as Henri tried to reach out to catch a butterfly. He sure had grown in the last few months, hard to believe how tiny he was when born. Jess let her thoughts float back to that day. It all seemed so perfect after Brent left. Cory was there for her, through everything, even stayed with her the couple days she remained at the hospital. However, Brent threw him out once he brought her back to the apartment. Jess sighed, things could never happen between Cory and her. Brent would act very possessive of her and would not even allow her to talk to anyone especially Cory, but then he would also completely ignore her. Jess wanted out. Brent was supposed to be gone for the rest of the afternoon and she wanted to be cleared out of the apartment before he came back.

Hurriedly stuffing things into her duffle and some bags to take with her, Jess glanced at Henri cooing in his crib waving his little fists in the air, a grin on his face. Half way across the room Jess froze, she heard Brent and his thugs coming up the stairs. She turned as the door opened, eyes wide.

Laughing as he stepped through the door, Brent's expression darkened as he saw the bags packed on the floor. He rushed at Jess grabbing her by the arm in a painful grip. "Leaving me are you? Do you think I'd let you get away that easily?" Brent sneered, forcing her back onto the couch. "Scott, take the baby to the other room. Brian, come here and hold this ungrateful bitch down. I'm going to make sure she won't consider leaving this place again." An evil grin briefly appeared on his face as he stretched her out on the couch. Brian grabbed hold of her arms, trying to keep her immobile.

"Henri! NO!! Don't take him away from me!" Frantically she tried to free herself from the strong grip on her wrists. Lashing out she tried kicking Brent, who avoided her struggles easily. "What are you going to do to him?" Jess demanded staring defiantly into his face.

"Nothing if you do what I want," Brent loomed above her. "You better get used to this bitch. I ain't letting you go, and you will soon realize that there is no place to go where I won't be able to find you...or your child."

Jess's cheeks dampened with tears, knowing there was little she could do to fight him, but she couldn't give up, they had Henri and she had to protect him. "Please don't do this." She whimpered, emotionally exhausted, flinching as Brent's hands tore at her clothes. As she felt her shirt fall from her, she let out a piercing screech.

"Damn it! Shut up bitch." Brent backhanded her across the jaw.

Jess's vision clouded as the room spun around her, barely keeping conscious she tried vainly to fight. She could hear Brian chuckling at her efforts. He tightened his grip, causing pain to flash through her arms, making Jess almost nauseous. She could feel Brent trying to work her pants free. She squirmed under him wiggling one leg free she kicked out hard landing a blow to his chest.

Letting out a rancid stream of obscenities Brent picked her up off the couch and slammed her to the floor. Looking down on her pathetic form, "Think you're so hot now? You are nothing but trash. I gave you a place to stay and this is how you treat me, by running out?" He punctuated his tirade with kicks to Jess's ribs.

Brian recaptured Jess's flailing wrists and put a knee to her shoulder to force her to remain on her back.

Jess's stomach clenched, her ribs were on fire as she struggle to take each breath. The roomed darkened and her eyes swum with tears. She knew there was nothing she could do to stop them from raping her. Silently she started to sob feeling Brent once again concentrating on removing her clothes. Soft whimpers escaped her bruised lips as she began to yield to the darkness ready to consume her soul.

Brent looked down at the pathetic bitch under him. Insane with rage he started to tear the remaining clothes off her. *The ungrateful bitch is going to pay for trying to run out on me,* Brent thought viscously, unaware of the noise outside the door.

"Brent," Brian started, realizing they had company.

"Shut up and just hold her." Brent freed Jess from the last remnants of clothing. Just as he was lowering himself down to her the door splintered from the frame. "What the fuck."

"Go, go, go!!" Shouted the team captain as DEA burst through the door quickly surrounding the two men holding a girl on the floor.

"Put your hands up, now!!"

Brian quickly did what they said trying to ignore the

gun pointed at his head. He looked at the expression in Brent's eyes, a maniac lust looked back at him. Brian realized Brent was not going down without a fight. He hoped that he wouldn't be taken out in the process.

Brent hesitated, watching Brian pull back from Jess. He could see her arms tuck around her middle as she attempted to curl into a fetal position. He glanced at the DEA around him; incensed beyond reasonable thought, he attacked the nearest officer, struggling to take the gun from him. Brent had one thought in his mind: this was all Jess's fault and she was going to pay. Succeeding in wrestling the gun away from the cop he turned and sprinted down the hall. Bursting through the door to where Scott had taken the baby he raised the gun.

Bam! The cop covering Scott went down, shot in the back.

Bam! Bam! Shock filled Brent's mind, pain slowly spread through his chest. *I'm shot?* Brent slowly squeezed the trigger of his gun, unaware of his aim. Bam! Scott had turned toward him, holding Henri in his arms; the bullet had gone through Henri and hit Scott in the heart. Glazed eyes stared at Brent, as Scott slowly slumped to the floor dead, still holding Henri's now lifeless body in his arms. Brent fell forward, his blood intermingling with Scott's and Henri's blood. *Pay back bitch,* was Brent's last thought as life faded from his body.

The last of DEA came through the door hearing the gunshots. One of them grabed a blanket off the couch to cover the naked, shivering girl on the floor.

Startled at the touch, Jess lifts her head and her eyes flutter open to stare into familiar warm brown eyes. "Cory?" she whispered, unbelieving that he was there. Unable to struggle anymore she whimpers, "Where's Henri..." as her eyes closed and she succumbed to the darkness dragging her into a void free from the pain.

Cory stared as her face started to swell and turn color where Brent had hit her. Brushing back a stray hair, Cory whispered, "It will be alright Jess, I'll take care of you." His heart wrenched as she slipped into unconsciousness.

"Hey," Cory pointed to another one of his teammates, "Call an ambulance, she needs to be taken to the hospital right away."

"Already on its way, Cory." The older officer looked at Cory with concern. "Do you know her?"

"Ya, she lives here. I never would have though Brent would stoop so low as to rape her, but then he was always an unpredictable bastard." Consumed with guilt as Cory knew when he dropped her off here almost a year ago that it was a bad idea. Looking up to his teammate, Derek had a knowing look and a small wry grin on his face, Cory knew his feeling for Jess had been guessed. *Henri!* Cory thought suddenly. "Where's the child?"

Another officer stepped into the room holding a blood soaked bundle of blankets, "The child is dead."

"My God, no!"

Chapter Four: Courage

Four days later Jess remained at the hospital, still in a coma.

"Still here?" The doctor asked stepping into the room to check on Jess.

"Ya, I can't leave, she needs me." Cory didn't look up, he stared at Jess's face hoping for any sign that she was waking up.

"What are you going to do when she does wake up?" Doctor McConnell hated to push the young man, but he suspected the feelings Cory had for Jess could be her only hope in recovering.

"What do you mean?" Startled Cory looked at Doctor McConnell's grandfatherly figure.

"She will need someone to help her get through the loss of her son and the trauma of rape." Doctor McConnell smiled compassionately as Cory winced at his statement. "The question you need to ask yourself is whether or not you can handle being there for her. To do anything less would hurt her beyond recovery. Unfortunately, I have seen this situation before, and this time I hope for a better outcome."

Cory once again focused on Jess and asked himself, *Can I be there for her?*

Later that night Cory suddenly woke from dozing in the chair next to Jess. At first he didn't know what woke him. Sitting up he realized Jess was moving frantically under the covers of the hospital bed. The bed's rails were the only things keeping Jess from falling to the floor.

"Nurse!! Doctor!! She's waking up!" Cory called trying to grab one of Jess's flailing arms.

A keening wail released from her lips as Jess fought the hands holding her down. Panicking, she struggled, trying to free herself, twisting in the bed. Opening her eyes she tried to focus on the face above her; convinced that it was Brent, she lashed out with all her strength, still believing she was in the apartment.

"Jess, it's me, Cory. Calm down, Jess." Cory tried to dodge her blows, a few landed and he knew he would sport bruises the next day. He could see the wild desperation in her unfocused eyes. "Jess, can you hear me?"

"Leave me alone! Let me go!" Jess screamed. "Henri!!"

The nurses came rushing in to give Jess a sedative. Attempting to hold her down only made Jess struggle more. The screeches she emitted tore at Cory's heart, he knew then no matter what happened he wouldn't leave her.

"Jess, Jess!!" Cory raised his voice trying to get through to her. "Let them help. They won't hurt you. Jess! Listen to me!"

Vaguely, Jess heard a familiar voice, a voice she could trust. Distracted Jess paused in her attempts to escape, the nurse quickly gave her the sedative. Feeling the drug overwhelm her Jess looked towards the voice, focusing for a moment on the figure above her. "Cory?" she said slipping into a deep sleep.

"Jess?" Cory turned to the nurses, concerned. "Is she alright?"

"She'll be fine," the first nurse answered. "We'll will inform Doctor McConnell right away. He should be here within the hour. It will take a couple hours for the sedative to wear off, we will restrain her for the next time she wakes up."

"Do you really think that is necessary?" Cory looked down at Jess brushing back her tumbled hair.

"We don't want to take any chances of her hurting herself or anyone else if she wakes to another panic attack." The second nurse said as he attached the restraints to the bed and slipped them over Jess's wrists and legs.

An hour later, Doctor McConnell found Cory sitting in his usual chair next to Jess's bed. "Have you come to a decision?" Checking Jess's chart, he only needed to wait until she woke again.

"Decision?" Cory repeated thoughtfully. "Yes, I have. I love her and I will be there for whatever she needs."

"Good I was hoping that would be your answer." Doctor McConnell smiled at the young man. "Just make sure you tell her how you feel when she wakes up. She will need someone strong to pull her through."

Jess fought her way out of the darkness, blinking as she opened her eyes to the dim hospital room. Feeling someone clutching hand she looked to her left into warm brown eyes. "Wh-why can't I move?" Jess slurred still recovering from the dose of sedative.

"You are restrained. When you woke up before, you panicked and fought us. We had to sedate you." Doctor McConnell said from the foot of the bed. "It will take you a little more time to recover from the sedative, rest."

Doctor McConnell left the two alone for a moment as he summoned one of the staff nurses to take off the restraints.

"I don't understand," Jess said, looking up to Cory. "Where's Henri? I want to see him."

Cory took a deep breath, "Jess, do you remember anything that happened? You've been in a coma for the past four days."

Tremors shook her body as memories started to surface. "I remember Brian holding me down, and Brent..." Jess choked back a sob, "I remember gun shots, and...you?" She searched Cory's face, "Why were you there?"

"Jess, I'm a police officer sent undercover to take down Brent and his thugs and place them into custody. He was operating a fairly active drug ring in the city. Unfortunately you and Henri ended up in the middle of everything, there was nothing I could do. God, I wish I could go back and changes things to get you and Henri out before it was too late." Cory bowed his head guilt stricken.

"Too late? Cory, what are you not telling me?" Jess

struggled to sit up, but was unable to move with the restraints. "Where's Henri?" she demanded.

Cory grasped Jess's hand, rubbing it between his. "Henri's dead, Brent shot him."

"No! No, it can't be!" Racking sobs escaped from her. Jess felt life had failed her, nothing was left for her to live for. "Henri."

One of the nurses just entered the room, Cory motioned for her to take off Jess's restraints quickly. Once free, Jess seemed to pull into herself, curling up on her side away from Cory, her arms wrapped around her middle as she continued to sob. Cory got up and walked around the bed and pulled up another chair. Lowering the bed rail, he took hold of her hand and placed it in his.

Cory brushed back Jess's hair. "God, Jess if there was anything I could do to bring Henri back I would." Gently Cory place a chaste kiss on her forehead as he gathered her into his arms, rubbing Jess's back until she fell asleep exhausted. Cory eased her back to the bed and watched over her throughout the night.

A few days later Doctor McConnell released Jess from the hospital.

Chapter Five: Home

Listlessly Jess looked out the window of the car, not really caring where they were going. It seemed hours since she had left the cemetery where Henri was buried. All she could think about was Henri, his chubby little fists and angelic smile. Tears slid silently down her face. She would never be able to hold him again.

"Jess, we're here." Cory said gently bringing Jess out of

her listless state. Cory mentioned that he lived clear on the other side of the city and only took the undercover job as a special case. Cory told her that she was staying at his place; for how long she did not know.

They were parked in front of a blue rambler in a nice suburb. Jess smiled sadly at the white picket fence; this was a place she had always dreamed of living in. She looked at Cory getting her things out of the car, a newer 4-door sedan.

"Let's go inside and get you settled in," Cory said, taking Jess's hand in his and leading her up to the front door. "It's not much, just bought it a few months ago."

Jess silently followed Cory to one of the bedrooms.

"This will be your room. The people who lived here before had a daughter who left for college. It's a bit frilly, but I hope you don't mind." Cory babbled on trying to hide his nervousness. He turned to Jess, who was still standing in the doorway, a lost look on her face. "Jess, I told you that you could stay here as long as you want." Cory gently placed his hands on her shoulders, noticing Jess's slight jump. "Why don't you put your things away and I'll start some dinner. I'm not the greatest cook, but I make a passable spaghetti and sauce."

Jess numbly watched as Cory walked back down the hallway. Alone, she unzipped her duffle; on top of everything was Henri's teddy bear. Renewed tears escaped her eyes as she sat on the bed holding the bear to her chest rocking back and forth. "Oh, Henri, I miss you so much." She smiled at the noise coming from the kitchen, it sounded like Cory had dropped half the pans on the kitchen floor. Shaking off her melancholy, Jess started to methodically put her things in the proper place. Looking about the light and airy room and the frilly comforter on the bed and the shear curtains, she wished that she could stay here forever, to have a home. Sadly she knew this was only temporary, once her injuries healed Cory would help her find her own place and she would have to leave.

"Jess?" Cory called down the hall. "Dinner's ready."

Jess took a chair at the table, her stomach rumbled reminding her that she hadn't eaten any real food for days.

They ate in silence, each with their own thoughts of the future. Every so often Jess would look up and catch Cory staring at her, nervously she looked back down to her plate a slight blush creeping to her cheeks.

After dinner Jess retreated to her room to lay down and rest, her first day from the hospital had taken its toll on her.

During the night Cory woke from his sleep. Rubbing the sleep from his eyes he heard a thud as something or someone dropped on to the floor. Fully awake he realized the noise came from Jess's room. Cory crossed the hall to Jess's door, softly knocking he called out to her. Not hearing an answer, he opened the door.

"Jess?" Shocked he stared at Jess who was huddled in the corner of the room.

"No, no don't take him, don't take Henri." Jess repeated over and over lost in her nightmare. She clutched Henri's teddy bear to her chest rocking back & forth.

Cory cautiously approached Jess, trying not to startle her. Cory knelt in front of her and gently placed his hand on her shoulder to wake her.

Jess felt the hand on her shoulder and was transported back to the apartment and Brian was holding her down. A scream, filled with pain and terror fled Jess's lips as she tried to shrink away bringing up her legs in a defensive position and trying to back up from Cory. Tremors violently shook her body as she remained locked in her nightmare.

"Jess, please hear me." Cory said urgently in a low voice trying not to excite Jess into further hysteria. "Jess, focus on my voice, you have to come back to me. It's only a nightmare." Cory fervently repeated this to Jess, hoping it would draw her out of whatever darkness she was hiding in.

Slowly Jess's eyes became lucid, focusing on Cory's face. Tears fell as the nightmare faded, but the emotion remained.

Cautiously, Cory reached out to her again and gathered Jess into his arms. Lowering himself to the floor he sat holding Jess as her sobs subsided to murmurs. As she became quiet Cory helped her back in to the bed and covered her with the blankets, suddenly Jess reached out and grabbed his sweatshirt.

"Stay," Jess whispered, not opening her eyes, "please?"

Cory didn't have much of a choice as he was pulled down beside her. Jess snuggled up against him, laying her head on his chest. Feeling the steady heartbeat under her, she drifted off into an exhausted sleep.

Cory lay awake for many hours, smoothing Jess's hair and rubbing her back. As dawn lightened the room he knew that he had to tell her how he felt. Shifting slightly he felt Jess stirring against him. He looked down in to questioning blue eyes.

"Morning Jess," Cory started. "Do you remember anything from last night?"

Jess frowned, "A nightmare?" Dark memories lurked at the fringes of her mind, she tried to shut them out.

"Yes, and you asked me to stay." Cory clasp Jess's hand to his chest trying to reassure her.

"And you're still here?" Jess asked confused, no one had ever stayed with her when she was upset, not even Dave. Unable to decipher the look Cory was giving her, Jess laid her head back down. Listening to Cory's heartbeat she felt safe and didn't want the moment to end.

"Yes, I'm still here," Cory repeated, "and I won't leave you again."

"What…" Jess started.

"No, let me finish," Cory interrupted her. "I think it started the night Henri was born and the few days that followed. I fell in love with you." Cory looked down. Cory grasped her hand and held it to his chest. Silence stretched and Cory became nervous that he wasn't receiving any answer.

"Jess? Answer me did you hear me? I love you and I'm not going to let you go."

Jess looked into Cory's eyes seeing the truth in the words she couldn't believe. "I didn't dare to hope that you…I mean…" Jess stuttered confused.

"Does this mean that you love me back?" Cory held his breath waiting for an answer.

Pushing against his chest Jess turned to look at Cory, "I do. I love you, but it is hard to believe I won't wake up and this will be all a dream."

"It's no dream." Cory smiled as he reached up to kiss Jess, his lips barely brushing hers. "I have another confession to make. I called my family and they will be over later today to meet you."

"Family? Who?" Jess asked nervously.

"My mom and dad wanted to meet you. I called last night, after you went to sleep, to tell them that I was back home and you were with me. Of course they wanted to know all about you." Cory smiled remembering mom's reaction to his news.

"When will they be here?" Jess sighed not sure if she

was up to meeting anyone, at least the bruises on her face had almost faded and her ribs didn't bother her much today.

"Just before noon. Are you ok with this?' Cory asked, concerned that he was pushing her too much.

"Yes, I'm ok. It's just hard to move on. I miss him so much. I feel like there's a part of my soul gone, empty." Jess snuggled back up to Cory wrapping her arm tightly around his middle.

"Henri will always have a place in your heart, and in mine as well. For now, I want to take care of you and be there for you when you need a shoulder to lean on." Cory grinned at how corny that sounded, but it was the truth he wanted to help her deal with all the pain Jess had gone through.

Sitting on the couch while Cory was in the kitchen preparing something for dinner. He had refused to let her help claiming that she still needed the rest. Jess sat on the couch nervously switching the channels on the TV not wanting to think of the people she would be meeting soon. Jess was jerked out of her musings by the doorbell.

Cory gave an encouraging grin to Jess as he went to open the door.

"Cory!" Beatrice, his mom exclaimed as she held her son in a tight hug.

"Mom, jeez, let me breathe." Cory laughed.

"Don't you ever disappear like that again! Nary a call for four months!" Beatrice looked over to Jess as her husband, Cory's brothers and sister came into the room. "You must be Jess." Beatrice greeted her with a warm smile. "I'm Beatrice. Cory told us only a little about you. So sorry to hear about your son, Henri." She clasped Jess's hands pulling her off the couch into a motherly hug.

"Thank you," Jess stammered overwhelmed by the people crowding into the living room.

"Come, let me introduce you to everyone." Beatrice didn't let Jess go and turned her to meet Cory's family. "This is Cory's father, Bill. Cory's two brothers Mark and Steve and there is Cory's sister Katie, she's the youngest of them."

"Nice to meet you." Jess looked at Cory for support. Seeing the broad grin on his face eased her nerves.

"You are just in time for dinner," Cory said as he motioned them to be seated at the dining room table.

Cory took Jess's hand as he led her into the kitchen. Away from prying eyes and ears he leaned over to whisper, "They like you, I knew they would. I know this is probably overwhelming, but give them a chance. They are my family and let them be your family, too." Cory looked at Jess, uncertain how she would react.

"My family." Tears came to Jess's eyes, happy at long last her dreams had come true, true love, a home and family. Jess took Cory's hand and with a smile on her face, led him out to face her future.

Hazel Fugue
(or An Encounter with an Abraxas Flight)
Stephen W. Cote

PROLOGUE
"A Distraction from Their Troubles"

Until all vision had been obscured in the passing of a southerly tempest, Marshall Island was reckoned to lay some twenty miles East of Salem, Massachusetts. A wrath of nature had entangled many a ship's riggings and capsized others including the once distinguished Island Pride. Her wreckage was cast upon an unlikely breakwater of blackened rock to have her planks and masts tossed between swells and waves. Considered lost to the New England Pirate - a daring night of debauchery that thirty-first day of October, sixteen hundred ninety one - many considered auspicious her recent discovery. Such naïve hope was diminished the morning following her relocation for this particular tempest blew that summer eve; the nineteenth day of July, sixteen hundred ninety two.

Of the ships that departed on the eve of the tempest, a lone rowboat was the single vessel to ever see land and whose markings were consistent with the Island Pride. An unfortunate man of questionable countenance was curled in its prow with a specter of death laboring upon his weak exhales, and he was tended by a hapless cabin boy. The boy's behavior was shrouded by opaque fright while his health was unnerving in its wholesome purity.

By the following day, that is the twentieth day of July, sixteen hundred ninety two, Jacob Marrow would spy and approach the boy because he wanted desperately to forget the visage of the women dangling by their necks from the sturdy branch on Gallows Hill. Both his wife Aubrey and he awoke to an amnesiac delirium and would make about their business in a futile attempt to ignore the most recent past. By mid-morning, they would realize that neither could push the thoughts from their minds, perhaps never again be able to discuss those events, and so would take a long walk through one of Putnams' gangly orchards. They would see a boy on the sandy shore, decipher his name and a sense of urgency from his broken English, and find a fascinating distraction from their own troubles.

To behold the events that end with a bedeviled man and a spiritually cleansed boy at a shore near Salem, and that begun nine months prior when the Island Pride fell prey to the New England Pirate, suggests that Marshall Island existed and was a location where fantastic events transpired. Upon hearing such descriptions, as Jacob and Aubrey Marrow would be witness, a high degree of suspicion and disbelief would certainly be expected. If any truth was to be found then how might such truth affect the course of history for a small city in the midst of correcting rampant and unscrupulous behavior? Were this truth remotely believable, and thus highlight the wrongs of the accusers instead of the accused, would not this information be extremely dangerous?

On the other hand, it would be a lot less dangerous simply to disavow the existence of the island. And that is an easy task when its existence already was in question.

PART I
"*Descent of Man*"

July 20, 1692, Salem, MA

The storm had broken, and the leaky rowboat rocked on gentle swells beneath a predawn sky visible through scattered and fleeting clouds. Dimitri looked over the barely living body cowering in the prow and could see the sandy shore of the Massachusetts mainland. He crouched and untethered the oars from stowage. Though weak and feeble hours prior, he was surprised that his body felt invigorated and he now had the strength to lift one oar to the oarlock, and then the other. He gave little more than a cursory glance at the ailing passenger, gripped the oars firmly in his slight palms, and began to row.

Massachusetts Bay was peaceful with subtle swells, few ships and the telling signs of vessels thrashed by the recent tempest. A stiff morning breeze helped carry the boat towards shore, and gulls flying into the wind hovered motionless above before swooping down to inspect the boy and his passenger. Dimitri chased lingering gulls from the passenger but did not stop rowing for those that only passed by and pecked once or twice.

In truth, he had never felt so well in his life and for once enjoyed the chore of rowing on the open sea. His heart beat strongly and his lungs did not feel as though they would burst. He felt energized. As the boat traveled closer to the shore, he watched as Marshall Island dissipated into the fog. For a time it appeared to be no more than an uninviting rock, and then the island vanished. Passage from the island to the shore had given him time to contemplate the events that had transpired over the previous nine months.

Suffering and slavery were his life, and he recalled individual moments only as vacant holes in his thoughts where he had turned his mind away from the world. He could not imagine another defense a boy of ten years might muster. Then he was on the island, and his memory became clearer if for no other reason than a strange man kept the boy at his side, and the vile inhumanities of his owners were focused upon a strange young woman named Paris. For those nine months, she occupied his place in bearing their vicious wiles until Captain West shot her, minutes before succumbing to his own ills.

Dimitri slowed his rowing as he struggled to remember the cause of Captain West's demise. It was on the tip of his tongue for it affected the passenger he now ferried to land. He thought it queer that he could not envision the answer. Nor did he feel compassion towards Paris, for whom he fostered great despair all the while she was thrashed and used. Dimitri could visualize the missing memory because he refused to remember so much before the island. To have a complete memory for the first time in his life with recent and interspersed breaks attracted further introspection. It was as though a penultimate truth about her death, Captain West's death, and the ill passenger were interconnected in such a way and under such circumstances that compassion and mercy became foreign thoughts in their consideration. With but ten tears of wisdom, he saw that truth only as the missing memory.

When the boat was within a hundred yards of the shore,

Dimitri stopped rowing and reached for a leather parcel he had placed in the aft. He carefully unwrapped the skin, streaked with blackened mold from time and exposure, and took a hazel nut from the folds. It was the last nut of a small amount given to him prior to leaving the island. He turned it over in his fingers for now he could see its marvelous composure and form. When he noticed the passenger staring wide- and lusty-eyed at that one nut in his fingers, he quickly ate it and threw the fabric into the sea.

The last few strokes to the shore were the most difficult. Dimitri wanted to jump into the water and pull the boat over the remaining distance, but was unsure that his strength would prevail upon such weight. Instead he rowed the boat right up to the shore and then climbed over the side and into the surf. He wrapped his arms around a coil of rotten and frayed rope attached to the bow and struggled to pull the boat further onto shore. When he had availed himself to no end, he dropped the coil of rope onto the sand and returned to the boat.

The passenger appeared to be asleep, so he wasted no time in pulling a large leather satchel from the aft, pitched it to the ground, and drug it over the sand to a pile of drift wood dressed in rotten fish parts. He buried the satchel near the drift wood, took a long and careful look at where he was on the beach and where he had buried the satchel, and then hur- riedly returned to the boat.

The sun was creeping over the horizon, and the passen- ger looked ashen even in the magnificent auburn glow. Weak- ness and ailment crippled his eyes into a forlorn gaze and certain death was remarked upon by his expression. His crusty eyes cracked open and he raised a gray and gamely hand to touch his parched lips with a crooked finger.

"Boy," came a rasped whisper from the passenger's de- crepit mouth. "Water."

Immediate reaction rippled across Dimitri's chest and down his spine. He started to look for water but stopped himself and looked straight into the eyes of the passenger. He spit directly at the man's mouth.

The man's white and bloated tongue slithered across his flaked lips and licked the spittle from his finger and his mouth. "Please," he beseeched.

"Pray Death be thy mate, O'Reilly." Fresh hurt and anger boiled in Dimitri because, although he tried, he had not forgotten the harsh words, the hard strikes, and the buck-embraces. He felt raw heat smolder in his chest and took several steps back from the boat. O'Reilly was too weak to lash out at him, but Dimitri did not want to give him the opportunity.

"Pack mule," he stuttered and wheezed as he tried to speak harshly, "wretched beast of bidding. You are property, boy. Now fetch me water." O'Reilly made his demand in broken and weakly spoken words, in the only vicious tone he could muster.

Dimitri shook his head. "I bring you hither." He stamped his bare foot in the sand. He screamed at O'Reilly, "Now I find ears for your words." A hint of a smile crossed his lips, but he forced it away. "Then die, O'Reilly. Then be dead."

O'Reilly lay into the corner of the bow, turned towards Dimitri with one arm dangling over the side. His face contorted into a scowl. "And when I speak, consider what I may let slip of the treasure."

Dimitri's eyes widened but he said nothing.

O'Reilly coughed. Blood flecked his lips. "Fantastic wealth".

Dimitri thought of the buried satchel and wondered if O'Reilly had seen him. A memory then returned. Only hours ago, he had been colder and in a night that was blacker than he had ever known. Waves were crushing him against the shore and he had to fight the ocean because, for a time, it was his only refuge. Paris, speaking clearly for the first and only time directed him to the waves. Another voice from the pitch-black night had later instructed him with words to the effect of "Into the skiff, and take the passenger hither towards the light of the rising sun. Others must hear what he has to tell. They may try to help him, but when he speaks on the Fugue, as his telling will ultimately compel him, he will pass."

The Fugue. Dimitri thought that must be what is wrong with O'Reilly, and what happened to the others. He knew O'Reilly must say something about the treasure for that was his story. But then wasn't his story also the only reason he still lived? Dimitri was only sure that he didn't want to spend any more time alone with O'Reilly.

"I go find your ears," he said.

O'Reilly tried to laugh but was only able to make a sputtering sound. "You would leave me like this?"

Dimitri shrugged and started walking up the beach. He could hear O'Reilly complain and curse at him, but his weak voice didn't carry far and soon it was drowned out by the gently rolling waves. The beach was shallow, rising into a grassy berm fewer than a hundred paces from the water. At the top of the incline, Dimitri could see the port of Salem Towne to the south. To the north was a gentrified forest thick with oak and cedar, and to the east the forest was tamed into orchards and crops. He wasn't sure whether to walk towards the heavily populated area, or towards the orchards, so he started walking eastward, angling himself between the town and orchards.

"Boy!" When he had reached the top of the berm, he

had not seen anyone else, so was startled to hear any words. "I say, Boy!"

A man and woman, hands together, approached him and he thought that he must have confused them with the trees. He stood unsure of whether he was to approach them, or wait for their arrival.

"Boy," the man called again, though his voice was clipped and the word fell silent, just shy of being complete. The couple walked towards him, speaking in a hushed tone.

"I reckon he isn't some indentured boy, do you suppose Aubrey?" The man asked the woman. "You don't suppose he is a slave child?"

"Ask him," she said curtly. Both had an unkempt and tragic countenance.

"I say, boy," the man asked and then extended his hand, a gesture of welcome. "Jacob Marrow," he spoke in an overly masculine tone and gestured to the woman. "My wife, Aubrey."

"Name is Dimitri." He pointed to himself.

"Dameeshee?" Aubrey smiled, but only slightly.

"Dimitri," he said again.

"Ah, I think the boy is trying to say Damiter." Jacob smiled at his own intellectual prowess. "I say, you're a sight Damiter." He looked over the boy, nodding his head.

"Jacob," Aubrey nudged her husband. "Leave the slave boy alone."

Dimitri waved his hand towards the Ocean and spoke with a more earnest tone. "Pray follow me. Help."

Jacob stepped to the top of the berm and looked onto the beach. From his vantage, he observed the skiff listing in the surf and a man lain within. "I say, is that man injured?"

Dimitri nodded, and Jacob and Aubrey walked down

the berm and briskly crossed the beach towards the boat. The boat rocked in the light waves with O'Reilly sprawled across the bow.

"Thank you, Lord," O'Reilly wheezed when he saw the approaching couple, though he didn't think to include Dimitri in his momentary lapse into piety.

"Are you unwell, sir?" Jacob asked as he approached, though came to an abrupt stop when he could see O'Reilly more clearly. He held back his wife, who signed the cross and said, "Heavens, he's got the plague."

"Fugue," Dimitri said abruptly and approached the boat. He prodded O'Reilly with several sharp stabs of the finger as though the man were a tamed beast. "He not hurt you."

The Marrows were understandably skeptical, though Jacob became more accepting as he looked between Dimitri and O'Reilly. "I reckon the boy seems quite healthy. But, the gentleman's manner seems familiar." He exchanged a glance with his wife, but they were not ready to bring voice to the familiarity of O'Reilly's condition.

"Boy," O'Reilly gasped and tried to grab Dimitri's arm. When that failed, he pointed to indicate himself and managed to speak his own name. "O'Reilly. My name is O'Reilly. The boy," he pointed at Dimitri, "the boy Dimitri is my servant. Property."

Dimitri turned to the Marrows to protest, but Jacob smiled and clapped his hands together, then turned to Aubrey. "The boy's name is Dimitri." Then, to O'Reilly. "Sir, we best help you back to our home and pray you might recover from this unfortunate ailment of yours."

"Fugue," Dimitri muttered, but didn't belabor the distinction as he didn't know what, exactly, that distinction was. He felt as though his new-found strength had been momentarily knocked from his body, and wondered what was to become of him.

PART II
"Broken Spirits"

October 3, 1691, Marshall Island, off the coast of MA

A once kindly merchant swung by his neck from the yardarm, pitching and rocking in mid-air as waves and swells pushed against the hull of the Island Pride. The ship, recently refitted in Salem, had put out late September and within days came broadside with what the merchant thought to be a derelict schooner. The pirates were swift and ruthless in their naval lusts, and the Island Pride had been their target for months. Captain West plotted and connived with the yard crews to leave some rig affixed to the flanks to make it possible for his crew to anchor their decrepit schooner alongside the larger ship. Though a merchant ship on a short jaunt to evaluate a new crew, and therefore without cargo or funds, it was everything Captain West had desired. His ambitions required cargo space.

As the Island Pride's new and salty crew negotiated the ship towards a tiny cove on the Northern face of Marshall Island, Captain West came to terms with the island's very existence. Charts he had drawn earlier indicated a breakwater and outcropping of blackened rocks, but no island. He didn't recall a spec of green on the rocks, and certainly not an island the size of a small country. He had sailed the schooner to this same position mid-September.

The crew fought to bring the ship into the calmer water of the tiny cove as the ship was upset by swells. As they labored, the Captain's door rattled against the frame and then opened. Dimitri stumbled from the Captain's quarters, onto the deck, and to the rail. He walked with obvious pain to his gait and seemed altogether unsteady on his feet.

Captain West emerged on the deck with a particular swagger, still tying his britches. He put his hand on Dimitri's shoulder and shoved the boy in the direction of the First Mate.

"'bout a pop before shore?" Captain West asked loudly.

The First Mate, Redlung, grinned a mouthful of rotten teeth, and grabbed the boy's loose-fitting tunic. "Don't mind if I do, Cap'n. Much obliged."

A man who was not part of the crew, at least as far as Dimitri could tell, interceded. The strange man was not quite as tall as Captain West or as burly as the other swells, but carried himself with a capable countenance.

"Not the time for tomfoolery." He peered at Dimitri and said, "Boy, fetch my kit to the skiff."

Captain West's face reddened and he grabbed the man's arm, though the man seemed to easily slip from the Captain's grip.

"Captain, I wish to wait no longer."

The Captain drew a stiletto from his sleeve in a heated move and held it against the man's throat. "Never intercede in my vices or those of my men, or I'll cut your throat myself."

Unphased, the man looked passed the stiletto and directly at the Captain. "Need I remind the Captain that the treasure is not secure?"

"You needn't," The Captain said and sniffed, returning the stiletto to his sleeve. "I am aware." He snarled at Dimitri and shoved him against the rail. "Be off then and fetch his kit."

The Captain turned and sneered at the man, then his face became more pensive and his tone more suited for business. "I figure with the load we'll need every warm body we can get."

The man nodded in agreement. "If we're to move the lot in one go." He looked out at the island. "You recall that I told you it would take us several months."

When the Captain didn't respond, the man continued. "Supplies."

"We have supplies for a few weeks. But no powder onboard, and we used every grain we had taking it." The Captain appeared dismayed, though was absolutely sure not to display his expression to any of his men.

"We'll find bounty of food further inland," the man assured.

"I don't trust you," The Captain said plainly.

"You didn't trust that I'd bring you to this island. Continue not trusting that I will bring you to the treasure, and well-fed at that." The man laughed aloud in confidence, then made his way to the skiff.

Captain West's crew anchored the Island Pride in the cove by noon, and the remainder of the day was spent ferrying the crew and supplies to the shore. The shore was little more than a narrow swatch of rocks that dipped in a steep incline to meet the water. Supplies were left at the bottom of the incline and the crew already on land humped the packs and kits up to a level clearing.

The sun had melted on the horizon when Captain West arrived at the clearing. Dimitri tended to a fire, though spent most of his time scurrying out of the crew's way. Redlung made one attempt to draw him into the woods but was intercepted by the strange man. The man tasked Dimitri to carry his kit, as well as a heavy burden of the supplies, and otherwise instructed him to stay near his side.

For the first time in his life, Dimitri felt a vague sense of relief, though only until Captain West arrived.

The Captain kicked him away from the strange man. He glanced around and started to say what Dimitri thought was a name, but the man silenced him. "I don't like this. Something doesn't feel right. This island is not supposed to be here."

The man shrugged. "Captain Shaw drew the map. Take it up with him."

Captain West growled. "Which way will we go?"

The man pointed towards a clump of trees. "A mountain trail, a steep climb, then a river valley and another climb. At least two weeks to get to the far side of the valley. Another few weeks to get," he paused and extracted a parchment from his finely tailored shirt. He unfolded it, then tipped it to let the Captain read it. "Here." He put the tip of his finger on some location of the parchment.

The Captain nodded. "We best get an early start. We have a long ways to go."

. . . .

Dimitri had never walked so much in his life. The supplies and the strange man's kit weighed him down considerably, and his feet ached and bled from the leather strips he was given for shoes. All of the crew were weighed down, so he was not the only one to fall behind, though he was the one most often punished. His eye was still swollen and purple from a brutal swat the Captain had given him when, four days into their journey, he had tried to pull Dimitri off behind a shrub but the strange man intervened again. The two got into a heated argument and the Captain delivered the stinging knuckle-slap to the boy's temple.

. . . .

Then came the matters of the food, the pistol, and the young woman. Twelve days of marching and everyone's spirits were up. As the strange man had foretold, a bounty of food was to be found. Nuts, berries, and fruits on every tree and bush. The weather was pleasant, if not unseasonably warm, and though Captain West had expressly forbidden Dimitri from eating any of the fresh fruits, berries, and nuts, Dimitri didn't mind. For once, there seemed to be a reason that Dimitri agreed with. He was carrying a load of foodstuffs, and the more he ate, the less he had to carry. Dimitri had enough smarts to realize that he would have to pack something else, but for the time his pack started to get lighter.

The woman and the pistol both appeared at the same time. She lept from a bush and pointed the pistol at Captain West, then began to yell and scream in an incomprehensible language. She pointed behind her, in front of her, and had a look of dread and unquenchable fear haunting her entire being.

She looked only a few years older than Dimitri, and wore a simple and tidy dress. Dimitri was not able to study her for more than a few moments because one of the crew pushed her off balance and Captain West picked up the pistol. At first, he seemed more interested in the pistol and smacked her with the butt.

"Powder? You have powder?" Everyone seemed to completely ignore the question of how she might have gotten so far inland of an island that wasn't supposed to exist.

She yelped at the strike, and tried to stand up but was struck down again. She jabbered away, though the only word Dimitri could come close to understanding sounded like 'Pyreesh'

Apparently the Captain thought the same because he muttered, "Your name is Paris, then, is it?" She jabbered, but no one could understand what she was trying to say, or what dangers or information she was trying to impart with her gestures. "Paris, I'll ask nicely just once more. See, we all want more powder like what you have here." He held up the gun, then inspected it to see if it was loaded; he immediately moved the barrel away from his face intimating a ball, patch, and grains where rammed. "Where did you get the powder?"

The strange man said softly, "Do you suppose she can't understand us?"

Captain West handed the pistol to one of his trusted crew, O'Reilly, and sucked in his ample gut. "I'll tell you what, I'll talk in the universal language." He smacked Paris again and then took hold of the collar of her dress and drug her into a grove of trees. Dimitri looked at the strange man to see if he would stop the Captain, but he didn't.

From the trees, the woman's babbling became anguished cries.

The Captain returned after several minutes, wiping his damp forehead with his hand. He nodded to Redlung, who dashed into the woods.

"I don't think she has any more powder," the Captain said to the man with a laugh of accomplishment. "We'll camp here for the night, and give the men a taste o' vice."

The man shrugged and cast a brief glance towards Dimitri, who could only watch his feet. He knew what was happening in those trees, but couldn't understand why the man didn't prevent it from happening.

Later, in the twilight hours, the men lay drunk and sated around a raging fire. Dimitri tended to a smaller fire and ate a portion of the rations. The crew had taken turns going into the trees all afternoon, and now Paris stumbled back into the camp. Her face was bloodied, she had to hold her dress together at the bosom to keep it from slipping off, and her body was scratched and bruised.

O'Reilly stood when she walked by him and he grabbed her arm and pushed her towards Dimitri. "Don't try runnin'," he slurred, then collapsed back to the ground.

Paris stumbled and fell at Dimitri's feet. He looked at her, at the men camped around the fire, and then with some hesitation extended his hands to help her up. She surprised him by reaching out and grabbing his shirt, and pulling him close to her face. She studied him very closely and said more unintelligible words in a hushed though earnest whisper. To Dimitri, it only sounded like she was saying her name. "Pyreesh. Pyreesh."

When Paris saw the Dimitri didn't understand her, she lay down by the fire and bit her lip to muffle her cries.

Dimitri looked up and over the camp, and saw the strange man had been watching.

. . . .

Twenty-seven more days of marching. It seemed as though the nuts, berries, and fruits tasted better with each passing hour. Not a daylight hour went by when Paris wasn't pulled off behind a bush or tree by one of the crew. Sometimes, at night, they didn't bother going anywhere.

On the fortieth day, the crew reached the place of the parchment that the strange man had shown to Captain West. Dimitri arrived having been untouched by the crew or Captain West for the entire trek. The strange man had seen to that. The strange man did nothing to help Paris.

PART III
"*Just Another Salem Witch*"

July 21, 1692, Salem, MA

Jacob and Aubrey Marrow occupied a fit house just out-side of Salem. The house was cobbled together with heavy maple planks, and was tucked by a freshwater stream that had thus far been unclaimed for irrigation. At the time, the geopolitical location of the house was about as ideal a place for a fusion of the reigning politics and Wiccan traditions.

One day had passed since Jacob and Aubrey had en-countered Dimitri and O'Reilly. Dimitri's health was unwa-vering in its purity, while O'Reilly continued to fare worse. Neither preacher nor doctor had been able to identify the cause of the ailment, and Jacob wisely consulted the judiciary coun-cil about the matter. The council representative, Peter Th-ompson, spent the morning observing O'Reilly while he told the Marrows about the trip inland on Marshall Island to the grove. The strange man had given O'Reilly the parchment, which O'Reilly produced to show where a large black 'X' was blotted on a clump of poorly sketched trees.

Peter looked up from where O'Reilly lay near the hearth, and walked across the tightly jointed floorboards to the plank table where the Marrows and Dimitri were seated.

"He's a witch," Peter said bluntly.

"We figured as much, Mr. Thompson, and that's why my husband and I consulted with you." Aubrey seemed very nervous.

Peter lay his hands on Aubrey's and Jacob's shoulders. "You folks did the right thing in coming to us right away. The boy there seems Godly enough, so I figure we can rule out some infectious ailment that rends the soul into a Witch. A few things caught my attention, though, in listening to his blathers."

"Yes, the poor woman." Jacob said, and signed the cross.

Peter nodded. "That, yes, though I admit I've heard that is the sort of scandalous behavior one must expect of his sort." He tipped his head towards O'Reilly.

"Pirates, yes," Aubrey agreed.

"It was the food that caught my attention." Peter looked at their quizzical expressions, and then back at O'Reilly. "Could you say again what you ate while you were there? And describe it for us as best as you can?"

O'Reilly had fallen into a great amount of pain and suffering, and could only speak in short bursts before succumbing to bloodied coughing and tormented wheezing. "Berries, fruits, nuts. A lot of nuts. Mostly hazel nuts. They were big and very tasty. Big strawberries and juicy huckleberries. Blackberries. Peaches. Apples of many sorts."

"Nuts, yes." Peter reached into a pocket and withdrew a square of white linen. He unfolded it and Dimitri could see a single hazel nut in his palm. Almost identical to the hazel nuts he had been given, and the ones he had seen the rest of the crew eat.

Peter approached O'Reilly and showed him what was in his hand.

O'Reilly's eyes widened and he coughed, then in an unexpected burst of speed snatched the nut and shoved it into his mouth. He quickly chewed it and swallowed it.

Peter recoiled his hand and looked perturbed, though also interested for O'Reilly convulsed almost immediately after eating the nut and his condition took a turn for the worse.

As Dimitri looked on, he had to blink several times for

he thought he saw a spark of light near O'Reilly's neck. Even thinking about having seen the spark brought back some of the memories that had been missing, and he became very nervous.

"Why do you suppose he did that?" Jacob asked. "Not a very neighborly act."

Peter dabbed his forehead with the square of linen and put it back in his pocket. "Jacob, Aubrey, I don't want to bring up any undue unpleasantness, but what we just observed seems to be common amongst those accused of witchcraft. The illness, the fantastic stories of islands that don't exist, and these hazel nuts. My well-learned opinion is that witches crave hazel nuts, this particular type of hazel nut to be precise."

A knock came upon the door and everyone turned to look in its direction. Jacob slowly rose and approached the door, waited a few moments, and then opened it.

Dimitri's jaw dropped when he saw the strange man standing in front of him.

"Ah, speaking of witches," Peter said acidly.

"Mister Barrymore," Jacob said and shot a cold look towards Peter. "What chance brings you to our house on this day?" Jacob extended an invitational gesture for Mr. Barrymore to enter.

Mr. Barrymore entered and tipped his head towards Dimitri. "I heard you had encountered a strange pair on the shore, and the descriptions of a particular boy piqued my interest. Ah," he looked directly at Dimitri. "I've been in search of you, Dimitri."

"You know this slave boy then?" Jacob asked.

"Indeed," Mr. Barrymore said, "though he is no slave. He was one of my wards, taken from my care by some brigands a number of months back."

"I don't recall that you announced such a heinous event," Peter said.

"I did, though this was Boston and I didn't think to send the news up here."

"Ah," Peter said with much skepticism.

Dimitri was quiet and could only look at the always well-dressed Mr. Barrymore. Now, after so many months, he knew his name.

"We were just listening to this man's confession," Peter said in an attempt to dismiss the new arrival.

"Ah, perhaps then another pair of learned ears might be needed as you do not appear to be keeping a record of the confession," he said, glancing around for any sign of scribing.

"Of course," Jacob said. "A very interesting story, tis. Though, I do warn you that Peter has vouchsafed this man as a witch."

Mr. Barrymore nodded and looked at O'Reilly, who could only look back with a perplexed expression. "By the looks of it, we'll soon be less one witch."

"Yes," Peter said anxiously, "Now if you don't mind, I am trying to find out the source of their demonic power. It seems to have something to do with those nuts we found on Tituba, Miss Parris and Miss Williams. We also found similar types of nuts in the homes of Miss Nurse, Martin, Howe, Good, and Wildes. We watched this man," He nodded to O'Reilly, "ingest one of those very nuts just moments ago."

"Pity," Mr. Barrymore said. "Pitiful fool." He walked over to O'Reilly and said in a soft, mercy-soaked tone, "You're out of time. Finish it now."

"Yes, we found the gold." O'Reilly gasped. "So much wealth. Gold, gems, pearls, silver."

"And what happened to everyone who was with you?" Mr. Barrymore prompted.

"Dead." O'Reilly said. "They're all dead."

"How did they die?" Peter asked in earnest, for all could tell that O'Reilly was in his last throws with death. "Was it an enclave of witches, then?"

Mr. Barrymore looked at Dimitri and rolled his eyes.

Dimitri bit back a light smile.

"It was the f…" O'Reilly started to say, but then exhaled his last breath.

. . . .

"The Fugue," Dimitri said later that evening after O'Reilly's body had been taken out back and, per Peter's instructions, burned. "It was the Fugue."

"This is all rather ridiculous, isn't it?" Peter asked. "Islands that aren't on any map, enough treasure to buy the whole of France. Plentiful and tasty foodstuffs at every turn."

"I want to know what happened to that poor girl," Aubrey asked.

"And how is it that you are not sick?" Jacob asked.

"I don't think you'll believe," Dimitri mumbled sullenly.

Mr. Barrymore sat at the plank table beside Dimitri and across from Peter Thompson. "Peter, perhaps the boy is right in thinking his words may be misconstrued with fantasy."

"Because everything the pirate-witch O'Reilly spoke of was ludicrous," Peter said. The Marrows nodded in agreement.

"Yet you acknowledge the existence of some particular hazel nut, and that nut must have come from somewhere. If there is witchcraft working in Salem," he paused to let the most recent events and his words intermingle with those at the table, "then perhaps the existence of such an Island, as the deceased witch and the boy have described, is not so far-fetched. As you suggested, it could very well be the source of witchcraft in Salem."

Peter narrowed his eyes, and after some intense thought nodded in agreement. "Yes, precisely as my keen and learned intellect prevailed upon me."

"All I am saying is let the boy answer your questions, but don't hold against him his exposure to these apparent witches. I would be remiss to not assume you would form the opinion that he is some witchcraft-plague carrier." Mr. Barrymore nodded at his own words. "Besides, whatever he has to say couldn't be any less believable than the entire notion of witchcraft," Mr. Barrymore added with a sharp look at Peter.

"What would you have me say?" Peter asked after some length of silence.

"That you would declare him not a witch nor in league with witchcraft before you have him say another word," Mr. Barrymore put bluntly.

"That seems rather backwards, wouldn't you say?" Peter argued.

"I would think the boy said enough to decide one way or the other," Jacob remarked.

"Fine. He's not a witch," Peter conceded.

"I'd prefer that you put your mark next to it, if it's all the same to you," Mr. Barrymore said. He withdrew a quill and parchment from his pocket and handed them to Peter. "I don't want this conversation to be twisted out of reason and be revisited upon the boy, or on me, some weeks or months hence."

Peter grimaced and took the quill, then held it up. "And you would have me sign in blood, I take it?"

Aubrey laughed nervously and fetched a pewter ink well. "Certainly not, Mr. Thompson." She set the ink well beside the parchment and Peter quickly scribbled a note declaring the "boy who is not a slave but of indenturement or wardship to one Mister Barrymore to be cleared of having any consortment with any known elements or persons having any such relationships with the evil tidings now termed witch craft."

"Satisfied?" Peter asked and handed the parchment to Mr. Barrymore.

"Quite." He offered only the slightest perceptible nod towards Dimitri.

"Then tell us about the source of witchcraft," Peter said with earnest.

Dimitri looked quizzically at Mr. Barrymore.

"What happened after the pirates found the treasure?" Mr. Barrymore asked.

PART IV
"*The Fugue*"

Captain West and the crew located the treasure, some of it buried, some of it tucked into knotholes, and the rest locked in heavy chests, close to where the map indicated. They wasted no time in separating out the best parts and assigning loads to each man. Dimitri, who still carried a part of the rations, could only carry a satchel of gemstones. His weight of rations was further increased as he took on the loads from the rest of the crew. Captain West instructed him through a serious of explanative kicks, shoves, and cuffs not to look inside the satchel.

The crew camped for several more weeks in the grove, basking in the warm weather and enjoying the incredible bounty of nuts, berries, and fruits. The strange man, who Dimitri would later learn to be named Mister Barrymore, distanced himself from the crew and was not to be seen for most of the time. He must have given very explicit instructions as to Dimitri's care, though, as none of the crew bothered him apart from the usual kicks and shoves.

Paris received the brunt of the crew's attention. She spent most of the time lashed to a tree, and Dimitri rarely saw her. A day before the crew broke camp for the return journey, she was freed. She returned to her spot next to Dimitri, curled into a fetal position, and lay quiet.

Her vacant expression and battered body reminded Dimitri of himself, but during the journey on the island, he had slowly distanced himself from those feelings under the watchfulness of the strange man. Just as Paris was reduced to his previous state, so did he feel his constitution rise.

Dimitri found himself enjoying the long periods of quiet, and he didn't mind having to eat the otherwise bland and spoiled rations instead of the succulent and aromatic foodstuffs. He had contemplated many times sneaking some for himself, but didn't want to tarnish the experience of being free from the crew's advances.

The morning the crew broke camp, the strange man returned. He spent several hours speaking with Captain West, and repeatedly pointed to the map. Several times, Captain West asked the strange man where he had been but he never answered. When their conversation finished, the crew started the journey back to the Island Pride.

The journey back grew increasingly less enjoyable than the journey in. The availability of food became scarcer and less tasty. The weather was not as pleasant, and the crew began to complain. Two weeks into the return journey, it became much worse.

. . . .

"Piss in the wind!" Redlung swore and slapped at his neck, his eyes watering and his nose starting to run. He jabbed his finger at his neck. "O'Reilly, what the hell is that?"

"A bit of odd color, I guess. No swelling." O'Reilly studied Redlung's neck then shrugged. "Haven't seen a mosquito or any other pest the whole while."

Redlung slapped the back of his neck and cringed. "There! It happened again. What was it?"

O'Reilly looked at him with a strange expression. "Nothing. There's nothing out here." He saw that Redlung's neck had another patch of discoloration. The skin looked gray.

Redlung continued to complain loudly for another half hour before Captain West called the march to a halt and approached Redlung. "What is this caterwauling 'bout back here? Suck it up and lets get moving."

"Mosquitos, Cap'n. They're eatin' me alive," Redlung complained boisterously.

Captain West grabbed Redlung's collar and yanked the man close to his face. "Look around you, you addled fool. Show me just one mosquito."

Redlung looked around but saw nothing. However, he felt another stabbing pain, one after another, this time on his arms. "Cap'n" he begged, near weeping, "I don't see them, but look at me. Look at my arms!"

The Captain inspected the man's arms and glanced at his neck. The discoloration had become quite noticeable and his skin was a patchwork of gray splotches. "Maybe something you ate," he observed. "Keep moving."

Throughout the day, Redlung suffered from his elusive mosquitoes, and began to fall behind. Others started to complain of stinging sensations as well, and bore the same skin discolorations.

"Your humors are imbalanced," O'Reilly suggested to Redlung. "Chew some of those weeds, maybe, and rub them on your forehead." Redlung snapped at O'Reilly, and attempted to shove him, but instead fell to the ground. He was quickly incapacitated and unable to move.

O'Reilly summoned Captain West. "Should we carry him?"

"Lose his load of the treasure, and another load to carry him? No. If he can't walk, we leave him." For the number of years Captain West had known Redlung, he had dismissed him entirely without a second thought.

Captain West looked at O'Reilly with much contempt. "Do be sure to redistribute as much of his load as can be carried."

. . . .

Throughout the night, and the next morning, others continued to complain of the same symptoms. They described feelings akin to exquisitely painful mosquito bites, but nary a mosquito was to be seen. Two men were unable to stand that morning, and another fell by noonday.

Thirty five men, plus Dimitri and the strange man, and later Paris, made the trip to the grove. Now, four of the thirty eight treasure hunters had fallen.

Captain West consulted with the strange man, and it was decided to quicken the pace so as to distance themselves from the fallen. They also decided to move anyone complaining of the illness to the back of the line. If anyone fell back, the healthy travelers would not wait for the others.

By following the map, the return trip took them along a different path as the one they had followed inland. Had they taken the return path inland, they would have encountered the skeletons two months earlier. The skeletons were scattered along the path, as though they had once been stragglers who had fallen apart from the main group, and their remnants bore telltale indications that they were Captain Shaw's crew.

Captain West pulled the strange man aside and furiously chided him. "The map says nothing about any sickness, yet it is plain to my eyes that Shaw encountered it and did just as we are doing. Obviously Shaw didn't make it off the island with the treasure, and now I have doubt that he made it off at all."

"Shaw must have made it off the island. How else would we have the map?"

"Shaw hasn't been seen in over a year," Captain West whispered angrily. "We picked up the map from a bloke who in turn lifted it from one of Shaw's crew he thought to have been addled-drunk. But you alone knew its markings, which tells me you must have been here before, or at least knew of this strange ill that now plagues us."

"Rubbish," the strange man spat. "You came to me with the map and I knew how to interpret its signets and markings, nothing more. Everything I've told you has been based on what you yourself gave to me."

The pistol Paris had once held was tucked in Captain West's sash, and he now withdrew it and jammed it under the strange man's chin. "I'd be better off if I put a ball into this filthy liar's mouth."

"Better be sure," the strange man said with a wry grin. "If I was here before, and I'm not claiming I have been, but supposing I was, then at least I made it out. Besides, you might want to save that one bullet."

"Yeah, and what for?" Captain West asked.

The strange man whispered something and nodded towards Paris. Captain West's eyes widened and he nodded, then said, "Yes, that does seem to make some sense to me."

The man easily pushed the barrel away from his chin, and added, "but you may want to wait until you're closer to the shore. More treasure that way."

. . . .

Four days from the Island Pride, and the crew was running under the full weight of their treasure. Eleven more men had fallen, leaving their numbers at twenty crew, Dimitri, Paris, and the strange man. The further they progressed, they encountered more skeletons from Captain Shaw's crew. And the more the illness seemed to affect them. Two more crew fell on the fourth day and third day, and three more on the third day. Thirteen crew remained by the time they reached a clearing where the Island Pride could be seen.

A steep incline lead to a sandy beach. To the northern end of the beach was the tiny cove where the Island Pride was anchored, blocked by an outcropping of sharp rocks. The crew had run for such a distance that the men were barely able to stand, and though eager to depart the ills of Marshall Island, they had to rest.

When the crew set their packs down, they noticed that the white rocks in the short grass were not rocks at all, but a mass of bones. Only then, and in their momentous alarm, did they observe a swarm of brightly colored wings and gleaming metal stingers bearing down on their position. At first glance, the insects looked like large, wicked mosquitoes, but as they flew closer, the crew could see their assailants for the first time.

The strange man grabbed Paris' and Dimitri's collars and pulled them down the steep embankment to the sandy beach. Captain West followed as the rest of the crew were engulfed in the swarm. Some of the crew threw themselves down the embankment and onto the beach, bringing the swarm with them.

The strange man left Paris and Dimitri on the beach, and Captain West raced over to them. He snatched at their necks and took hold of them with a tight grip in an attempt to use the two bodies as shields against the onslaught.

PART V
"An Encounter with an Abraxas Flight"

Thousands upon thousands of fairies poured over the steep embankment onto the beach. Each fairy was adorned with tiny, intricate-designed armor, had a pair of beautifully colored wings, and wielded a silver pike twice as long as the fairy was tall. Dimitri could only watch helplessly as the fairies jabbed their terrible pikes into the bodies of the crews. Wherever their pikes pierced the skin, it looked as though a small part of life was drained from the victim's body.

As the fairies closed in on Captain West, he could see that they had no immediate interest in either Paris or Dimitri. He looked around for the strange man, but did not see him anywhere.

Captain West let go of Paris and Dimitri, then pulled out the pistol and pointed it at the boy. "I'll not let my beasts live if I must die," he swore and cocked the pistol. Then, remembering what the strange man had told him more than a week prior, he pointed the pistol at Paris and snarled. "I was told you to be a witch who cursed us with this ill wind, and now I see it to be the truth."

Captain West fired the pistol and Paris crumpled to the ground. As Paris fell, she pulled Dimitri down with her. With his anger and only shot spent, he was left alone with raw panic. Captain West started to run towards the Island Pride, but had been boxed-in by the fairies.

Dimitri found himself laying across Paris' chest, his tunic becoming drenched in her blood from the wound in her stomach. Her arm drew his ear close to her mouth.

"For you boy," she sucked at the air, blood flowing from her mouth. For the first time, her words were clear. She took his chin in her trembling hand and turned his head then fully kissed his lips. "One last kiss upon your innocent lips" She lay her head back against the sand and her eyes became vacant. Her face contorted in pain, and Dimitri could feel her entire body writhe and lurch beneath him. He pulled himself away from her chest and sat beside her. Fairies swarmed around their heads, though ignored them and seemed to be concentrating on Captain West.

Captain West looked at Dimitri and Paris, and screamed.

Dimitri looked up at Captain West, but saw that the fairies had not set in on him yet. He looked back at Paris, but what he saw startled him and he scooted back in the sand several feet.

Captain Shaw lay dying in the sand where the young woman he knew as Paris once lay. Shaw was dressed in the remains of a woman's simple dress that had been tattered and torn from the abuse of Captain West and his men.

Shaw reached towards Dimitri, his eyes tearful and his voice pleading. He didn't try to apologize for the evils he had imparted on Dimitri before the boy had been given to Captain West. Instead, he pointed towards the water, and said, "Now, to the sea, Dimitri."

The fairies started in on Captain West.

Amidst Captain West's shrieks, Captain Shaw said as loud as his dying breaths permitted, "Run now to the sea, quick before West falls! Stay off dry land until you see no life t'all; only a dead rock and nothing t'all of this island."

Dimitri looked between Shaw, the water, and the fairies swarming around Captain West.

Shaw sputtered and retched. "Boy," he said in barely a whisper. "Run now to the sea. Stand fast against the surf until all is dead. When you see nothing alive and the fairies have subsided, only then emerge and I promise you this boy, for these fairies have bound me to say it," tears welled in Shaws eyes and he wept into the sand. "I swear to you boy you will be cleansed of all wrong brought to bare against you."

He turned in the sand so as to touch Dimitri, and tugged at his arm. "You must go now, boy. Run now into the sea, and you will be made right again."

Shaw exhaled and went still.

Dimitri climbed to his feet and saw that he was surrounded by a wall of fairies. Whatever they were doing to Captain West made him shriek, and his words began to become garbled and unintelligible. Dimitri gave Captain West a wide berth, but was not sure what to do. He started to walk on uncertain legs towards the Island Pride, then towards the slope leading inland to the island.

From atop the slope, the strange man appeared and pointed to the water. "That way boy. Run!"

Dimitri looked back towards the water and started to run across the sand. He ran into the water, and then looked back at the beach. A young woman of similar build and appearance to Paris stood amidst the flight of fairies. The fairies started towards the water and Dimitri stepped back further.

It looked to be a wall of fairies at the edge of the water; vibrant hues and majestic life. The fairies thrust their pikes into the air at the edge of the water, though did cross over the water.

Dimitri could not see Captain West, only the dead body of Captain Shaw and a confused young woman who spoke nonsensical phrases. Every so often, over the din of the flight of fairies, he heard her cry aloud, "Pyreesh. Capeesh. Capwaa. Pyrwee." Only then did it occur to him what Paris had been trying to say when she spoke 'Pryeesh'. She was trying to say "Pirate Shaw."

. . . .

Cold seeped through his clothes, skin, and muscles until his bones ached. Waves crashed at his back and threw his body onto the shore. He scrambled back into the cold, dark ocean every time. Hours passed, the night was long, and a storm had arisen to blow overhead. Alone in this dark and perilous place, the wrongdoings afflicted upon this innocent boy were crushed from his body with each wave and gust of wind.

At any other place or time, he would have died from exposure and cold. He would have grown weary and drowned. He would have given up and succumbed to the ocean.
But each time he was thrown to the beach, swallowed by the waves, or smacked by a gust of wind, he stood up again and felt stronger.

Dimitri felt like every bad thing that the pirates had done to him was being beaten out of his body.

. . . .

He wasn't sure how much time had passed, but it seemed to be considerable. Longer than an hour. Perhaps longer than an entire night, or even an entire day. Eventually, the waves were no longer as high, the wind stopped blowing, and the water felt less cold. A soft amber light radiated on the horizon as though the sun were about to rise, and Dimitri could see that Marshall Island was nothing more than a small outcropping of blackened rocks,

What looked to be a glowing orb of light arose from the rocks and floated towards Dimitri. He wasn't sure what to make of it, but as it came closer, he could see a beautiful female fairy in a golden gown and with springtime-colored wings. She bore a lantern in one hand and in the other a pike as long as her wingspan.

Dimitri heard her voice from all directions. "Come away from the water child, for I mean you no harm."

Dimitri walked out of the water and climbed onto the outcrop of rocks. As he emerged from the water, he could feel himself become dry very quickly and was surrounded by a pleasant warmth.

The fairy flew close to him, and he could see her present him with a paternal smile. She was quiet for some time, and at last spoke. "All that has transpired before your eyes and ears you may tell," the fairy says, "but you must never speak to the fate of the female you called Paris, nor of the change upon the male you knew as West. Though we could take this from your mind, we wish to return you to your land renewed and fulfilled, for you have endured more than any child should, and we shall leave you that knowledge so that you might contemplate upon the fates that befell those who had wronged you."

She flew towards him and Dimitri held out his palm. She lit upon his hand, then perched herself upon his finger-tips. "What are you?" he asked.

She smiled. "We are fairies. Beings that are beyond the wills of man, and move with nature itself. We live in no particular time and in no particular place. The winds we choose

to follow have taken us from France to this island, and perhaps we shall return to our homeland, or continue onwards to
New England. We take our land with us when we move, and
all worldly possessions brought to our land remain lost."

Dimitri looked around, and saw no sign of any other life
except the smashed remains of the Island Pride, and the skiff,
which appeared to be intact. The fairy lead Dimitri over the
rocks to the skiff, and he saw that O'Reilly lay in its bow.

"Child," the fairy said, "you must return this vessel to
the waves now, and take this wretched man back to your world,
for he must impart his story upon another. You must stand by
his side to be sure he speaks all that was experienced. Remember to be vigilant for he must not speak on West's or
Paris' fate."

"What happened to everyone?"

"My dear child," the fairy said softly, "it is a tangled
web of events that lead humans to our world. Once the living
arrive in our world, they eat of our food and in doing so consume our spirit. When you eat the food of fairies, you become infused with fairy magic. But we could not let them
take the magic from our land, so we took it back."

"You killed them," Dimitri protested, though meekly,
for he was not altogether unhappy that they were dead.

"They ate of the food infused with the fairy spirit. Their
bodies were so saturated with our energy that our reclama-
tion of that energy left them with no remaining sustenance to
support their life." Then, she smiled up at him. "We have our
own reasons for what we did, and if you consider what has
happened here you will realize that this was not mere chance.
This was not the first time it has happened, nor will it be the
last. Though we did not expect you to be here, we took pre-
cautions to make sure that you would be safe once you arrived."

"The strange man," Dimitri said to himself, thinking back on what had happened.

She lit from his palm and landed on his shoulder. "Yes. You will soon see him again. And we had the other human guide you towards the water. Understand that we must closely guard our magic, particularly when humans come in contact with it and inadvertently spread it throughout their world." She set the lantern down on his shoulder and touched his cheek with her small fingertips. "But, as we seek to protect our magic, so may we choose to allow some to be infused with it. In consideration of how we might help protect you from all the wrongs you have experienced, we have chosen you to be infused."

She picked up the lantern and flew from his shoulder to the boat, and landed atop a piece of rotting and worn leather. "In these folds are nuts that will bring a small part of the fairy world into your life, and help return to you the health and innocence that others have taken. Live true to yourself, and you will always find benefit from their sustenance. Do that, and the fairies shall not seek to reclaim it." Then, her tone became a warning. "But you must consume them before touching upon the mainland, for then the food will become poison and other fairies will lay claim to its magic and extract it from you." She indicated O'Reilly. "Nor must you give any to this man for it will prematurely cause him great and terrible pain."

"Will he die?" Dimitri asked.

"Indeed," she said with utmost assurance.

"Will I ever see you again?"

She smiled. "Once you have eaten the nuts and are infused with fairy magic, you will find that fairies are never far away. And, one day many years from now, though for us it may be as though no time has passed t'all, we may call upon you for your assistance, and I hope you shall remember our kindness and repay it in kind."

Dimitri nodded slightly, and then she flew from his hand and disappeared amongst the rocks. He heard her say to him, "Now board the boat, eat the hazel nuts, and you shall find your way through the storm and to shore with much ease."

She never once remarked upon the satchel of treasure he still carried strapped to his back.

Part VI
"Of Witches and Fairies"

Though he recalled the events quite clearly, Dimitri was careful to excise any mention of Paris' and Captain West's ultimate fates. When he fell silent, Peter Thompson yawned and rubbed his eyes. "The boy can spin an interesting yarn, but I wouldn't worry about anyone confusing his flights of fancy with more evil inclinations."

"Good," was all Mr. Barrymore said.

"Of course, the map would be helpful as evidence pertaining to the pirate-witch." He studied Mr. Barrymore as he spoke.

Mr. Barrymore surprised him by simply shrugging. "If you think it will aid your case. It may even be helpful for the others who stand accused."

"Yes, I believe it will," Peter agreed hastily. He picked up the map and tucked it inside his shirt. "It seems that I've learned all that I could here," and he nodded to the Marrows, Mr. Barrymore, and Dimitri. "I should be returning now."

Peter Thompson left in a hurry, his hand pressed to his chest where he had tucked the map.

Mr. Barrymore looked at the Marrows and then Dimitri. "I'm rather curious what you good folks think about what has been said."

Aubrey looked at her husband and raised her hands. "I don't think I have much of an opinion, really."

Jacob put his arm around Aubrey and nodded. "All this talk of witches, mysterious islands, and fairies. It all seems like a lot of nonsense. Yet, I do find myself drawing a connection between the island and the most recent trials because it is the only instance where a claim was made to identify what may in fact be the source of these witches' power. And, where the source of that power is not attributed to the Devil. If there are indeed witches, why not fairies and vanishing islands? Or, if not fairies and not vanishing islands, how might one purport that witches exist yet fairies do not? Better the connection not be made t'all I suppose, lest we find ourselves defending our good names from accusations."

"Still," Aubrey added, "if one were inclined to believe this tale of islands, treasure and fairy magic, then it does cast a pallor over the recent trials as it raises doubt as to whether the witches were in league with the Devil." It was the first time she had mentioned the accusations or the trial since the whole matter had begun, and she felt all the more better after hearing the tale of Marshall Island and the fairies because it put the other events into a perspective: sheer madness.

"A very dangerous supposition," Mr. Barrymore remarked. "Mister Thompson now has the proof and I imagine the whole affair is best left to those most polarized by the subject."

The Marrows nodded, though appeared slightly confused by the cryptic comment. "I suppose," Aubrey began, "that they'll simply say nothing more of magic nuts, fairies, Marshall Island, or witches for that matter."

"Who then wouldn't assume that witches were just addled by some fairy fugue?" Jacob offered.

"I think we shan't hear anything further of the fairies, the island, or the fugue," Mr. Barrymore said. "And if our Mister Thompson is dutiful, I'd wager you'll never find record of a vessel in dock at the Salem shipyard with the name Island Pride. Unfortunately, I don't think the issue of witches will be so readily dismissed by simply burying knowledge that could otherwise be helpful."

Dimitri remembered the satchel, and looked at Mr. Barrymore. "I left something on the beach. I should fetch it now."

"It's rather later. Best to wait till the morrow," Jacob said.

"This one time, perhaps let the boy fetch his misplaced article." Mr. Barrymore smiled knowingly at Dimitri.

When the boy left, Mr. Barrymore looked between Jacob and Aubrey. "I am wondering whether the boy might be better raised by some well-meaning parents instead of a bachelor such as myself."

They looked uncertainly at Mr. Barrymore. "Is he not a slave then?"

Mr. Barrymore pursed his lips. "I suppose folks must be bound by the reigning standards," and fell quiet for some time and didn't offer any further response or explanation. When Dimitri returned, satchel in hand, he stood and nodded to them. "I do appreciate your time and hospitality, Mister and Missus Marrow. Dimitri and I shall, perhaps, try our luck up North."

As the two walked down the road leading away from the Marrows' quaint cottage, Dimitri looked inside the satchel and caught a glimpse of a treasure unlike any treasure he could have imagined.

"Where do we go now?" He asked Mr. Barrymore.

"North, Dimitri, we'll go North, and see what kind of life a boy who is pure in heart can lead. And," he whispered into the night air, "a vast fortune, a healthy heart, and a little fairy magic certainly can't hurt."

EPILOGUE

History remembers no slave child named Dimitri who was thrown to the abusive care of pirates and later saved by fairies, or a man named Barrymore. There is no account of a vessel with the markings of Island Pride, a couple on the outskirts of Salem by the names of Jacob and Aubrey Marrow, or a court councilor named Peter Thompson. There was no landmass off the coast of Massachusetts named Marshall Island, and there never were New England pirates named Shaw and West.

According to known history, the Salem Witch Trials ended when the last hangings took place on September 22nd, 1692, and the court overseeing the trials was dissolved in October, 1692. Any connection between the antics and ailments of the 'afflicted', who were the pivotal accusers in the witchcraft brouhaha, and a fugue brought about by becoming infused with fairy magic is purely circumspect.

Rather than suggest a vaudeville conscription to conspiracy, one only has to believe in human nature. Peter Thompson, upon taking possession of the map, probably had no intention of using the evidence to stop the trials, and instead organized a crew of ruffians and went in search of pirate treasure on the hitherto non-existent Marshall Island. Once there, he and his crew most assuredly encountered a comely woman whose name they gathered to be Paris, and a bounty of food unlike any they had experienced. This seemingly innocent and pure young woman would most likely be subject to a rank vileness that could only be born of the human spirit. It could further be suggested that Peter Thompson would later become intimately familiar with the woman called Paris in ways that would forever change him. As someone who simply disappeared, Peter Thompson's name merely became disassociated with the trials.

Had the Marrows not been so instilled with the social attitudes of the time, though one cannot necessarily fault them in light of their own social prejudices and inclinations, they may have enjoyed a productive and footnote-worthy life as the parents to a very special young boy. Alas, under the judicious eye of Mr. Barrymore, they would simply fade into obscurity.

As with Mr. Barrymore before him, the fairies most likely called upon Dimitri. In repaying their kindness, Dimitri became a part of the fairy world, which exists outside of our own time. Of course history would record neither the life nor death of a man named Dimitri. Yet, if one were to encounter a child or adult by this name, they might be brought to pause in consideration: could this be the same Dimitri who was enslaved by pirates, freed by fairies, aided by a man named Barrymore, and who now may be moving backwards and forwards through time as the world of fairies is want to do?

Skein

Richard Gazley

A dry ticking consumes me
bit by bit
each second's blade slices
wide
as the string unravels
the ball grows small
and one can imagine its end
to stand on that last step
with no more string to pull
and then to fall
free
better to try pulling slower
better to close one's eyes
better to dream
that the ball is still full
and one's days unending
than to stare at that nearing tip

Say Anything My Ass
Russ Unger

One of my all-time favorite movies is "Say Anything…". For no really good reason, I must say that it is merely a hairline fracture behind "The Princess Bride".

Through the years, I've had a lot of time to ponder "Say Anything…", as I've been known to be somewhat of a romantic throughout my youth, and I'm admitting that reluctantly now. I'm old and married and married men scoff at romance (and secretly plan and plot romantic events anyway).

I'd like for you to take a moment and ponder with me. Remember back in 1989—or whatever year you saw it in, for that matter—and how you thought about how incredibly romantic John Cusack's Lloyd Dobler was. No, really. I don't care if you're a man or a woman as you read this—you did think that Lloyd Dobler was a romantic man.

If you were a guy at all like me, all you wanted to do was to be Lloyd Dobler.

If you were a girl, very much unlike me, all you wanted was a guy like Lloyd Dobler to come into your life and sweep you off of your feet, complete with "whooshing" sound. You wanted your very own Lloyd to have all kinds of quirks and odd mannerisms, career goals in kickboxing and you wanted him to show up outside of your window at 5:00 a.m. with his boombox blaring Peter Gabriel's "In Your Eyes".

You know that, if nothing else, I am spewing the truth here. You can deny, deny, deny it all you would like. You can make up excuses that you're not old enough to remember the movie or that you've never seen it—but you will see it. You will hope it. You will dream it.

And I will tell you this: **You. Are. Wrong.**

Let's analyze this movie and this situation just a little deeper, shall we?

If you are Diane Court, played by Ione Skye, you're one of those hot little high school chippees that has only dated older guys with nice cars. You've been attending college while you're still working toward that high school diploma, earning yourself a little contempt from your high school peers. You're smarter than most of the rest of the planet and no one in your high school really knows you—and if they pretend that they do, it's only so they can get close enough to you to nail you (guys) or get some dirt on you and crap on you later (girls). Your yearbook is probably loaded with catchy little phrases like "I wish we had more time to get to know each other better" and "Good luck in the future!" and nary a "BFF" in sight. Hey, I just call 'em as I see 'em, okay?

If you're Lloyd Dobler, you're looking for an "in". Let's face it, the guy isn't hip with the latest trends, he's interested in kickboxing, which, with the exception of a Jean Claude Van Damme movie, I'm not too sure what became of the sport. You live with your older sister and you nephew in a small apartment that doesn't afford you much privacy. Your parents are all over the planet, in the military I think, and they're not really "there" for you. Basically, you're a loner. A rebel. People know you, but they don't really know you. You hang with 3 chicks, one of whom is a nutjob still clinging to an ex-boyfriend that continues to mess with her brain ("He… likes gi-irls… with names like Ashley… and Tamerlain… THAT'LL NEVER BE ME! THAT'LL NEVER BE ME! THAT'LL NEVER BE ME! don't you even think it!").

For a lot of the "loser class" (you can refer to anything I've ever written at www.unrealisticexpectations.com in which I've discussed my high school years), we had these girl "friends". No, not the girlfriends we wanted—and a lot of them probably could have been girlfriends, but it was either weird, or in all honesty… Well, look. It's a well-kept loser-geek secret that we had this "trophy chick" mentality and we wouldn't let a lot of the really cool girls be our girlfriends, even if we could have figured out what to do with them. We were the nerds who wanted the girlfriends of the [insert team sport here] players. No one ever falsely accused too many high schoolers of being too together, you know.

No, instead, we had to be all Miss Amanda Jones (that's an 80's reference to the movie "Some Kind of Wonderful", in case you missed it) about it.

The only noted exception to that rule is that I thought Mary Stuart Masterson was way hotter than Lea Thompson.

Anyway.

Lloyd pulled off the impossible; he landed the big fish. He got the trophy girl—by simply being himself, no less. Most of us can't figure out how to manage this feat until we're at least 25 years old, after we've finally come to terms with our inner geek. Embraced it. Molded it. Taken owner-ship of it enough that we no longer need to tape our glasses or snort when we laugh.

Well... At least we no longer fold our jeans in such a way that there's that faded line right smack down the middle of your shin. Most times, at least. Damned mothers and their folding of the jeans.

As with all good tales, there is an adversary for Lloyd: The Father. (queue dramatic theme music) Diane's father strongly advises her that kickboxing Lloyd is not in the same league as her and that she should be focusing her time on someone...better. Diane dumps Lloyd, leaving him with a pen that he can use to write with her while she's in school overseas. At least she could have left him with a bunch of stamps, too. Talk about not having any class. Sheesh!

A lot of us have been there. We've dated the person with parents that didn't think that we were the right person for their child. Sooner or later, if we don't elope, we get dumped. In my experience, it's almost always for the best and when you reach your destination, you'll have no regrets. Nerds *can* get cheerleaders in the end, just remember that!

In a move that's completely understood by anyone who's ever had their heart ripped to shreds, Lloyd goes a bit psycho.

Time out. We've all done this same type of thing, unless you're that freak-of-nature who has won everything you've ever participated in, has never received a speeding ticket and has had a bad day in your life. If I've just described you, you might just as well skip the rest of this, settle back in your comfy chair and punch the clicker on over to TGIF.

When you get dumped, not only do you feel an incredible sense of loneliness, but you also feel a loss of control over your life. You wig out.

That's all there is to it.

You stop seeing life as clearly as you used to. You want your life back the way it was. You have one motivation and a one-track mind—and sometimes it's so strong that when you finally do get what you want...

Well, let's just say that it doesn't always seem as great as you were hoping for. That, however, is a topic for someone else to figure out.

And if you're Lloyd Dobler, you park your butt outside your ex-girlfriend's bedroom window, turn up the boombox in order to crank out the song that was playing the first time the two of you figured out you were in love or lust (or whatever it was).

Ladies, I implore you to stop your sighing. Guys, stop acting like this is so righteous.

There are very basic rules to relationships being over-looked here, and they have to brought out. When you dump someone, the **last thing** that you want is to have the ex show-ing up and performing some sort of psycho-stalker event that has you wondering where they're going to be next. Think about it.

Some of you have done this (don't look around or we'll know it's you)—or something similar—to try and work your way back into the relationship.

The best thing you can do right now is to simply cringe as I mention it—the same sort of embarrassed cringe you'd do right after someone tells you that you've been singing the wrong words to Manfred Mann's Earth Band's "Blinded by the Light" (originally written and first recorded by Bruce Springsteen) for the last 10 years of your life. The very same kind of embarrassment you get when you watch Corey Feldman crying on some reality show.

In real life, does any of this behavior salvage your rela-tionship?

Hell no!!

In fact, if anything, all it does is rack up tons of "loser" points with the girl, all of her friends, their boyfriends, some parents and/or teachers and you just look like some dumb dork without an ounce of emotional maturity.

Does she come back?

Hell no!!

Does her dad go to jail for ripping off old people?

Hell no!!

The only thing that really happens is that some studly dude comes cruising in and sweeps her off of her rebound-ready feet, leaving them to live happily ever after. You, on the other hand, make a mix tape that has "In Your Eyes" on it—like 32 times or something—and sit in your dark, stank-ass room with paper plates all crusted-up with old pizza and empty coke cans everywhere.

My advice is simple: Watch the movie.

It's great. It really is. It's hands-down one of the greats of the era, but don't go and think it's the Holy Grail of relationships.

Don't go thinking that all that mushy crap is going to help you get the girl. Sure—it might, but how long will that last? How long will it be until someone else tops your grand romantic gesture or you run out of ideas on how to top yourself?

If anyone's going to land that dream significant other, it's going to the "you" that you really are and not the storybook/movie person.

Unfortunately, it usually takes going through the "Lloyd Dobler" thing (and for some, a few times at least!) before you can figure it out.

Snowbound

Carolyn Collins Petersen

Snow had been falling since noon with no sign of letup. Rachel looked out the window at the blanket of heavy, wet stuff weighing down the branches of the trees. Another hour at this rate and there'd be no way anything other than an ambulance or fire truck would get up the driveway. She hoped it wouldn't come to that. Well, Dana would be back soon and he was bringing the Jeep. She sat back on the sofa and gazed into space, absent-mindedly rubbing her belly. *If it's a girl, I'll name her Keri,* she thought dreamily.

There — she could feel the movement under her skin. It was an insistent bumping, followed almost immediately by a hard, cramping contraction. She breathed through it, her thoughts focused on the mental image of a beached whale, blowing and flopping around. As the pain eased, she slipped her feet onto the hassock and snuggled deeper under the comforter.

It was warm beneath the quilted softness and she drowsed for what seemed like hours, dreaming of snorkeling at Hapuna.

Hundreds of tropical fish flowed around her, their darting shapes like blurs of color in the crystal clear water. She happened by a turtle watching her dispassionately from atop a coral outcrop. She floated over to touch its shell and bumped her belly on the rough surface of the reef.

That slight movement touched off another cramp that dragged her out of the water and back to the snowbound house. This one seemed to go on forever, and it took all her breathing and concentration to get past the discomfort.

Damn it, Dana! Where are you? Keri's coming!

In the immediate aftermath of the contraction, the sudden lack of pain left her dazed and sleepy. It wasn't bad, really. She wafted back to the dream lagoon, and let herself be carried out to sea on the relentless tide. Maui wasn't so far away — she could swim there in a few hours...

Rachel stroked effortlessly through the waves, her distended stomach slipping through the water like the bottom of a boat. It was surprising how her ungainliness disappeared in the water. She reached down to cup her belly, and was astonished to find a flat, slim stomach. She stopped and treaded water, wondering where the baby had gone. *Where are you, baby?* Pain constricted her throat. *Keri, I've lost you... I've lost the baby,* she thought, and tears poured out of her eyes in grief. *Dana??? Why aren't you here to help me?*

"Mom!" It came from a voice she thought she recognized. She turned her head and looked at the green hills shimmering in the distance. The voice seemed to come from that direction. It wasn't far away, but she was too tired to swim. She just wanted to rest, and so she cradled her head in her arms and drifted away.

"Mom! Wake up! Please??" the inexplicably familiar voice called. *Who was it?* Rachel looked across the water and saw a tall, slim woman with long, black hair running along the beach, waving and shouting. She looked familiar, but who was she? Curiosity got the best of Rachel and so she summoned up the strength to keep going.

At last she felt sand beneath her feet. *I made it! I made it!*

Nothing else mattered; the long swim was over. Rachel looked for the woman who had urged her on, but she was gone. In her place sat a toddler splashing playfully in gentle waves creaming up onto the sand. *I have to get to her,* thought Rachel. *Can't let the tide take her away.*

She rose out of the water and headed for the baby, but the child had disappeared. Rachel sank to her knees, rubbed her empty belly and cried for the loss of the baby. And cried for Dana. And confused in her loss, she cried for the unknown woman who called her "Mom."

****

Keri stared out the hospital window, watching the snow piling down out of the sky. There was so much of it she couldn't tell her car from the other white-covered lumps in the parking lot. Next to the window, Rachel lay deathly still. A tangle of tubes and wires stretched out from her body under the covers to a collection of bags and beeping machines. Hours earlier, Keri had returned from a hurried lunch to find her comatose mother in silent tears, her hand rubbing her stomach over and over again.

No, it wasn't a sign that the coma was lifting. Keri had been through this so many times since the accident that took her father's life and shattered her mother's body. If Dad had lived he'd have held out undying hope that Mom would come out of it. Keri knew better. She read the charts, talked to the doctors. The broken pelvis and leg and arm could be healed, but the long coma and erratic brainwave activity told a different and more ominous story. Everyone understood the outcome, but that didn't make it any easier to bear. So, Keri stayed on as if waiting for the end of a long and difficult birth, instead of the death she knew was coming.

I wonder what's going on inside her head? It was a thought that crossed Keri's mind a hundred times a day. And she'd never know. All she could do was wait with her mother, wait until her life had run its course. At least Mom wasn't going alone. Keri settled into a chair beside the bed, wrapped herself in a hospital blanket, and stared out the window at the silently falling snow.

***

The morning sun seemed unnaturally bright when Rachel stopped crying and opened her eyes. She didn't remember it being this brilliant. *Thank heaven the snow is gone,* she thought. *But of course it would be – it doesn't snow here!*

She realized she was still on the beach, lying alone in the soft sand, not far from the edge of a fragrant rainforest. A faint breeze tousled her hair and as she stood and stretched, she heard the words *I'll always love you, Mom* wafting through the breeze. Whoever was saying it didn't matter anymore. Rachel was free. No pain, no curiosity, no memory of her past. It was time for her choose a new path. Unhesitatingly, she stepped toward the trees and disappeared into the snowy white light of the Sun.

She Waits
Stargazer

She catalogs the pain
marking the dates
writing down names

She tries not to feel
when she looks through the columns
weighing and measuring the days as they fade

She wants to forget
but can't stop remembering
the people who cut her pieces away

She tried not to see all the sad down turned faces
the friends and the lovers
who fought her to stay

She's adding up the pain
looking for an answer
waiting for a chance to float far away

J. Grady's Iggy
In
To Hell With Sex
J. Grady

"So, Mr. Neutron, we meet again," Iggy spoke boldly in his very best superhero voice.

"Hopefully, we won't have to do this anymore," Mr. Neutron's voice was loud and hollow when coming out of his gas mask.

"We shan't meet again, cause I will stop you from dumping radioactive toothpaste into the water supply, you foul fiend!!"

"Try as you might, you cannot stop me. My robotic suit gives me super powers. I am stronger than you."

" You may be but I know your weakness," Iggy scoped the ground for a weapon; he found one. Distracting the villain by dancing the Jig, he rolled on the ground, picked up a rock and threw it.

The rock bounced off Mr. Neutron's robotic fedora, "That was pathetic. There is nothing that can stop me now, ha-ha-ha-ha, etc, etc."

Iggy reached into his black trench coat and pulled out two rather large, rather silver handguns.

Mr. Neutron stopped laughing, "That might do it," He reached into his gray trench coat and produced a tiny capsule. Throwing it to the ground, a loud pop echoed through the silence of the night. Billowing smoke arose from the capsule, engulfing our superhero and even our super villain. Iggy was lost in a sea of gray smoke, but figured it was still safer than breathing the city air.

Twenty minutes later, the smoke started to disappear. Iggy was stunned; Mr. Neutron was gone. "Holy smoke, Mr. Neutron is gone!!"

As he searched the area for clues, he hear the sound of a car starting, "That's the Demon One," He said to himself. Iggy ran toward his tan and simulated wood paneled station wagon with fins on the back. He found Mr. Neutron trying to steal it, "Uh. Iggy? Your car's not starting," Mr. Neutron said whilst sitting in the driver's seat.

"Give it some gas," Iggy replied.

Mr. Neutron did as he said, the engine roared to life. Iggy smiled, "That always works," he smiled as the Demon One roared out of the parking lot. Iggy suddenly realized something bad just happened. He ran after the escaping Mr. Neutron, "You gotta let the engine warm up first!!" He cried, but his cries were left unanswered.

Walking to a nearby gas station, Iggy called his sister, who answered the phone while laughing, "Hey Iggy, how's it going?"

"Fine, sis," he muttered, listening to all the laughing and giggling in the background, "Are you having another slumber party?"

She hesitated, "uh…no."

"You know I told never to throw parties at my mansion, I've told you this a hundred times."

"I know," she said sheepishly, "but the final episode of Let's Date a Super Villain is on and I promised my friends I'd let them see it in your secret crime cave."

Iggy shook his head, "fine, just don't spill anything on my computer, I can't fight crime without it."

"Fine, be a spoil sport," She said as she hung up. Iggy wasn't happy; not only was his sister ruining his crime cave, but he also forgot to tell her that he needed a ride.

After two hours of walking, Iggy was at the front gate of his mansion estate. He pressed the button on the front gate intercom, "Did the Demon One break down again, Sir?" Burke, his loyal butler and aerobics instructor questioned."

"Just open the gate," Iggy muttered.

Inside his luxurious house, Iggy walked down to his crime cave, stepping over crayons and pictures of the latest teen heartthrobs. Pushing cute little stuffed animals off of the gigantic crime computer's keyboard, Iggy slumped into his crime chair.

Suddenly, the crime computer's huge monitor flickered on, startling Iggy.

It was Chief Inspector Larry, the chief of police, "Iggy, get down to the hospital, hurry. There's no time to explain." Iggy sensed the urgency in his voice; "I'll meet you there."

"Oh, I'm not going, Iggy," The chief suddenly got all nervous, " I have to return some videotapes."

"Fine, I guess I'll go alone…again," Iggy replied as the giant screen faded to black, a slight popping sound was heard as the screen finally went dark.

"Sir, I prepared your new Demon One, affectionately named Demon Two," Burke said cheerfully as he handed Iggy the keys.

Iggy's eyes widened "Where the hell did you come from?"

" I appear as the writer sees fit, it's all top secret hush-hush James Bond type stuff, sir," He said as he disappeared into thin air again.

A circle formed in the grass, spinning slowly at first and then getting faster. The circle sunk into the ground, it rose up again with the Demon Two. The sleek black car roared in the moonlight as Iggy pounded the gas to impress his sister's live-n roommates.

Cruising on a lonely stretch of highway winding itself alongside a river, Iggy thought about the night's earlier events. He wanted revenge so bad he could taste it. He also wanted a strawberry milkshake so bad he could taste it. He pulled into the 24 hour Strawberry Milkshake Warehouse and got one of his wishes fulfilled.

Jumping back in his car, he raced down the highway only to get stuck behind an elderly gentleman driving a Cadillac. He was going 25 miles under the limit and his right turn signal was permanently stuck in the "on" position. Iggy glanced at his crime clock; Gasp, the hospital was only twenty minutes away.

Iggy tried to pass him, but the road was separated in the middle by the dreaded double yellow line. Iggy could not cross it, for if he did he could incur fines of up to and including fifteen dollars.

An hour later, Iggy pulled into the hospital parking lot, setting his eyes on his favorite cop on the force. He saw that Constable Melanie was sitting in her squad car, and decided he must talk to her. Iggy's heart started beating faster with every step he took towards her. His pulse raced, he was sweating like a sumo wrestler running a quarter -mile sprint as he drew closer to her. His whole body seemed to shake as he approached her car door.

Melanie saw him and she smiled softly, "Iggy, I heard that Mr. Neutron got away. How did it happen?" Her worrying about him made him feel all tingly.

Iggy smiled, ignoring his quickening heart rate and faster breathing, "He tricked me as only the master of deception can," He smiled, wondering why he was feeling this way.

"Well, never fear, we found Mr. Neutron and your car. The car was wrapped around a tree. Mr. Neutron was wrapped around a fire hydrant. Both are in critical condition." She walked towards the entrance of the hospital, passing a sign advertising Green jelly Tuesdays in the cafeteria; Iggy followed thinking he should check himself in to see what was going on.

Heart rate and all other bodily functions returning to normal, Iggy followed her to the elevator. "Which room is he in?"

"Room 143567. It's on the third floor." She looked at him seductively, " You know, Iggy, I never got a chance to thank you for saving me from that maniacal tow truck stealing murderer," She undid the top button of her uniform as she kissed Iggy's cheek.

"Hey Baby, I want you," She smirked as she ripped open her shirt, revealing a black lace bra. Iggy kissed her as his hand gently squeezed her....

"Iggy, wake up," Melanie said anxiously, "You passed out in the elevator as soon as the doors closed." I thought you had a heart attack or something."

Iggy got up off the floor, "It was just a dream?" He asked as he stood to his feet.

Melanie straightened her uniform " Must've been a good

one, you were saying wakka-joo-wakka in your sleep. What was it about?"

Feeling nervous, Iggy replied, "Uh.........nothing," and walked into the room. Iggy stopped dead in his tracks just after walking through the door

"Oh my god," Melanie exclaimed as she followed behind, bumping into him. (Iggy, not God. – Ed Note.)

The room was torn apart, the bed ripped in half. Cabinets overturned, papers were strewn all over, blood and green jelly splattered on the walls, and the bathroom faucet was left running. Iggy immediately headed for the bathroom, shutting the door behind him. Constable Melanie approached an officer already at the scene. She examined the mess on the ceiling. Blood and jelly dripped onto her shoulder.

"What the hell happened here, Officer Schweinhalt?" She inquired.

"Far as we can tell," He looked around the room at the carnage, "something awful." A toilet flush was heard as Iggy stepped out of the bathroom, "Where's Mr. Neutron?"

"There's nothing left of him." Melanie turned to Iggy, "He's dead."

"Mr.; Neutron is a master of deception," Iggy stated matter of fact, "Do you know how many times he's faked his own death?"

"No, how many?"

"One," Iggy walked to the wall, "That's a lot of blood." Tracing a line in the blood with his finger, then touching it to his tongue, "Dah-ha!! It's not blood, it's ketchup," He tasted it again, "And green jelly. There's only one place that would sell both ketchup and green jelly on a Tuesday." He looked at Melanie to see if she knew the answer.

"The All Night Jelly and Ketchup Depository on Fifth and Market?"

"No. The hospital cafeteria! The villain must be there!" Iggy ran to the window, "Mel, you take the lift. I'll meet you in the cafeteria."

"Okay, Iggy, don't be late," Her smile warmed Iggy's heart as she exited the room heading for the elevator.

Reaching to his belt, Iggy pulled out a gun shaped device with a hook on the end, he stuck the hook into the window frame and attached the rest of the device onto his belt. Jumping out the window the line attached to the hook tightened as he slowly descended. Iggy checked each of his guns, making sure they were fully loaded and ready to go. On the way down he also had time to finish his crossword puzzle book, check his hair in the high tech crime mirror attached to his belt, floss his teeth, check his email, and look at his watch.

Once on the ground, Iggy detached the line and ran inside. The cafeteria was busy with many people coming in and out; Iggy scanned the room. He noticed a strange figure sitting in the corner; this person was wearing a hooded cloak and reading a fashion magazine.

Melanie was already in the cafeteria searching for Mr. Neutron when she spotted the hooded fiend, she drew her gun, "Hold it right there, you hooded fiend," she said.

The man rose up out of his chair and smiled. Under the shadow of his dark cloak a line of white sharp pointed teeth could be seen.

"Oh shit," Melanie muttered under her breath. Saying out loud, "Put your hands above your head or there will be...." she was cut off as the man removed his cloak, revealing his red fur covered body. The wolf-man lunged at her, grabbing her gun, turning her around and looking at Iggy.

Melanie was caught by surprise that she finished her line with just another mutter, "trouble."

"Iggy!" The creature shouted, "I have your girl," he taunted.

"Put her down you.... you carpet sample," Iggy shouted as he pulled out his guns

"Carpet sample? Don't you know who I am?" The wolf lowered the gun a bit

Iggy shrugged, "Not really,"

The monster dropped Melanie, "C'mon, you have to know me. I'm the evil villain Red Wulff," His eyes showed sadness.

"Doesn't sound familiar, sorry," Iggy lowered his guns as well.

"I was the one who slashed the police chief's tires." He replied.

"Still not ringing a bell," Iggy was trying to recall any memory.

"How bout the time I kidnapped the old Mayor and wanted ten million dollars?" Red looked into Iggy's eyes

"Can't say I remember that either, sorry," Iggy said. Red Wulff dropped his gun and fell into a chair. His sharp claws covered his tear filled eyes. Iggy ran over to him, "What's wrong?"

"I'm sorry," Red looked up, tears sliding down his face, "It's just been a tough year. My wife died, leaving me to care for our son Franklin. He misses his mother all the time now. And he just broke his leg playing full contact hopscotch and I have no medical insurance. I'm out of work, barely making ends meet and Christmas is coming. He wants a new bike, and every time he asks for one I break down and cry. I can't even afford to put food on the table, let alone keep him happy. He's such a good kid, never asks for anything. I feel like I let him down. And now he may never walk again," Red collapsed on the table, crying loudly.

Iggy put his hand on Red furry shoulder. Red lifted his head, "Can you help me and Franklin? Can you? Please?"

Iggy lifted the furry man-wolf out of his chair and looked into his doughy eyes, "As God as my witness, Red Wulff, I will help you. You and Franklin both."

Red put his hand on Iggy's shoulder, "Thank you, friend."

Melanie, Iggy, and Red waited for Franklin to get a cast. They wheeled him to the Demon Two and put him in the back seat. Then they went for ice cream and Red Wulff agreed to become a hero instead of a villain. He was now Iggy's partner.

Meanwhile, in the vile cybernetic gangster's secret hideout and laundromat, evil doings were transpiring.

"So you are interested in joining our little establishment?" Praxus, the cybernetic gangster, sat at the end of a long table, over looking his comrades, "Is that right…. Mr. Neutron?"

"Yes it is, I need someone who can take care of Iggy for me. He has thwarted my plans time and again and, frankly, I'm sick of it," Mr. Neutron sat at the other end of the long table.

Praxus smiled, "Very well, you're particular brand of villainy may compliment my little brood. Welcome aboard. May I introduce you to the rest of my crew?" Praxus pointed to the person sitting next to Mr. Neutron, "This is Anonymous Bob, he is my confidant and general jack of all trades. He is also the world's only mildly evil genius."

Anonymous Bob turned to Mr. Neutron, "How ya doin'?"

Mr. Neutron looked around the room, except for them and a wall lined with washing machines, it was empty, "Will I be meeting the rest of your crew later?"

Praxus shrugged, "What crew? This is it."

"Oh, okay." Mr. Neutron slumped back in his chair.

"Boss, I have a plan that will make us famous," Anonymous Bob jumped up in his seat, "I will build a device capable of destroying the city unless they give control of city hall."

Praxus smiled, his bright white teeth practically blinding his crew, "I like this plan, it's devious and yet practical. Very well, make it so"

"Okay boss, I made a list of the items I need for the device," Bob passed him the list.

Mr. Neutron looked it over, "Hmmm…dynamite, fuses, several pounds of C4, a broom handle, pixie sticks, and an unknown substance known as Tang?"

Praxus gazed at Bob, "And these items are what you need to perfect this device?"

Anonymous Bob shook his head, "Oh no, this is my shopping list," He reached into his pocket and pulled out another piece of paper, "This is the list."

"Very well, we must start at once." Praxus smiled gleefully.

"Well, I hope you're happy in your new home Franklin," Iggy smiled as the kid hobbled up the stairs, "Ah, to be young again, " he thought.

"Sir, there was a message tied to a rock," Burke the butler said as he walked over carrying a tray with Gummi Bears and a rock on it.

Iggy grabbed a handful of candy and grabbed the note, "Thanks Burke,"

"No problem sir,"

Melanie looked at the piece of paper in Iggy's hand, "What does it say?"

Iggy looked at the pink piece of paper, it smelled like

roses, "Dear Mr. Iggy, we have a device that will blow up the city. If we do not have control of city hall, a million dollars, and a gallon of milk by ten tonight, we will activate the device. We you have what we desire, you will know how to find us by answering this riddle. What has four legs and barks?" Iggy crumpled up the paper and threw it to the ground.

"What's up Iggy?" Melanie and Red Wulff walked over to him.

Iggy shook his head, "Mr. Neutron's not dead, and him and some friends are going to destroy the city unless we stop him."

Melanie was stunned, "Where do we find them?"

"They gave us a riddle, we get the answer, we find out where they are."

Red looked nervous as well, "What was the riddle?"

Iggy looked at him, "What has four legs and barks?

Melanie jumped in, "A dog!"

Iggy started pacing around the room, "What do dogs like to do? Run, just like…trains. Trains are always on time, just like the news. The news has anchors, boats have anchors," Melanie and Red just stared as they tried to follow his line of reasoning, Iggy still paced in a circle around the, " Boats are used in family vacations and family vacations include children. Some people regard their pets as children. Some pets are dogs. Dogs like to bark…that's it!" He stopped and shouted.

Red and Melanie just looked at him, "What's it?"

"He's at the abandoned dog pound," Iggy rushed to the crime cave. Mel and Red followed closely behind, "We need to get to the dog pound to stop them, but first we need some reinforcements," Iggy ran to his gigantic crime computer and pressed a button, "Iggy to the Legion, Iggy to the legion," He repeated.

The screen suddenly showed the picture of an old man, "Iggy, how are you doing?

"Captain Bloodloss, I'm glad to get a hold of you, I've got some bad news,"

"What is it?"

"What? Bad news? It's the kind of news that isn't good, but that's not important right now. Praxus, Mr. Neutron and Anonymous Bob are planning to destroy the city."

Captain Bloodloss' tone changed and his eyes slowly shifted back and forth, "Wow, that is bad news, gee I wish I could help...but...er.... I'm tied up with...uh...aliens.... of some sort...trying to....er...somethingororder."

"But what about that beer you're men are carrying, I can see it in the background?"

"Beer?" The Captain turned around quickly and then turned back just as quickly, "Uh...that's not beer. My men just got back from...uh...fighting the super villain...um...Kegger. Oh wait, too much interference, I'm losing you," The picture faded to static as Iggy turned around, "Well, I guess it's up to us now."

"What about the Phantom Pansy?" Melanie walked up to him.

"Can't get him, he's in San Francisco working a case," Iggy shook his head.

"Well, what are we waiting for, let's go save the city," Red yelled as Burke walked in, "Here are your keys, sir, please bring the car back by six. It needs to get inspected."

Piling into the Demon Two, they tore into the night headed for the old abandoned dog pound. They pulled up to the building and exited the vehicle. Iggy walked to the trunk and opened it, revealing a cache of weapons. He picked one up, "Now Red, this is a powerful weapon so when you fire it make sure that this end is pointing away from you."

Red nodded, "Right," and took the weapon. Together all three walked to the door. Iggy kicked it in. Guns drawn they stormed into the dog pound and looked around. Red shouted after checking the entire area, "There's nobody here."

Iggy looked at Melanie and shrugged, "I guess we were wrong."

A monotone beep punctured the silence of the night, Iggy jumped, "The crime phone!!" He exclaimed as he reached into his back pocket and answered the phone, "Hello?"

"Iggy, this is Mr. Neutron, where the hell are you?" Mr. Neutron sounded impatient.

"I figured out your ruse, Neutty. I cracked your riddle and made it to the abandoned dog pound," Iggy sounded proud of his detective skills.

"Well, that's nice, but you were supposed to come to the old abandoned laudromat," Mr. Neutron shook his head.

"I knew that," Iggy snapped back," I am looking for the device."

"I have the device, Iggy,"

"Can I have it?"

"No," Mr. Neutron hung up the phone and looked at Bob and Praxus, "Make some room on that couch for me. I don't want to miss my stories."

Iggy put the phone back in his pocket and looked at Melanie, "I need you to get Chief Inspector Larry for me, "I might not be able to solve this by myself."

Melanie took off for the car and in a flash was racing up the street to the precinct. Red cracked his knuckles as they both headed across the street to the old abandoned laudromat.

All the windows were painted black and Iggy could not see anything inside. He knocked on the glass door that claimed they store was empty. Nobody answered the door. He knocked again, still no answer.

"Oh well, nobody's here," he shrugged to Red, "I guess we can go home," He started to walk away when he heard the sound of someone unlocking the door. The door swung open. "You must be Iggy," Mr. Neutron said, holding a very convincing shotgun, "Why don't you step inside, both of you."

Iggy and Red entered the door and were quickly thrown against the wall, "So you thought you can exterminate my egomaniacal dreams," Praxus pulled Iggy up by his collar, "You shall soon find out that it is you who will be exterminated," He dropped Iggy to the floor and looked at Mr. Neutron, "Tie them up, I have a plan for them." He smiled all mean and evil-like.

On the other side of darkness, Melanie alerted Chief Inspector Larry, but he didn't care. He had more videotapes to return. Melanie hopped back in the car and raced to the laudromat. Melanie got back into Demon Two raced down the highway only to get stuck behind another elderly gentleman driving a Buick. He was also going 25 miles under the limit and his right turn signal was permanently stuck in the "on" position.

"Screw this," Melanie muttered as she crossed the double yellow line. The elderly gentleman was just a blur as the Demon Two roared with enthusiasm. The wind blowing in her hair, Melanie didn't notice the red and blue lights behind her.

"Damn cops," she yelled as she slowed down and pulled over to the side of the road. The police cruiser stopped behind and a constable made his way to the Demon Two's driver side window. Melanie took this time to check her hair, adjust her bra, put on some lipstick, and spray some perfume.

She was just about done when the officer knocked on the window, "You crossed the double yellow line, let me see some identification," His solemn expression did not change.

"Why do you want to blow up the city?" Red struggled against the nylon ropes.

"Because," Praxus pulled up a chair and stared at Iggy and Red, "I'm sick of never being able to get what I want. I'm sick of never reaching that final step or catching that last train. I want to free myself of the burdens, the troubles, and the odor. This city is a wasteland, almost as bad as Detroit. That is why the city must be destroyed."

"Oh geez," Iggy rolled his eyes."

The sound of a door opening gained everyone's attention, "I have a box for Iggy," Mr., Neutron smiled, although no one could tell as his face was covered with a gas mask.

Praxus clapped his hands, "Oh goody," He put the box on a table and pushed in lengthwise into Iggy and Red's knee-caps, "Say good night you two," Praxus remarked as all both.

As Praxus closed the door and switched off all but one light, Iggy and Red replied, "Good night you two."

Red looked curiously at the box, which was starting to move, "What do you think is in there?"

"Something diabolical, I'll bet. Praxus was always a sucker for some elaborate death trap," He stared at the boxed, thinking of the time be bought something on the Internet and forget what it was when it arrived at his doorstep.

The cardboard boxed rocked back and forth for a few minutes. Iggy was worried, he didn't know what was in the box but was sure it would mean their doom. The box stopped moving and silence shrouded both our heroes.

Red started to fall asleep, but was jolted awake by a strange noise. He looked at the box and saw a knife stab through the box top. Suddenly, a brown furry paw punched through the box. Iggy stared in disbelief as two leather-clad teddy bears with eye patches and switchblades jumped out.

"Oh god, not again," Red muttered as the bears drew closer, swinging their blades wildly. Iggy and Red struggled against the ropes, trying to free themselves from the impending doom.

"So this is how it ends?" Iggy grunted as he was trying to get loose, "Stab to death by crummy puppets." The swinging blades swung closer, as the bears approached with eerie calmness.

Red growled in pain as one of the blades sliced his shoulder, "That's going to leave a mark,"

"Stay calm," Iggy snapped back as blade swung right by his nose, "There's no reason to panic." The bears were now close enough to deal a fatal blow, "okay, now it's time to panic."

A loud bang turned Iggy and Red's, as well as the teddy bears heads, to the main door. The door fell to the ground with a dull thud, as Melanie rolled into the room with guns drawn.

"What took you so long?" Iggy said while dodging the swinging knife.

"I crossed the dreaded double yellow line," Melanie quickly stood up and shot one of the bears. The other bear threw his switchblade right for Melanie's head.

"Look out, "Iggy shouted, as Melanie caught the knife. She raised her gun and aimed for the teddy bear's cute fuzzy head, "When you get to Hell, tell 'em Melanie sent ya," she pulled the trigger. The bear bent backwards as the bullet whizzed past him and cut the rope that bound Iggy and Red. Instantly, they both got up and ran over to Melanie.

"That was amazing," Iggy shouted as he hugged her.

"It's not over yet," Melanie pushed him away as she threw the switchblade right for the teddy bear's cute fuzzy tummy. The bear flinched as the knife went through him, a mix of stuffing and blood fell to the floor.

"I'm glad that's over," Red replied as they stared at the gruesome, yet cute sight.

"Now let's go get Mr. Neutron," Melanie said as she headed for the door.

On the roof of the abandoned laundromat, Mr. Neutron worked alone, his cohorts having left to read children's books at the local hospital. "I just love working with my hands. That should be the last wire," Mr. Neutron talked to himself, as he was often found doing, "Very well, there is no escape." He connected one last wire to the device.

"Don't make a move," Iggy said loudly as he stepped off the ladder onto the rooftop.

"Iggy, you're just in time, " Mr. Neutron grabbed the device and turned to Iggy, "Here it is, the pinnacle of human achievement."

"I can't let you do this. If you destroy this city, I wouldn't be able to go to that all night chili bistro I love so muc,." Iggy pulled out a gun and aimed it for Mr. Neutron's robotic head

"I won't have to, if you join me," Mr. Neutron walked closer to Iggy.

Iggy took a step back," No,"

"Don't you know what we can do?" Mr. Neutron showed him the device.

"Yeah, but it's not right," The protagonist shook his head in an attempt to be negative.

"Exactly, we can run the world," Mr. Neutron raised the device into the air, "We can rule the world together, as a family."

Iggy's eyes widened. Lowering his gun, the darkly dressed superhero took a step forward, "What are you saying?"

"Iggy, I am your father's only son, and I am here to avenge your death," The gas masked villain breathed deeply, "We can crush anyone who rebels."

A million thoughts raced through Iggy's head. He thought about his parents, who died before he was born. He thought about he relationship with Mr. Neutron, the many times he foiled the villain's most foul schemes, he remembered that day they called a truce to their fighting and went to a live taping of the Cosby Show. Neutron just looked at his watch.

"I can't join you, Neutty," Our hero shook his head and raised his gun again, "Momma always said that evil is like a box of cookies, eventually they all disappear,"

"Not today, Ignatius," Mr. Neutron activated the device, "If you won't join me, then I'll kill you and have to settle for that."

Iggy shouted, ran, and tackled Mr. Neutron. The device flew off the roof.

After struggling for what seemed like five seconds, Mr. Neutron pushed Iggy off of him. Standing up and dusting himself off, Mr. Neutron stared at Iggy, " Gee thanks, all that work and you throw it off the roof, I can't believe that! You are such a jerk," He began to walk away.

"We're not finished, I'm bringing you in," Iggy pulled out his other gun, because he did not know what happened to the one he had before. He stood up and looked around, but Mr. Neutron was gone. Twenty minutes later, Iggy heard a noise coming from behind him; he spun around to see whom it was. He lowered his gun; it was Melanie and Red.

"Is everything all right?" Melanie ran over and hugged Iggy, "I was so worried about you."

Iggy pulled her hand of his shoulder and pushed her away, "What took you so long?"

"Red was scheduled for a tick bath and a rabies shot," She replied looking all sad and rejected. She started to walk away when Iggy grabbed her hand and spun her around. They were face to face,

"Melanie, if I didn't love you, I'd probably love somebody else." He used his very best smooth hero voice.

"Oh, Iggy," Melanie sunk into his arms as their lips drew closer.

Just as they were about to kiss, Red walked up with the device in his furry yet neatly trimmed claws, "Hey, I wonder what this big red button does."

Sibling Rivalry
Jonathan Cross

Kris saw the short man emerge, running, from the alley. He clutched a package protectively to his chest as his torn, bulky, brown clothing threatened to trip him with each step. The man paused at the edge of the sidewalk and looked behind him. A tall, muscular figure appeared right on his heels, his arms outstretched as if he were getting ready to tackle.

The short man's eyes widened as his pursuer lunged. He secured his brown fedora with his hand, took a breath, and jumped into the street, narrowly evading the muscular man's grasp. Cars honked angrily at the as they whizzed by. The short man danced through the traffic, his attention locked on his pursuer. He stepped in front of the carriage's path, and Kris pulled hard on the reins. The horse shrieked in protest, reared up, and the carriage shuddered to a halt.

"What the hell do you think you're doing?" Kris shouted as he scrambled out of the carriage.

The horse whinnied and stamped its feet in annoyance at the abrupt stop. Kris walked around the horse, patting it to calm both it and himself down. Irritation bubbled within him. What was that crazy pedestrian thinking? His passengers weren't going to be happy.

Kris stepped in front of the horse to help the old man up, but he was nowhere to be found. Now, where is he? he thought. The space in front of the carriage was empty. He got to his hands and knees to look underneath the carriage, but found no trace of anyone. As he was standing up, he noticed a round charred spot on the underside of the carriage and sighed. He'd have to tell Charles about that. He definitely wouldn't be happy.

Remembering the short man had a pursuer, Kris peered into the alleyway for him. Through the passing cars, he saw no sign of the taller man either.

Kris stood up and scratched his head, feeling confused. "Now where did—"

"Where did you learn to drive?" yelled one of his passengers. He'd poked his head out of the side of the carriage. "A stop like that could have thrown us off and broken our necks."

He continued insulting Kris's driving ability as Kris sullenly climbed back into the driver's seat. Tourists, he thought. Still, he couldn't blame the guy too much. He'd paid for a romantic ride through the city with his new wife, and that braking job was anything but romantic.

Kris shook his head and started the horse moving again, doing his best to keep the acceleration smooth. Whoever that short man had been, he was nothing but trouble. Trouble for his passengers, and trouble for him once Charles heard about the damage. He sighed, pushing his worries into the dull and noisy background of the busy streets, along with the two disappearing men. The horse's hooves clopped against the pavement, and he wished for what seemed like the hundredth time today that he had never taken this job from his brother-in-law. The things he put up with to put food on the table.

***

The elevator doors opened, and Kris stepped into the waiting room for his brother-in-law's office. He was nervous, afraid that his report of damage to the carriage would end with his head ripped off. Butterflies fluttered in his stomach as he stood looking over the office. A bank of filing cabinets was on his right and a couch was on his left. He glanced around the room for his wife. There she was, at her desk beyond the filing cabinets, next to the door to Charles' office.

"Hi, Elizabeth," he said. "Could you tell Charles I'm here to see him? I need to talk to him about some repairs to the carriage."

Elizabeth cocked her head, her blue eyes examining Kris. "Are you all right?"

Kris shrugged, not wanting to let her see him worried. "Yeah, I'm fine. There was just some minor stuff that I'd like to get repaired."

"Good," said Elizabeth. She turned to her intercom, and Kris sat down on the couch to wait. "Charles, your brother-in-law is here to see you," Kris heard her say. He picked up a magazine, expecting to wait a few minutes.

"Tell him to come on in," came Charles' thin voice in reply.

Kris replaced the magazine on the coffee table and stood. He looked at Elizabeth in surprise. She shrugged her shoulders, and returned to her work. Kris walked to the door, gathered his strength for the tirade he expected, and entered Charles' office.

"Stolen? What do you mean, 'stolen?'" Kris heard Charles bellow as he entered the room.

Kris waited by the door, glad that he wasn't the recipient

of Charles' for a change. He didn't want to make eye contact, so he surveyed the elegant luxury of the room. The size of the office always impressed him. The room ended thirty feet from where Kris stood in a wall of windows. The office was the penthouse of Brown Savings and Loan, Charles' bank, and the windows gave a magnificent view over the city. To-night the sun was turning the sky a gorgeous azure and magenta as it set over the river. Located in the center of the window was Charles' desk. He stood behind it, talking to someone who sat on the couch in front of his desk. Charles managed to catch Kris's eye, and held up a finger to indicate he'd be just a minute.

Kris nodded, acknowledging Charles and turned to examine the violently colored paintings hanging beside the door. He hoped that maybe Charles would expend his energy on whatever was vexing him before it was his turn.

"I'm disappointed in you, Horace," Charles continued with the man on the couch. "I gave you this task because I believed you could do it. What you lost must be reclaimed. Now make yourself useful and actually help me for once."

Kris heard the man rise from the couch and turned to watch. He saw the man, rather tall and dressed in a black suit, following the elegant red carpet to the other door on the opposite side of the room.

"Kris!" exclaimed Charles, his green eyes shining as he made eye contact with his brother-in-law. "How long has it been? You don't come by as often as you used to."

Kris walked slowly to Charles' desk and sat down on the couch. "It's been a while, but I haven't had anything to report."

"That's all right. News can sometimes come slow," said Charles. "So how's that horse and buggy been treating you?"

"Actually, that's what I'm here about," said Kris, running his hand through his long dark hair as he talked. "The carriage somehow got a burn or something underneath it. I was hoping you could fix it for me."

"A burn?" asked Charles, his eyes suddenly narrowing. "How did that happen? Were you attacked?"

"I don't know," answered Kris. "I don't think so. A crazy old man ran right in front of me and just disappeared. Then I found the charred mark. I don't think it was The Society, though."

"Ah. Good. Thanks for letting me know."

Charles reclined in his chair and rubbed his dimpled chin, apparently thinking hard about what Kris had said. The man was quite paranoid. His paranoia about this so-called "Society" had begun about two years ago. He'd insisted on having Kris roaming the city searching for "odd occurrences." Kris's role as a horse and buggy driver for tourists had been born.

Charles had never offered any more details for what constituted an odd occurrence. Kris thought it was strange then, but didn't argue. He'd had troubles finding a job after dropping out of college, and Elizabeth's job wasn't quite enough to support both of them. The money Charles had offered for this job made their lives a lot easier. They didn't have to cut as many corners to live now. So, knowing the boon it would be for his family, Kris had agreed, and Charles provided the horse and carriage. He'd been busy ever since, working 10 to 12 hour days regularly with only a day off here and there.

"Well," Charles said, breaking his silence, "put the buggy in the garage. I'll have someone take a look at it later tonight. It should be ready for you tomorrow."

"Thanks," said Kris, shocked that Charles hadn't blown

up at him for some perceived negligence. He leaned forward outstretching his right hand across the desk.

"You're welcome," said Charles, returning the handshake. "I'll see you later."

Kris felt relieved as he stood. Charles hadn't been mad at him! Maybe it wasn't going to be such a bad day, after all. He saw Charles wince and rub his right hand as he turned his attention to his computer screen. Kris turned and walked to the door, looking at the colorful paintings again as he left.

The door shut behind him. "How did it go?" asked Elizabeth from her desk.

Kris hesitated, momentarily at a loss for words. "Better than I thought it would," he finally said. He kissed her on the forehead. "He usually blows up and blames me for the smallest mistake. This time, no blame. He's even going to fix the carriage."

"That's wonderful," she exclaimed. She looked up into Kris's eyes, and pulled him closer. "With the carriage broken, maybe we'll get some time alone tonight. I could arrange to get off work early."

Kris smiled down at her. "That is an excellent idea. I'll be home just as soon as I can put the carriage away."

She stood up, and they hugged. Kris closed his eyes and smiled. Charles not mad at him and a romantic night alone with the woman he loved. This day was going to be great.

It had been so long since they'd had an evening to themselves. He thought back, battling his memory that so often failed him. In all of their two-plus years of marriage, he could recall only their honeymoon night as their last moment together. Since then, life had been constantly busy: business for Elizabeth at the bank and Kris's special assignment.

Kris sighed, forcing thoughts of the past trials of his life away from his mind. Tonight would be a perfect evening between him and his wife. Right after he put the carriage in the garage.

***

"Move, dammit," Kris cried as he threw his weight into the carriage one more time. The carriage slid a couple of inches across the cement floor, screeching as the wheels refused to move.

Kris stopped and wiped his brow. What was wrong? The start had been easy enough. He'd pulled the carriage in with the horse to a point where he could push it himself to where Charles had specified. After taking the horse to its stall, rubbing it down, and feeding it, he'd returned to situate the carriage. But the carriage wouldn't budge. The wheels were locked, and Kris couldn't figure out why.

He looked at his wristwatch and sighed. He was already late meeting with Elizabeth at their apartment. Frustrated, he gathered up all of his strength and pushed the carriage with all his might. With a crack, the wheels suddenly started moving, and the carriage slammed against the wall of the garage, then rested in its place.

"Well, it's where Charles wanted it," Kris said, hoping no further damage was done. Maybe there'd be enough time to be with Elizabeth after all. He sprinted forward to inspect the carriage, crying out as he tripped and nearly landed face-first on the floor.

He looked to his feet to see what he'd tripped over, and found a shoebox shaped package, covered with an oil-stained brown cloth. Perplexed, he moved to inspect the object. He picked it up, surprised at its heaviness, and removed the cloth, exposing a dirty box underneath. He opened it and was amazed to see a shining piece of gold. Strange black symbols encompassed the object, looking like a combination of Chinese ideograms and Mayan hieroglyphics. The object was oblong, with what looked like indentations for hands on the sides. Different from the rest of the object, they were silver and lacked the black symbols.

Kris just stared at the image for a time. Then he placed it back in the box and closed it, thinking that if this wasn't something out of the ordinary, then nothing was. He contemplated taking it to Charles right then, but decided against it. This might be one of the last chances he had to spend the evening with Elizabeth for a while. He'd show the strange thing to Charles tomorrow.

***

Kris arrived home to find a darkened apartment. From the entryway, he saw the flicker of candles on the dining room table. "Elizabeth, you shouldn't have," he murmured.

"Why shouldn't I?" she said as she appeared out from the kitchen and slid into Kris's arms. "I love you more than life itself. A beautiful meal is the least that I could have done."

"Forgive me for being late," Kris said as he was led into the dining room. "I had problems dealing with the…" He trailed off as Elizabeth's hand was placed over his mouth.

"Uh uh," she said, "no talking about work, or there won't be any dessert for you." She winked suggestively.

She left the room and shortly returned with steaming plates of pasta shells. A ricotta, onion, and spinach filling seeped out from the ends of each shell, and an appetizing marinara sauce covered the tops. Kris licked his lips and followed her into the dining room. She set the plate on the table.

"This looks great," Kris said. He reached to serve himself, but Elizabeth playfully slapped him. He exclaimed as he withdrew his hand quickly. He smiled and looked at his wife as she served his food. Her blue eyes sparkled with the obvious enjoyment she was deriving from the company with her husband. Her blond hair was down—usually she wore it on top of her head in some fashion—combed behind her small ears and displaying its beautiful curls. He liked it better as its natural honey brown color, but the blond was very attractive, too.

"What are you looking at?" she asked coyly, breaking him out of his train of thoughts.

"Just the most beautiful woman in the world. That's all."

"Good answer," Elizabeth said. "Eat. Your food's getting cold." She walked over to the opposite side of the table and served her plate. Then she turned to leave the room.

"And just where do you think you're going?" Kris asked.

"To slip into something more comfortable," she replied, slyly. "Now eat."

Elizabeth left the room for the bedroom. Kris watched her depart, remembering the first time they'd met about two and a half years ago. He'd been standing on a corner, waiting for the bus. He was late for class and was in a bit of a hurry. When the bus arrived, he had rushed through the door, not waiting to let the exiting passengers out first. He'd thrown his bus fare into the machine and turned down the aisle to find a seat. Then he crashed into someone, felt a prickling sensation on his head as he fell, and passed out. When he awoke, he was in a hospital, and she was caring for him. He'd suffered a concussion in the collision and ensuing fall, and she'd brought him straight to the hospital, where they fell in love at first sight.

His life sure had changed since then. After four months of dating, they were married. He had dropped out of college, going from a single, poor student to a happily married man working for his brother-in-law driving tourists through the city in a horse-driven carriage. He liked the changes.

Kris speared one of the pasta shells with his fork and brought it to his mouth. He took a bite, and the delicate shells broke away, releasing their ricotta and onion filling into his mouth. He swallowed, and the feeling of relaxation characteristic of Elizabeth's pasta dishes washed over him. So he just sat back and enjoyed the food whenever she had the time and felt the desire to make it. Kris cleared off his plate, then took a drink of wine.

The bedroom door clicked as it opened, and soon his wife appeared. Through his sleepy eyes, Kris saw the lingerie he had given her for Valentine's the year before peeking through her low-cut gown. It was a lacy, pink outfit that showed off her cleavage. Pink fishnet stockings were visible where the gown ended down by her ankles. Kris smiled. "You are *so* sexy."

She strode forward to where he was sitting and sat on his lap. "You finished all your food already?" she purred. She began caressing his head and kissing him all over. Kris reached his arms around her waist and started kissing her back. As she kissed him, his eyes drooped closed and the world faded to black. He felt someone gently place his head on the table.

Dimly, Kris heard a loud commotion from the door. He fought to open his heavy-lidded eyes, vaguely seeing Elizabeth running out of the room. Soon she was back, but terrified. Kris felt her hands on his right temple, massaging him. A warming sensation began in Kris's head, and the world started swimming around him. Then the room exploded.

Everything that Kris saw, felt, heard, smelled was fuzzy. His wife was gone; the spot where she had been was replaced with gray smoke and flashing lights. Violent winds buffeted him from all sides, roaring in his ears. The smell of the food still lingered, mixed with smoke and charred wood. He tried to get up, but his body refused to respond.

He battled his eyes to stay open to search for his wife. All he could make out were brilliant flashes of light flying all through the apartment. Wherever they touched, they left black scorch marks. A beam flew towards him, grazing his head.

"He knows what you're doing, Elizabeth," Kris heard a gravelly voice say as he lost the fight to stay conscious. A sticky fluid was flowing over his outstretched arms. Then he heard what he thought was his wife's voice screaming, but he couldn't understand any of the words. There was one last brilliant explosion of light before he passed out, realizing how similar the designs on the tablecloth were to the object he'd found by the carriage.

***

"Kris, wake up, honey. You're going to be late for work."

Kris groaned as he slowly opened his eyes. His wife was busy folding laundry and putting it away into the closet. "Are you okay?" he asked her.

She turned from what she was doing and looked at Kris. One of her brown curls slipped from its place on top of her head and fell in front of her eyes. "I'm fine," she said, looking perplexed, as she smoothed the hair back into place over her ear. "Are you all right? You look a little worse for the wear."

"I—"

"You had a nightmare again, didn't you," Elizabeth consoled. "Well, I warned you. You know what happens to you when you eat too much of my good cooking." She smiled as she turned back to folding and putting away the laundry. "Now hurry up. Charles won't be too happy with you if you're late."

Kris shook his head as he got out of bed. He knew something didn't feel right, but he couldn't remember what. He thought back to the day before, remembering the day of work driving his carriage. Charles had wanted him to patrol the city because he had had a feeling the Society was up to something. Kris remembered the strange burn mark on the carriage, the conversation with Charles, the discovery of the strange object, and the romantic evening with Elizabeth. Hadn't there been something more?

He buttoned up his shirt and walked into the bathroom to shave, comb his hair, and brush his teeth. He saw his reflection in the mirror, noticing the dime-sized dark red mark on the right side of his head, near his temple. The mark had been there for years now, a scar that served as a permanent reminder of the first meeting with Elizabeth. Today it looked fresh, almost as if it had been opened again recently. He lifted his hand and touched the spot with the tips of his fingers. Pain shot through his head, and he withdrew quickly, wondering why it hurt so much.

"Are you ready yet?" his wife called.

"Almost," Kris replied. He quickly finished up and left the bathroom, trying to put the mysterious head injury out of his mind. It hurt to think about it.

Grabbing an apple from the kitchen counter, he glanced around the house as he left the apartment. Paintings filled with swirls of brightly colored strokes he didn't remember were hanging on the living room walls. "Are those new?" he asked Elizabeth as she joined him at the door.

"What? Those paintings?" she said. "No, we've had those for ages. I was thinking about taking them down, though. I'm getting tired of them."

Kris opened the door and stepped out of the apartment,

waiting for Elizabeth. She exited next, closing the door and locking it behind her. Kris thought he saw light flash through the door cracks as she removed the key from the lock.

"Come on, let's go," Elizabeth said. She walked quickly from the door down the stairs to the car. They piled into the car, Elizabeth in the driver's seat, and drove off for work.

***

"Thanks for driving me to the bank this morning," Kris said as they left the elevator from the parking garage to the penthouse. "I need to talk to Charles and see if the carriage has been fixed."

Elizabeth paused at her desk, setting down some papers and turning on her computer. "I'd like to talk to him before you, if you don't mind."

Kris shrugged, and Elizabeth disappeared into Charles' office. Kris sat down at Elizabeth's desk to pass the time. He was feeling better; his head pain had calmed down.

"Does Kris know?" Kris jumped at the sudden mention of his name. He whirled his head around, scanning the receptionist's room, but saw no one. Then he realized the voice was Charles', coming from the intercom. Elizabeth must have left it turned on.

"No," Kris heard Elizabeth say. "I know you worry because I married outside of my race, but you shouldn't. He doesn't know, and he never will. We've been together for more than two years. If he were going to find out, he would've by now. Besides, I'm too careful."

"Very well," said Charles, "I'll trust your judgment, little sister. For now. But I'll be keeping a close eye on you."

There was a pause in the conversation, and Kris's world began to swim. The red injury on the side of his head started throbbing, and his head felt as if it were going to explode. He rested his elbows on the desk and placed his hands on his forehead. The voices coming from the intercom stopped speaking English or any language he had ever heard before. Kris had the distinct impression that this was all too familiar, and he closed his eyes, praying that it would pass quickly.

"Kris?"

Kris turned his head toward the voice, trying in vain to focus his eyes upon whoever stood before him. "What?" he stammered.

"For the third time, I said that Charles will see you now, Kris." The world calmed itself a little, and Kris finally found the ability to focus. His wife stood with her back to him, putting papers away in the file cabinet. "But you better be careful, he's not in a very good mood."

"Thanks," Kris said as he stood up, glad to see the ground underneath his feet was sturdy. He grabbed the package containing the strange object and walked into Charles's office.

"Good morning, Kris," called Charles when he saw Kris come through the doorway. "Have you checked the repairs made on the buggy yet?"

Kris let the door shut behind him. He saw the paintings with their splashes of bright colors and thought Charles and Elizabeth certainly did have similar tastes in art. "No," he answered and walked to Charles's desk. "But I did find this. I thought you might be interested." He quickly opened the package and placed the gold and silver sculpture on the desk.

Charles' eyes widened, though whether in fear or amazement was impossible to tell. "Where did you find this?"

"Last night after I parked the carriage where you told me to, I tripped over it. It must have gotten lodged somewhere and then fallen out as I put the carriage away."

Charles tentatively reached for the object. It began to glow. When his hand was about an inch from touching the metal, the object zapped, and Charles jumped back. Before Kris's eyes, the appearance of his brother-in-law shifted. Suddenly his hair was dark brown, his nose was somewhat hooked, and his ears started growing. But only for an instant. Kris blinked and Charles appeared as his normal self with his blond hair, slim nose, and small ears.

"Whoa," exclaimed Kris. "What happened?"

"I'm…not…sure," Charles stammered. His brow furrowed, and he started putting distance between himself and the object. His stammering disappeared as he walked away from the object. "My guess is it was a failed attack by the Society. Those burns you found yesterday on the carriage were probably caused by this object. It seems to be a bomb of some sort, but it's a dud. I mean, it didn't explode."

Kris looked at Charles in shock. A bomb? Had he almost died? When he started this special assignment for Charles, he hadn't realized his life would be in danger.

"Did you tell anyone about this?" asked Charles. He raised his gaze from the object to look at Kris.

"No, of course not. You know you ordered me never to tell anyone about my assisting you, not even my wife."

Charles nodded as he stopped walking to stand beside Kris. He started examining Kris's head injury. "Your scar looks worse. Did something happen?" He raised his hand to touch it.

"I don't know," said Kris. He flinched away from Charles' touch, expecting the same pain to wash over him that he had experienced when he examined the injury after getting out of bed. Instead, Charles' touch was calming, decongesting Kris's brain.

"It looks like it's been reopened," Charles said as he removed his hand from Kris's head. "Do be careful in the future, Kris. I'm going to ask that you return to your horse and buggy driving today. The repairs have been made, and I believe some surveillance today could prove useful."

"But what about this bomb?" asked Kris. "Will I be safe?"

"Yes. I'll have it looked at and taken care of. Thanks for bringing it to my attention. Good day, Kris." With that, Charles dismissed Kris with a wave of the hand and walked to the other door in the room.

Kris looked bewilderedly at Charles and slowly backed out of the room. His wife was waiting for him outside the door.

"How did it go?" she asked.

"Um, good," Kris said, hesitantly. Realizing he needed to lie to his wife about what had happened in the office, he racked his brain for something, anything to say. "You were right, Elizabeth, he was in quite a mood today. You know yesterday how he had said he would take care of the repairs to my carriage? Well, it's going to come out of my paycheck. I argued with him, probably more than I should have. At the end, I was afraid he was going to fire me."

Elizabeth grabbed Kris and hugged him. "Don't worry, it'll be okay. Just be more careful in the future."

**

Kris saw the short man emerge, running, from the alley. His torn, bulky, brown clothing threatened to trip him with every step. Without pausing, the man ran from the edge of the sidewalk into the path of Kris's carriage.

"Hey, watch it," Kris shouted, feeling a bit of déjà vu.

The short man looked straight at Kris, giving him warm, friendly smile. Kris started pulling on the reins of the horse, when the short man mumbled something and disappeared.

Kris dropped the horse's reins in shock. The horse slowed down to a trot, and Kris looked wildly around the street for the disappeared stranger. Suddenly the odor of rotten fruit hit his nose and he felt a hand around his mouth. He looked down to see nothing. As he tried to scream, the invisible hold only increased. His attempted scream was stifled, along with his ability to breathe.

"Don't," Kris heard from behind him. He turned to find out who was holding him, but saw no one. Another invisible hand smacked him across the head. "I can make that red spot on your head hurt more than you could ever imagine," the voice said. "Now, don't try to struggle. Just do what I say, and everything's going to be all right. Drive us to someplace secluded, a nice dark alley somewhere."

Kris tried not to panic. He picked up the horse's reins and guided it to the first dark and empty alley he saw. All the while, the odor of burning, decaying garbage coming from the invisible hand on his mouth urged him onward.

Kris's mind raced as the carriage entered the alley. As much as he tried, he could not accept that an invisible man was holding him hostage. A trick, that's what it is, he concluded. Elizabeth or Charles, or both, are playing a joke on me, he thought. Thoughts of the Society and the strange bomb from earlier that morning flashed through his mind. He pushed them away, instead clinging to his belief that it was just a prank. He started to relax a little. Then the carriage stopped, and the hand covering his mouth was removed.

"You don't know me," said the voice, "but I know you. I've been watching you for quite some time. You might say we have the same business associates."

"You mean Charles and Elizabeth? They can come out now. I think this joke has gone on long enough," Kris insisted, still hoping that it really was nothing more than a prank.

"You've had a tough day," the voice continued, ignoring Kris's outburst. "I'm sure you've got lots of questions. I'd like to answer them all for you—I hate the way you've been dragged into this—but I have neither the time nor the liberty to do so. I can tell you this: like I arranged for you to hear today, your wife is a different race than you.

"I know you don't understand that or anything that's going on around you, and that's why I came to see you to-night. I wanted to assure you that you will be safe. The Society will not harm you. And that's straight from the horse's mouth. I don't think you should be harmed, and the Society agrees with me. You might say you've got your own little guardian angel. So try not to worry too much.

"Also, let me fix that wound on your head for you. That's been there for far too long, and it's time for something to be done about it. This will cure slowly during tonight and to-morrow. As it heals, many of your lost or confusing memo-ries will also return."

Kris squirmed as he felt the invisible hands touching his head, rubbing both temples, and delicately pinching the skin. He felt electrical current start flowing from the hands through his head, then he saw brilliant flashes of color. He closed his eyes to keep from being blinded. Then the hands and the lights stopped.

Kris opened his eyes and looked around. He was still in the darkened alley, but he could just barely make out a small figure bundled in a bulky brown coat standing in front of the carriage. He touched his right temple and felt no pain, but the red scab remained.

"One more thing," said the short figure, holding up his index finger. "The scab will remain as a safe-guard, if you will. We wouldn't want just anyone knowing that you've been cured." With that the figure vanished again.

Kris sighed, unable to make sense of anything that had just happened. Who was this man, and why did he keep jumping in front of his carriage? Why did people keep saying his wife was not of his race? He yawned as he backed the carriage out of the alley. A wave of tiredness hit him, so he decided to head home for the night.

***

The first thing Kris thought of when opened his eyes the next morning was the similarity between the tablecloth and the strange object he'd found.

He got out of bed, dressed himself, and headed into the dining room. The tablecloth was still there, just as he had noticed it after his wife had vanished in the flashing lights. Then he remembered the wind and the colors that had flashed through the apartment leaving black stains on the walls. He walked out of the dining room into the living room. The paintings with the randomly colored paint strokes remained on the walls, covering the black spots the light beams had caused.

He tried removing one of the paintings to look behind it, but his fingers went right through the frame and canvas. At his touch, the painting dissolved into snowy television static, flickering as he'd seen from the door cracks when Elizabeth closed the door the day before. He briefly saw the wall where the painting had been charred black before the painting returned. He quickly checked all the other paintings. They all turned into snow, flickered, and returned to their status as paintings when he touched them. Behind every one were black stains.

He moved to the center of the room, bracing himself for the inevitable swimming the world was about to do. Except that it didn't. The ground remained solid; his mind remained clear.

Then other details of the day that he'd forgotten or never noticed returned to him. He remembered shaking Charles' hand, removing some of Charles' skin with a tiny metal device in his hand. Then he saw himself walk out to Elizabeth and slip it to her when they hugged.

He remembered the changes in Elizabeth's hair color: from blond before the romantic dinner to brown the next morning when he awoke.

He wanted to cry, to force the onslaught of memories to stop. But more kept coming.

He remembered the explosion as his wife kneeled over him after he'd fallen off the chair. The weird language, the strange lights. He remembered sitting with his head on the table in a pool of his own blood. He remembered someone shooting bolts of light at his wife. He remembered seeing his wife sending bolts of colored lights forth from her hands in return. He remembered seeing her hair slowly change from blond to brown the more she fought. He remembered her brown hair whipping around her in the wind, revealing her pointed ears.

Kris sank to the floor, realizing that both Charles and the strange short man had been right. His wife was of another race, and his whole life was a lie.

Kris sat, numb and unsure of what to do. This was too much. He couldn't handle all this. He almost wished the world would start swimming and his head would start hurting again. But it didn't. Nothing was blocking him from dealing with his life now.

Kris picked himself up off the floor, feeling a resolve grow that he hadn't felt since he'd been a college student. He was determined to confront his wife and get some answers. He searched the apartment only to find a note that she'd left.

"Dear Kris," she wrote, "Forgive me for leaving you before you woke up, but Charles wants me in at work early today. He told me that he didn't need you today, so I decided to take the car. I'm afraid that it'll also be a late night of work for me. Try to have a relaxing day at home. Love, Elizabeth."

Kris wadded up the note and threw it on the floor. He stormed out of the apartment to find a cab to the bank.

***

The elevator doors to Charles' top floor office opened, and Kris stepped out. Seeing Elizabeth wasn't at her desk, he assumed she was inside Charles' office with him. He walked to the office door and opened it.

He blinked. The same colorful lights he'd seen the evening of the romantic dinner were flashing around the room. He saw Charles standing just a few feet in front of him, too involved to have noticed his entrance. But it was not the Charles he was used to. Charles' hair had changed to brown, his nose was bigger, and his ears were pointed, like when he'd touched the strange device the day before. Kris saw another figure with brown hair whipping around in the winds on the other side of the room. He was pretty sure it was Elizabeth.

Charles and Elizabeth stood facing each other down. They were both shooting bolts of light at each other, while trying to block the attacks of the other. A tall, muscular man stood nearby Charles. It was difficult for Kris to make him out with the brilliant blinding light, but he thought it was Horace, the man who Charles had chastised earlier.

"How dare you challenge me?" Kris heard Elizabeth scream. "Father had left the elven throne to me before he disappeared."

Charles laughed. "You know you have no right to the throne," he said arrogantly. "And why should I believe you didn't knock off dear old dad yourself?"

Elves? Kris thought. His wife was an elf? And here he was in the middle of a magical battle between two of them. He ducked back through the door, hoping that no one had seen him. He could hear Elizabeth screaming something in the strange language he'd been hearing a lot of lately. He rested against the wall in Elizabeth's office next to the open door.

"Horace," he heard Charles scream at the top of his lungs.

Kris slowly poked his head around the edge of the door. Elizabeth had managed to injure Charles. Blood was flowing freely from his forehead. He saw the muscular man lumber towards Charles, take an attack stance, and start attacking his wife with the flying bolts of light.

He looked at his wife fearfully, barely able to see her at this angle. He hoped she would be able to handle both attacking her at once. But as Charles' henchman added his power to the fight, Elizabeth's defenses started failing. Suddenly Charles and his henchman both broke through at the same time. Elizabeth was knocked back against the wall. She fell down onto the ground, splattering blood as she went.

Kris lost control of himself and burst into the room, screaming. The lights had stopped flying through the air once she had fallen, so Kris was able to safely run to her. He knelt by her side and grabbed her head, cradling it in his arms. He looked down at her blood-soaked body. "I love you," he said through tears. At that moment, he did, even with all her lies.

He felt a hand on his shoulder. He looked up and saw Charles and Horace behind him. Kris whirled around to face them. "You killed her," he shouted. "She was my wife." Kris began pummeling Charles. Horace grabbed Kris, pulling him off his brother-in-law.

"Stop," Horace said in a deep, gravelly voice. Kris looked

at him and remembered him. He was the one who had attacked his wife two nights ago.

He tried to kick and punch the man, but to no avail. Horace, unhindered by Kris's feeble punches, scooped him up like a sack of potatoes and flung him across the room. Kris landed on Charles' desk and groaned. His back felt as if it had a stone in it the size of…

Kris rolled over and saw the strange golden object. He looked back up to see Horace coming over to finish him off. As Horace neared, Kris reached back with his right hand and grabbed hold of one of the silver handles.

Horace walked up to him with one arm outstretched. "Stay," he commanded. When he was near enough, Kris swung his arm around and hit the man with the device as hard as he could. Horace staggered back. He opened his mouth in a silent howl. He brought his hands in front of his face, and they disintegrated. Horace screamed as the rest of his body exploded.

Shards of burnt, bloody flesh flew across the room, coating Kris. He wretched, and saw Charles storming towards him. "Horace," Charles bellowed in agony. He looked at Kris, his face a mask of rage. "I should have killed you on the bus when I had the chance. You would have died, too, if it weren't for my damn sister. Nothing ever good comes from interactions with humans." Charles flashed a glance back at his sister's crumpled body with the last remark.

He grabbed the device by the free silver handle and ripped it out of Kris's hands. "Let's see how you like dying like that." Charles started chanting, holding the object out toward Kris. Kris tried to get out of the way, but knew that it would be useless. He prepared himself for the impact and his certain death.

Charles stopped chanting; Kris inhaled sharply. The

object fizzled, but did nothing. Charles looked at it curiously. Suddenly he found himself lying on his back next to where his sister was. The golden device flew from Charles' grasp and bounced on the floor.

"You always did get it wrong," a voice said sadly. The golden object floated up from the floor, into the air. A cloth appeared and started wrapping itself around the object. Slowly the short man in the bulky, brown clothing materialized. He finished the folding and buried the object somewhere inside his brown coat.

At the sight of the old man, more memories hit Kris. His mind traveled back to more than two years before, to when he'd stepped onto that bus without looking to see where he was going. No, that was wrong. He remembered now, he had looked. He had seen bright lights emanating through the windows of the bus as it slowed for its stop. He had climbed on slowly, looked down the aisle, and found dozens of faces with pointy ears staring at him. He remembered one of them, a short old man, pushed him aside to run through the bus door. One man, without hesitation, turned, raised his hands, and pointed them toward the door. Bolts of light left his fingertips, nailing Kris in the head instead of the short old man who was now safely away. Kris remembered falling, looking up into the cold green eyes of Charles.

He remembered lying in a hospital bed. He remembered Elizabeth standing above him, arguing with Charles. He remembered her forcing Charles out of the room, coming to him, and placing her hands on his head. He remembered a tear falling from her eye as she kissed the newly formed red scar near his right temple.

At the thought of Elizabeth, Kris snapped out of his flashback and pulled himself to Elizabeth's side, looking bewilderedly at the short man the whole time. When he touched her cheek, she opened her eyes and looked at him, smilingly sweetly. "I'm sorry I got you involved in all this," she said faintly.

Kris looked down at her, angry, full of questions, and scared she was going to die all at the same time. "Please don't die," was all he managed.

Her eyes closed, and Kris felt a hand on his shoulder. He looked up to see the short old man standing behind him. "Let me," he said, smiling.

Kris moved to let the man kneel beside his wife. He placed his hands on her body, and he started glowing. The blood smeared along the wall and floor flowed slowly back into Elizabeth's body. The gashes on her skin sucked at the blood as they closed themselves. Soon her skin was again perfect, unmarred.

Elizabeth stirred, opening her eyes to gaze at Kris first, the old man second. "Who?" was all Elizabeth could say.

The short old man stepped closer, removing the brown hat on his head and unwrapping the dirty scarf that still partially obscured his face. His wrinkled, leathery face exposed itself, followed by a bald head with wisps of white-blond hair. And long pointy ears.

"Daddy," gasped Elizabeth. "Charles said that you were dead."

"Charles tried to have it that way," the short old man stated. "But he wasn't all that successful. Thanks to this young human here, I was saved."

"But why did you go away?" asked Elizabeth as she sat up. Her voice was strong and sounded angry. She had clearly regained her strength.

"Let's just say that I thought I should lie low for a while," the old man said with a twinkle in his eye. "Me and my Society watched for the right time to deal with things. I would've come back sooner, but I thought it would be a good time to see how you two would do governing our race." His happiness erased from his face as his tone became somber. "You disappointed me, Elizabeth. I know you loved Kris, but he's a human, and we have rules that must be followed. And you never should have involved him in our affairs like that, having him take a sample of your brother's skin for the Submission spell. You should be ashamed of yourself."

"I'm sorry, daddy," said Elizabeth, lowering her head.

Charles groaned and his eyelids fluttered beside her. "Father?" he exclaimed when he saw the short old man.

The old man turned his parenting to Charles. Kris heard him chastise Charles for his various deeds, having Horace steal the golden device, trying to use it to destroy his sister, usurping his sister's authority, trying to use the elf-only device on a non-elf, the list continued, but it faded from Kris's hearing as he looked into Elizabeth's beautiful blue eyes.

She looked up at him with tears in her eyes. "I'm sorry for what I put you through. I used you, and I know you'll never be able to forgive me. I promise you that you'll never have to put up with this again."

She interrupted her father's tirade of Charles: "Daddy, will you please?"

The short old man nodded. "It's time for you to return to your college career," he said.

"I really did love you," Kris heard Elizabeth say as his eyes closed themselves.

The last thing he heard was the strange language being chanted.

***

Kris saw the short man emerge, walking, from the alley, his torn, bulky, brown clothing flapping in the light breeze. The man paused at the edge of the sidewalk, looked behind him, and put a hand on his brown hat.

"Be careful," Kris shouted, inexplicably overcome with the feeling that the man was going to jump in front of the carriage.

The short man snapped his blue eyes to Kris. He smiled a toothy grin, and held a dirty thumb up into the air. Kris gave a friendly wave back to the stranger. Then he sighed, dreaming of having a real job, a real family, a real home one day soon when he finally finished college.

My Sushi Adventure 2: The Voyage Home
Rob Montanaro

Prologue

Thinking back, I ponder the wisdom in buying *The Tiny Book of Sushi*[1] for Kristina this Christmas. I thought to myself "This would make a nice joke gift to give to Kristina."

My wife, Shree, found the same kit a few moments later. "We should get this for Kristina".

You don't say.

As a rarity I didn't actually say what I was thinking. "Okay" was all I could come up with. After all, we had just been Christmas shopping.

The Sunday before Christmas arrived before we knew it, and my wife and I humbly exchanged gifts with Kristina and Charlie . We gave her the little book, and some fake and not-so-fake jewelry, and immediately she became entranced by the little sushi book. I thought to myself, "It's not 802.11b but at least she liked it." So we went off to our usual weekly sushi and ate ourselves into oblivion and promptly forgot the little book.

Time passed until New Year's Eve morn came around.

"Call Kristina & Charlie and see if they want to do anything tonight," my wife said.

"Why can't you?" I replied.

"Because I'm at work."

"You were able to call to tell me to call them, but you can't call them directly?" A lot of our conversations go this way; I'm not sure why I bother to ask.

"I was just making sure you got out of bed to go to work."

Ouch. Well, she's just jealous I can stumble into work anytime I please. "I'm not still in bed and I resent the implication."

"I gotta go. Just call them and find out."

"Fine." So I hung up the phone, got out of bed and got ready for the day. It was a cold morning, so while the car was warming I whipped out my handy dandy cell phone and hit my speed dial.

"This is Kristina."

"It's Me. Shree wants to know if you want to do anything tonight — yah know the whole New Years Eve thing."

"I dunno, I have to ask Charlie." Hmmm. Standard line, but that's ok, the playbook calls for Charlie not caring so long as he doesn't have to leave the house. In this regard, Charlie is very wise indeed. Anyway, I'd already long ago accepted the necessity of going to their house. They had a severe case of Renodistancenosis where a journey to the corner drugstore is too far and well, to my house is right out being 4 miles and 8 turns away. Actually, our working theory is that they are some new form of vampire and they can't cross under freeway overpasses.

"I'm thinking about trying to make Sushi tonight." Her voice brought me back to the moment.

What her voice said caught me off guard. "You're going to make Sushi?" Kristina? I wasn't sure if Kristina could make Pop Tarts to tell you the truth. Much like my wife, she has pawned the food preparation onto her husband. Which is not a bad thing, he makes a mean swordfish (Broiled that is). Its just...unusual... "Do you have everything?" I asked probingly

"No, but I'll be going out later."

Hmmm. Not only is she going to make a food item, she's going to go out to get the ingredients. I know for a fact the Asian market is more than 4 miles away. Dark and mysterious forces were at work here. For her own protection I felt I needed to be there. "Ok, well I'll give you a call after work."

The day passed uneventfully and around five I left and headed towards the Asian market, whipping out my trusty companion, the cell phone. The events of that evening I will not go into since they have already been well established[2].

SushiRob Residence
8:45 PM Friday, January 25th

Three weeks had passed since that fateful night. What's more, the next day promised the riches of exploring a new Asian Market. I love Asian Markets, they have wacky things you can't read. Their junk food is totally different in style and in taste. My wife and I often would go to the market for fun on a weekend during leaner times because it was cheap and it was strange. Think of it as a small cramped amusement park that only allows single file lines.

I knew we were going to attempt to make sushi again, tomorrow. The first time around had been a surprise — I was caught off guard on the way to work. I only had time after work to stop at the Asian market and get essential items. I had to improvise. That's ok, because cooking is cooking and it usually comes down to preparation. Of which in this case there was none. But it was New Years and the little book of sushi said it was FUN. and EASY. Kristina is no dummy either, I'm sure she spent a few dozen hours on the net researching. I mean, that's just standard operating procedure.

But this time, this time would be different. This time I knew the face of my enemy and I knew the time of our battle. This time I would be.

Prepared.

"Let's go to Barnes and Noble," I told my wife. She was immediately suspicious. She loves bookstores and well, I never take her to them anymore since I prefer to buy off the net. So my volunteering to go to one from out of the blue sent up red flags.

"Why?"

"I need to get a book on Sushi making". Books are a good thing(tm). If I'm going into battle, I want something more substantial than *The Tiny Book of Sushi*. I knew if it came down to it, that little book wouldn't take the bullet for me. I had to have reinforcements. It was my only chance for my cuisine to reign supreme. So off we went and soon I was confronted with row after row of not-so-neatly organized cookbooks. Organized alphabetically by author.

Wars are fought and won on Information. Fortunately for me that night, the shooting hadn't started, for in my rush to be prepared I had forgotten to go online, and well, get prepared to be prepared. I should have made a nice list of books to evaluate.

Did I mention the books were in alphabetical order by author? I sighed and settled down to the fact this was going to take longer than I anticipated. Nevertheless, I pushed on. After a little searching I came up with my first volume

Sushi[3]. I quickly looked it over, and was quickly disappointed. It was one of those glossy, full-page color photo, one recipe per page cookbooks. I never trust those, they never deliver. The authors name was Yoshii. Hmm, Yoshi, that's a Nintendo character. No this would not do at all.

The next find *Japanese Food and Cooking*[4] was a beautiful book. Indeed it captured the essence of everything I needed, and then some. But it was a little large, a little unwieldy and it did go into non-sushi aspects. Although I sense this becoming part of my library in the future, today, I would move on. *[As it turned out, I did indeed purchase this fine book a few months later.]*

I went through about a half a dozen books I could find before I settled for *Sushi: Taste and Technique*[5]. Here was a title one could appreciate. Taste? Yes it's quite tasty. Technique? That's what we're looking for alrighty. It was hefty, but more of a standard hardbound size. The text was clear and concise and not too big, not too small. An abundance of photos go along with it, but the photos didn't try to replace the text. Yes, this was a tome that could guide me in the dark art of sushi making.

It only took a couple hours to find, too! We made our purchases, and home I went to begin to study.

SushiRob Residence
9:30 AM Saturday, January 26th

The morning had arrived. Sometime in the afternoon I expected to receive a call from Kristina that would initiate our assault.

But first I needed to assemble my gear. No 1957 steamer that can only make 2 cups of rice this time, baby! No way. I broke out my 14 cup Salton Steamer. That should do the job nicely. Not as nice as one of the really cool electric rice cook-ers, but I don't cook rice very often and have yet to have the excuse to buy a high quality one. Of course, now that I'm making sushi, I'll have to re-evaluate that stance.

Also, draining the rice was a problem, so I figured I would bring my splatter guard for frying and use it. That way the water/starch could run off without the rice ending in the sink.

The whole rice-tossing thing went horribly last time. I didn't have a Hangiri, the traditional wide flat wooden bowl that is used to apply the salt/vinegar solution to the rice, but maybe I could acquire one today. As for the rice paddle, I figured I could use one of those pasta measuring plastic things you get free as a promotional everywhere. You know, plastic paddle with hole marking portions for spaghetti? Totally useless, but it seemed to be a good shape for such a task.

For good measure, I grabbed my egg slicer. Why you ask? Well, if you were a follower of Alton Brown you would know. Quite simply, it's probably the most versatile tool in your kitchen for evenly slicing foods.

My eye then fell on my 5000-foot roll of plastic wrap. Yes, that would indeed come in handy. Kristina buys cling wrap, which while it is indeed clingy it was fairly annoying to work with.

Yes, things looked ready, and now I need only await the call to come in to initiate deployment.

SushiRob Residence
4:30 PM, Saturday, January 26th

I was slowly conquering the galaxy of my latest strategic war game on my computer and as such things are likely to happen, forgot the time. It wasn't until 4:30 that Kristina called. "You know, it's getting too late to make sushi, by the time we shop and make rice and everything it will be 10:00 before we take a bite."

My heart sank. My one chance for true happiness, wasted, and for what? Building a fleet of warships to take over neighboring virtual worlds. At last I understood what they meant by War being Hell. Desperate to remedy the situation, I formulated a new and improved plan.

"I guess you're right." Admitting defeat is always difficult. "But we can still go to different Asian markets and see what we can find together? You know, you with your magic kanji reading skills and me with my experience. Could make for a fun outing. Also a new store just opened where Grand Auto used to be! It will be FUN!" in the back of my mind I thought it would be EASY too. "Then we can make sushi tomorrow."

"Well, I guess we could do that." My heart quickened. "But isn't it getting too late? Won't they be closed?"

"Oh no! They'll be open till at least six."

I lied.

I had no clue how late they would be open. However I wasn't going to ruin my chance at salvation over a little thing like store hours. "We'll be over in a few minutes." I hung up before she could change her mind.

New International Market
5:00 PM, Saturday, January 26th

We arrived and surveyed the scene. It was a big store but it was only half full. For some reason they still ensured that you could only have one person in an aisle at a time. Must be some form of regulation they must adhere to in order to be an Asian market. Along one wall was some strange vegetation imported from God-knows-where. It didn't look entirely appealing. Next to it was the fish freezer, which REALLY didn't look appetizing. Scary looking fish with clouded eyes looked back at us.

"Definitely not Sushi grade," I said. Kristina nodded with agreement.

I heard a scream come from the freezer section. We rushed over to my wife who had discovered and apparently touched a container of some animal blood.

"What do you make with blood?" my wife shivered. I honestly didn't know for once, and more importantly I didn't want to know. Why would someone use Pork and Beef blood in a recipe?

"Oh Look! Green Tea ice cream!" My wife, having recovered from the shock, was looking in the next freezer. She loves green tea ice cream. "I'm going to get one."

"Get me one too. Charlie will like it."

It was getting a little crowded so I went off to search for sushi practical items. For instance, ingredients to make Miso soup. Technically not a sushi item, still a damn fine appetizer. It was easy enough to find the Miso paste in the refrigerator section. Of course then I had to make the big decision of whether to get light, medium or dark paste. This wasn't the first time I was perplexed by such a problem, and as before I took the easy route, medium.

Next I needed to find the ingredients for the broth, or Daishi. Bonito flakes and Kombu, a type of dried fish flakes and kelp (with natural MSG!) respectively. I knew this would be more of a challenge, so I summoned forth the Kanji abilities of Kristina. "Help me find Kombu & Bonito Flakes. Or anything that says Dashi" I began rummaging around the store. The kelp I figured would be easy, it would be in the seaweed section (Yes, for those who have never been in an Asian market there is a seaweed section, usually taking up many shelves with different varieties.)

A few minutes later Kristina asks me from another aisle. "What were you looking for?"

"Bonito Flakes. Kombu. Dashi"

I continued rummaging around and came across the Kombu. Score. Still, $6 for seaweed? Well, that's ok I guess. I put it in my little shopping basket.

"What were you looking for?"

I raised my eyebrow. "Bonito Flakes. Dashi". Onward I pressed on my quest, staring at little strange symbols on packages. Eventually I found the Bonito flakes. Ouch! $16 for a package.

"Were you looking for Dashi? Here's something labeled Hon-Dashi," my wife said helpfully from down the aisle.

It was a little round container. I took the little container. It was like $3 and had difficult instructions such as boil water and add 2 tablespoons of Hon-Dashi. I stared at my hard-gained bonito flakes and kombu. My face grew pale. I realized this must be *instant* Dashi.

"Instead of spending $25 on that stuff, why don't you just get that? It's not like you always make miso soup: that will work just fine," Kristina helpfully suggested. "I mean it's just the Miso soup."

I felt like I had been slapped in the face. Dare I use *instant* Dashi instead of the real thing? *INSTANT?!* "I can't do that! I may as well just buy the instant Miso soup packets if I was to do that!"

"Good idea. We should get these instead." My wife helpfully holds up a couple packages of microwave Miso soup mix.

"We can't do that! *What's the point of making home-made Miso soup if it's just a package mix?*" I tried to reason with them but they just didn't get it. I realized this was a one-man crusade, and not one that I was going to win. Reluctantly, I put my precious finds back on the shelf. After all, spending $25 to make miso soup for 4 wasn't exactly practical. But damn it, I had to maintain some pride! I kept the miso paste and placed the Hon-Dashi in my basket.

"This sauce says it's made with Conger Eel" my wife holds up a jar.

"Is Unagi made out of Conger Eel?" I asked Kristina.

"I don't know. Maybe. Unagi is freshwater eel."

"I know that!" I said exasperated, "But is Conger Eel freshwater or salt water?"

"Just get the Eel sauce Rob, it doesn't matter," chided Kristina. "I'm sure it will work just fine. Just fine"

We poked around the store for another half hour and Kristina stumbled upon a few more things. "Pocky Sticks!" the exclamation came. My wife found little square inch pudding like things that had cute little packages. I bought some pretzels wrapped in nori with a hint of wasabi. Still, we didn't find everything we were seeking. Not much of anything really. Certainly no hangiri, but I hadn't really expected it there since they had no other cooking implements. No sushi grade fish for certain.

"Lets go try the International Market near the mall." Ah yes, the infamous store where Kristina last did battle with the Dark Mistress. She was surprisingly agreeable to the prospect of facing her old nemesis. We paid our tab and off we went.

International World Market
5:45 PM, Saturday, January 26th

Darkness was starting to fall on the land as we made our way stealthily to the market. Market is kind of a misnomer. It was a big warehouse with all sorts of Ethnic foods and items. Where the first location had ample room, this 20000 square foot room was crammed with shelves head high and aisles 2 feet wide. Strange exotic plants, herbs, spices and vegetables in cans, bags and jars all lined up in chaotic order. It was amazing Kristina did as well as she did the first time. Still, anywhere that has a gallon jar of pure white MSG on an end cap isn't all that bad.

We started sauntering up and down the aisle, looking at strange packages, but realistically we had everything we needed. It was the freezers we were mainly interested in. That's where you get the good stuff. Or at least stuff you feel better about buying. Of course on the way to the freezer we passed the refrigerators.

The refrigerators that had 50 cubic feet of gari, Kristina's ever so precious pickled ginger. The gari that had heretofore eluded her and whose bottle in the intervening weeks had grown in strange and icky ways in her refrigerator. Guess she shouldn't have found it on a shelf alone by itself, when it should have been sitting in this huge refrigerator with hundreds of pounds of its friends.

"How could you miss this much Gari?" I asked her perplexed.

"I didn't look in the refrigerated area," she responded.

"Oh, of course," I replied with a pained look. Since hers had somehow become a host to a wandering troupe of bacteria, we took a jar. "You know the freezers and the fridge is where the good stuff is."

Well, if not good then strange and bizarre things. This trip was no exception; there were truly bizarre horrors, horrors of which I dare not speak for your sake, beloved reader. I won't even mention the strange parts of cattle we found in there, but personally I think we solved the cattle mutilation mystery. We found fish, but none of it was something we were willing to try raw. Hell, cooked was questionable! The "Fresh" fish area was even scarier than the frozen section. At least the frozen section didn't smell like fish. Helpful safety tip: if it smells like fish, don't buy it.

I went in search for that ever elusive hangiri: I was sure I'd find it here. Surely it must be tucked away with the strange wooden steamers and woks the size of a small child. To my dismay there was no such implement on the shelf. Perhaps the dark mistress got wind of our arrival and hid the hangiri. Perhaps Kristina wasn't as delusional as I had first thought. I dismissed the idea and headed toward checkout.

On our way out we had to stop at the fascinating selection of candies and snacks and ended up buying lots of useless stuff. I paid the tab. I didn't want Kristina to relive her anguish with the Dark Mistress. That's just the type of guy I am.

Two stores down and we were still fishless, and we were having sushi. This absolutely would not do. We had to forge ahead, and so I pulled out my secret location, the market that had served me well in the past. Sure, they looked funny at me last time I was there, cell phone in hand, running from freezer to freezer. But damn it, they had fish I could count on!

Asian Market
6:00 PM Saturday, January 26th

My ace in the hole, my private little stash of Asian goodness. Our last stop was more the size of a 7-11 but for once, you could walk two abreast in the aisle. Apparently they didn't sign the aisle size pact, which may explain why they only get a fraction of the merchandise. Hard to say, but what they have is good stuff.

"Sac Sac!" Kristina squealed. "I haven't had Sac Sac since I was in Korea! I use to drink these every day!"

I turned around to find her hauling up a 12 pack of little iron cans. Apparently it was some sort of orange juice but with the pulp left in.

"There's individual cans for sale, I think I'll try one," my wife says from the refrigerator section.

"Get me one!" Kristina was way too excited over a 6 oz beverage.

"Umm, we're here for Sushi stuff…" I was looking in the wonderful freezer section where the ever so neatly vacuum-sealed pouches of slabs of fish were stacked. You could tell this store was smart, and organized their sushi stuff in one area. They had a strip of little sushi pictures along the door of the refrigerator. How can one argue when there are pictures of sushi on the door?

I peered through the glass and beheld at last, fish. There were all sorts of fish. There was Tuna, and albacore Tuna, and packages of sweet shrimp. Big packages of imitation crab, which is nothing like crab but still very tasty. Large purple slabs of Octopus tentacles were practically waving at me, screaming, "Buy Me! Buy Me!" in their cephalopod voices. There were packages of Mackarel with their sleek silver bodies bundled in their vacuum pack blankets. Round containers of Masago and Tobiko, the perfect compliment to any sushi roll. Fleshy white and red Tilapia peeked from under a pile of Cuttlefish, which I'd always thought was squid up till now at the sushi bar. Whatever it was, it was good, and besides that I thought the tilapia was red snapper, so it all balances out in the end. The ever present Unagi was there, tempting us with its barbeque goodness. There was even pre-made Tamago (Egg Omelet) — not that I would want egg in a sushi roll.

"OK, here's the fish, what are we having?" I asked Kristina.

"Unagi! Definitely Unagi," she said sagely. "After all, we have the Unagi Tare."

She was mocking me, I could just tell.

"Ok, and how about tuna, for spicy tuna rolls, and albacore for nigiri?" I said to her.

"Don't forget the crab, I'm all out of crab. But we have the Masago still. Do they have any yellowtail?"

Alas, yellowtail, hamachi, an ever so delicate treat upon whom we feast so greedily when we are at the sushi bar. "Unfortunately no, unless it's this here." I handed her a pound of frozen fish for $30 that was just wrapped in a clear plastic bag with some foreign characters on it. "Last time I was here I think the guy said this was yellowtail, or maybe he just meant it was yellow, I don't know. Can you read it?"

She looked at the fish carefully. "No, it doesn't make any sense to me, and it's pretty expensive and not vacuum packed."

I had to agree with her, it would be one thing to know for sure, but being an expensive random fish – well, that wouldn't work at all. So with our basket filled with tuna, albacore tuna, shrimp, crab, and mackerel, and tofu, we were well stocked for our adventure.

I went in search for my hangiri, and at long last I found one. "Look!" I called Kristina over. We looked at the object of my desire, a perfectly beautiful hangiri, 20 inches wide and with the proper paddle. With this we could easily turn out the rice.

"$80 for a bowl?" Kristina looked scornfully at it.

"But it would be perfect!" I stared wistfully at the bowl. I could have bought it, but then I realized I'd have nowhere to put it. My cupboards have a hard enough time with a 16" platter let alone this monster. I knew this hangiri was not destined for me. Still, it was with great sorrow I put it back on the shelf. I was considering the sleek little electronic perfect rice cooker next to it when Kristina pointed out a neat little sushi press box.

"We probably should get going before we start buying stuff we don't need." I said.

"Start?" my wife asked contemptuously.

"We need to make one more stop, we need avocado and cucumber."

We were on our way home, Kristina and my wife drinking their SacSac and I drinking some other ice mocha sort of beverage in a steel can. The whole steel can thing was disconcerting to me. But that's what all the drinks there seemed to be in, so apparently steel is more widely used outside our country. Such is the wisdom gained from the Asian market.

So we ended up at the Raley's, a local grocery store. Since vegetables aren't my thing I let Kristina pick them. English Cucumber —apparently they have less seeds — and a few nice avocados. We paid our bill and dropped our groceries off with Kristina.

We said good night.

I went home that night, read my book on Sushi, meditating on the task ahead. Tomorrow, at last, we would truly do battle, virtual warships be damned!

Kristina's House
Noon. Sunday, January 27th. Zero Hour

I walked into Kristina's house, big box of gear in my hand, setting it clumsily on her dining room table. She looked at me kinda funny. But I've come to expect that from Kristina, especially in culinary matters.

"How much rice should we make?" Kristina said looking at my rice cooker. "At least a double batch," was my reply as I plugged the machine in. She started the long arduous process of sifting through the rice, rinsing off the starch and draining it. I pulled my grease splatter guard out of the box of equipment and walked over to the sink. "Let's try this". I took the bowl of rice: the guard covered it with room to spare. I then started pouring the water out and it worked like a champ, the water left, and the rice stayed. It even survived being turned upside down. After a few dozen rinses, the rice was ready to be steamed. We placed the precious morsels in the cooker, added water, turned it on and walked away.

The fish was still in the freezer, and frozen fish doesn't good sushi make. So I took a portion of each fish, put them each in a zip lock bag, and the bags in the sink with cool running water to thaw them.

We turned our attention to the vinegar and sugar mixture. "You sure you have the right recipe this time?" I asked.

"Yes!" she said, menacingly brandishing the sauté pan she was about to hand me.

I took the pan, and started adding the ingredients for a double batch of sushi rice. Rice Vinegar, Sugar, Salt. Very simple really, almost impossible to get wrong one would think. I wasn't going to mention that though. After all, the sauté pan was hot now and had warm sugar and vinegar. A few minutes later and the mixture was ready and cooling on the stove.

While waiting for the rice to finish I prepared the spicy sauce for the spicy tuna while Kristina prepared the wasabi. The cucumber was next to be prepared. After peeling the cucumber, I cut it up into cubes about 1 ½ inches long and an inch thick. Pulling out my egg slicer, I carefully laid the cucumber in place, and with a little effort cut through the cucumber. Laughing maniacally I turned them over, and cut them into perfect little square strips.

"You are such a geek." Kristina looked bemused.

"Alton is a god," was my only reply. I took the next piece: slice and slice and another perfect pile of cucumber was ready. I was feeling rather proud of myself by this point when there was a horrible snap as I closed the slicer on the next piece. In shock, I looked to see my egg slicer in two pieces, its hinges looking very out of place.

"Guess Alton uses a metal slicer, huh?" Oh yes, she laughs now. Some gratitude.

"Yeah well, it worked perfectly!"

"Until it broke."

"That's not the point!" I looked at my poor egg slicer and sighed deeply. "Let's get the rice done." Since we had not bought the Hangiri I brought out my old wide salad bowl and rinsed it to get it damp. Kristina turned the rice out into the bowl and I gave her my cheap spaghetti measuring paddle.

"You've got to be kidding."

"Just try it." I said as I spread a little of the vinegar mixture on the rice. She did, but we quickly discovered it was not a practical instrument. Oh well, another idea shot to hell. She continued to turn the rice with a wooden spoon, while I continued adding the mixture and fanning the rice. Not too long later, our rice was glistening in the warm glow of the florescent lights. We both tried a bit.

It was good. Damn good.

"Much better this time, you can actually still see the individual grains!" I said more enthusiastically than Kristina cared for.

With the rice ready, it was fish cutting time. I went over to the box to get my Sushi book. My sushi book, which should have been right there. "Does anyone have my Sushi book?" I looked at my wife and to Kristina and neither of them were any help.

Then I remembered.

I was reading it before bed.

My sushi book with sage advice and pretty pictures of how to cut fish was sitting next to my bed.

In my eagerness to make sushi I had forgotten to bring

it! Disheartened I went over to the fish, I would just have to wing it, again.

"Here's Chef Tony's knives," Kristina offered helpfully. I looked at the shiny set of miracle blades; all things considered they weren't bad. I took a boning knife and began to cut up slabs of the fish. Making those neat little square pieces for nigiri is hardly easy. I cut up several slices of the tuna and albacore and kept the pretty ones (well prettier ones) for nigiri and the rest were for rolls. I sliced up nice even pieces of the mackerel. Being a thin fish filet, there wasn't much of a choice for cutting it wrong. I chopped up the leftover tuna and mixed it with the spicy sauce.

We were at last prepared to roll the sushi. I wrapped the rolling mats in my plastic wrap, which promptly refused to stick. After making several inane attempts, I gave up and proceeded to use her cling wrap. "Good thing you brought all 5,000 feet of that stuff," she smirked.

"The rice came out perfect!" She had to grudgingly admit that. Carefully taking a handful of the rice, she placed it on the nori, gently spreading it. Deftly the nori was flipped over and she began lining up the ingredients for a California roll, the crab, cucumber and avocado fitting neatly into their designated place. Rolling it up was a bit more difficult but more than plausible. First try up and it was more or less a California roll. Since I was doing the knife work, I dampened the blade and cut it up into somewhat even pieces and laid the first of our creations on a plate.

"Not bad. Your turn," she said handing me a piece of fresh nori.

The rice went on first. It was fairly difficult to spread the rice without crushing the little grains: eventually I had a piece of nori with too much rice. I flipped it over, and began spreading the spicy tuna mixture. It became evident that I had put too much in as I began rolling. Sticky tuna oozed out of each end of the roll, and cutting the sushi was a nightmare, the pressure of the blade making the filling ooze out everywhere. Finishing, I tried to put them on the plate in a pleasing way, but in the end, it was just round things oozing with tuna.

"Maybe you should try making a different roll." She almost had sympathy for me, I think.

So I started another roll. Using less rice this time. I began filling the roll with albacore and cucumber, and before rolling, topped it with masago. Rolling it up had the nice effect of the masago clinging evenly to the roll. It was a much more dignified attempt.

"That's better." I turned the rolling mat over to Kristina while I began making nigiri style sushi. Who knew that making a ball of rice could be so tough? Either it was too round, or too long, or it fell apart. After several fumbled attempts at shaping, I began to get something close and put the fish I had prepared for them carefully on the mat, even so far as to trying to put the nice little ring of nori around it to hold it in place. It went around, but it hardly held it in place.

While Kristina finished up making rolls, I boiled the water for the miso soup. I still had a twinge of regret for the homemade Dashi that could have been, but this would do for now. I heated the mixture up, added the miso paste and stirred till it was a good color then added sliced tofu.

"We're forgetting something"

"Unagi! We need to make the unagi." Of course. Unagi. I took the unagi out of the freezer, and began slicing it on a bias. My pieces look pale and anemic compared to what they do at the sushi bar. The eel is dark on the outside, but is only about a ¼ inch thick. How they end up with strips of unagi an inch by three inches all nicely darkened is beyond me. I cut the pieces to be at least the right size, and microwaved it as directed adding the unagi tare we finally had acquired.

"Mr. Unagi, Mr. Unagi, I love you Mr. Unagi," sang Kristina.

I looked at her strangely.

"What?"

The microwave beeped and I decided it was better just to get the sushi on the plate and served before anything stranger happened.

Everyone was called to the table, and we proudly presented two plates full of yummy sushi treats. We managed to make about a dozen nigiri and 8 or 9 rolls. Even the kitchen sink roll which was huge and contained everything we had left over. It looked more or less like sushi.

Well, maybe sushi made by the criminally insane. Pieces of fish bled here and there, and it had to be handled very carefully while serving otherwise it would fall apart, but damn it, we made sushi. For the most part the sushi tasted really good too. I found I actually liked the mackerel quite a bit more without the vinegar they add to it in the sushi bar. Of course it took us about 3 hours to make what we normally get served in 5 minutes. Oh, and the miso soup was too strong for everyone but me and Kristina, and she didn't actually finish her bowl.

Within too short a period of time the sushi was gone. The general consensus: it was good. Sure, the sliced fish was either too thin or worse, too thick. Yes the spicy tuna bled out all over the place, but it still tasted like spicy tuna. The California rolls probably turned out the best. The plates were empty and everyone was hungry. Our efforts had made a nice appetizer.

So we did the only logical thing. We got in the car and drove to our favorite sushi bar and paid less for four people than we spent on ingredients, and we ate a lot more than a few rolls. It was fun making sushi. The experience was well worth the time and effort, if only to appreciate the artistry and skill that goes into the profession.

We had returned to our sushi bar home, and we knew full well the value we received from their service. Sure, I continue to dabble in the dark sushi arts, but for the real thing, I leave it to the professionals.

***

(Footnotes)
[1] Hyun, Victoria. *The Tiny Book of Sushi.* Running Press, 2001.

[2] Pfaff-Harris, Kristina. "My Sushi Adventure" *Boxer Shorts.* Inkblot Books, 2003

[3] Yoshii, Ryuichi. *Sushi.* Periplus Editions (HK), Limited, 1999.

[4] Kazuko, Emi and Fukuoaka, Yasuko. *Japanese Food and Cooking.* Anness Publishing, Ltd 2001

[5] Barber, Kimiko and Takemura, Hiroki. *Sushi: Taste and Technique.* DK Publishing, Inc., 2002.

Sam

K.A. Thompson

Whenever I think of Sam, I picture him standing in front of the big bay window, staring out at the snow, watching as it piled in huge clumps on his front lawn, the tree limbs heavy and white. He bitched and moaned about the cold and the sidewalks to be shoveled, yet when the first hints of winter brushed by he always waited eagerly for that first flake to strike the ground, for the air to fill with sights and smells of winter. He reveled in the watercolor gray of the skies, little boys wading through knee deep snow with their dogs and sleds in tow, snowmen dotting the streets and soft angels drawn impulsively just outside his front door.

There were the other things in life that Sam hated as intently as snowflakes dancing through the skies onto his side-walks; the sound of his daughter's awkward fingers tinkering over the piano keys, relentlessly, pursuing the perfection of *Twinkle Twinkle Little Star*; banana breath and sticky fingers reaching over the edge of the mattress to greet him just min-utes before the alarm was set to go off; his two year old son gleefully peeing up the wall behind the toilet, squealing with delight at the discovery of this simple ability. There were all the odd, quirky things that irritated and aggravated him that he kept tucked away in some private place deep inside.

Sam also hated his job, contending with all those sparks of curiosity flying from the eyes and minds of ultra absorbent five year old boys and girls, living through story hour and the wonders of science and, most important, Show and Tell. In ten years of silently suffering the kindergarten moppets, Sam had been Shown and Told it all. He hated all the laughter, recess patrol, listening as some mirthful prodigy reeled off his first ever joke.

"Mr. Moore, why does a lion eat raw meat? He can't cook!"

"Mr. Moore, why did the scientist turn off his doorbell? He wanted to win the No-bell prize!"

"Mr. Moore, what'dya get when you pour boiling water down a rabbit hole? Hot cross bunnies!"

Oh, Sam hated it all.

The children, the laughter, all the little firsts. They were too much like snowflakes. There once in a brilliant flash of beauty, and then gone.

"I know *Green Eggs and Ham* backwards and forwards," Sam sighed, a twist of tired laughter tinging his voice. "It's the first thing I read them during the year, and for the next week I'm Sam-I-Am."

"You tell them your first name?"

Sam popped open a Diet Coke, leaning back in one of the cheap metal chairs provided in the teacher's lounge. He nodded as he took a sip, looking at his new student teacher; this was the first time Sam could remember being assigned a male student. "No reason not to. It makes me human. They call me Mr. Moore, but they know that deep down I'm just plain Sam."

"So I should introduce myself as Tim?"

"Up to you. I usually introduce myself as Mr. Moore, and then tell them my first name is Sam."

"And then you pull out *Green Eggs and Ham*?"

"Exactly."

"'I do not like them Sam-I-Am.'"

"Be honest. Have you ever had green eggs and ham?"

"Not in this lifetime."

"Don't knock it till you've tried it. Theodore Geisel never wrote crap, you know."

Tim Anderson frowned. "Who?"

"Dr. Seuss." Sam took another swallow of the Coke. What human didn't know about Dr. Seuss? "This is kindergarten, Timothy. Seuss is the icon of great literature here. These kids know every book, every line, word for word. If you want to survive, so will you." He reached into his briefcase and pulled out a well-worn copy of *Horton Hears a Who*.

"Memorize this by tomorrow, Mr. Anderson. And then read it like you mean it."

The simple fact that he could reel off, line by line, with great dramatic inflection, nearly every single word of every single book written by Dr. Seuss, bothered Sam. His intention had been to fill their little minds with great facts of literature and mathematics and science. His reality was that *The Cat In The Hat* was high literature in the rugrat set, math was limited to memorization of numbers through ten, their phone numbers and addresses, and science was the wonder of how to make everlasting soap bubbles andvolcanoes out of baking soda, vinegar, and old newspapers.

He could explode the entrails out of any paper-mache volcano better than any other teacher in school.

His soap bubbles expanded and floated endlessly, disappearing out of sight before they popped.

He taught his students their colors and their numbers through song, he taught them how to write their first and last names, he taught them simple addition by using pennies they could keep when they solved the problem correctly.

The kids got rich.

Sam got tired. Very tired.

Sam, after ten years of cajoling young minds to open up, ten years of nursing hurt feelings and playing at recess and singing goofy songs at the top of his lungs, was ready to quit.

He hated it.

Really.

"Parent-teacher conferences," he told Tim, "are one of the necessary evils. Most of the mothers and fathers are alright—" he shrugged and sighed, "—there are the few demon seeds.

"'What?'" he went on, voice pitched high. "'Not little Johnny. Little Johnny is a genius, a perfect angel.'"

He crumpled his Coke can with one hand and sent it sailing across the room, landing neatly into the metal wastebasket. "I hate to tell you, lady," he said, mostly to himself, "but your little Johnny is saddled with so much of your cast-off emotional baggage that he's turning into a five year old walking S.O.B. headed straight for juvenile hall, if he's lucky."

Tim sat quietly, not sure what to say.

Sam looked up at him, smiling sadly. "You know what really bites? Deep down Little Johnny is probably a good kid. A redeemable kid. But Mom the alcoholic and Dad the workaholic don't even recognize the pot of gold living under their inebriated noses."

Sam didn't always hate things. Sam at twenty two was an idealist, full of life and ideas and was sure he could turn the world upside down.

Sam at thirty two realized the world had already been turned upside down, and he didn't like the way things scattered.

"When I first started this," he confided to his wife, late at night in the comfort of a completely dark room, "I wanted to give them the universe. Every little bit of wonder and every piece of magic."

"You still can."

Sam stood by the bedroom window, staring out at the night sky and the stars that winked back at him. "No," he sighed, "not really. Most of them don't want to know and those who do … they're too young to understand."

"Those little minds understand more than you know."

Sam nodded. "Brains like little sponges," he agreed. "But that's not it, not really. They need something else. Something I'm not sure is in me anymore."

Sam had known his fair share of gifted five year olds. Kids who grasped the concept of addition beyond the simple chanting of "One plus one equals two. Two plus two equals four." The pleasant surprises that came to him wrapped in brand new sneakers and jeans a size too big rarely stayed throughout the school year. They showed up in his classroom, their little heads already filled with the standard kindergarten education, and after a few weeks of trying to reach through their clouds of boredom, Sam reluctantly sent them on their way to first grade.

Deep down he knew it was for the best; the children weren't there to appease his ego as an educator. He understood that they were there to learn, and that he had a responsibility to teach the curriculum for the rest of his students.

But those rare prodigies, those were the students who most fascinated Sam. They gave him a glimpse into the futures of the rest of his kids. He had the chance to see how a young mind could progress and thrive.

Sam rarely saw his former students, other than passing them in the hallways or the cafeteria. He never knew if he'd given them the foundation he wanted and they needed, not unless one of their later teachers came asking questions. Consulting Sam was rare.

Sam often stood on the playground during recess to watch the kids play. There were, he told Tim, other adults hired to do that, and he could spend his time better by preparing for the afternoon class, or the next day, but he thought he might know them better as individuals by the way they played.

And sometimes, when the weather was good and the attendants brought out the big red rubber balls, Sam played a low key game of dodge ball with them.

"It doesn't have to last long. Just be their target for ten minutes, and they'll be happy the rest of the day."

But Sam hated the squeals of laughter.

Seriously.

Almost six months before Sam began to hate it all, on a bright winter day, just long enough after the holidays that the kids had begun to settle down, Sam welcomed a new student into his already over crowded classroom.

Shane Hamilton eased into this new environment as if he had been there all along. He was friendly and instantly well liked – a gregarious six year old, Sam mused – and brighter than any child Sam had seen in years.

He waffled over what to do with Shane; it was too late in the year to shove him out the door on his way to first grade. There was nothing he was teaching that Shane didn't already know, yet the boy never stared at him with glazed over, disinterested eyes. Shane didn't fidget with boredom or talk out of turn; he completed worksheets without complaint, quietly read books while others were still working, and never whined about how little there really was for him to do.

"He could be learning much more with a private tutor," Sam explained to Shane's mother. "Keeping him here is holding him back."

Sam Moore's kindergarten class, Mrs. Hamilton insisted, was exactly where Shane wanted to be.

Sam left it alone. If Shane's mother wanted him to flounder in kindergarten, far be it for him to interfere. He welcomed Shane's presence in his world from 12:00 to 3:30 every day. He simply didn't want to let the boy down.

At the end of Shane's first month in his class, Sam discovered that he was as musically gifted as he was academically. He'd sat quietly through countless other days of Show and Tell, but on a day when a hint of spring warmth was seeping through the last days of winter cold, Shane brought his guitar to school. He was the last to stand up in front of the class, and when he did he explained, in simple terms, all the parts of the guitar his father had given him when he was four years old.

On request, Shane began to play. He plucked out smooth

versions of kid friendly songs his classmates knew, and for the next half hour the room full of five and six year old kids happily sang along.

"Mr. Moore," someone asked, "can you play?"

Sam shook his head. "I never learned to play anything. I always wanted to, though."

Shane held his guitar out to his teacher, and offered to teach him two or three chords. Egged on by the pint sized crowd, Sam couldn't refuse. He learned three basic chords and clumsily plucked them out while the kids sang *Row, Row, Row Your Boat.*

"When you grow up," he told Shane, "you should be a teacher. You're pretty good at it."

It was the first time Sam saw a smile slide from Shane's face.

Worried that simple subtraction would bore Shane out of his mind, Sam borrowed workbooks from first and second grade teachers, and quietly set about teaching Shane math more complicated than his classmates were being introduced to. While they filled out their worksheets – not as quietly as Sam would have liked – Shane sat in a small chair beside Sam's desk, easily grasping the addition and subtraction of double digits, and he took to basic multiplication with ease.

"If we time it right," Sam said to Mrs. Hamilton after class, "he'll be prepared to go directly into second grade next year."

"We'll see," was her non-committed reply. "Shane may wish to stay with his friends."

Sam wanted to argue – if Shane was ever going to skip a grade, now was the time to do it – but she smiled brightly, took her son by the hand, and walked away.

~

Some evenings, Sam watched his baby son squirming in the play pen, and wondered what Shane's parents had done to foster their son's intelligence. He listened to his daughter giggle as she played with her dolls, and wondered if, whatever it was, it was too late to begin with her.

"Maybe," his wife said, "they did nothing special, and Shane is just an exceptionally bright kid."

Sam allowed for that possibility, and wondered if he'd had students in the past who blossomed as well once they moved beyond the confines of kindergarten.

It wasn't ego, he told himself, but he deeply, truly, hoped there were many.

Shane missed his first day of school in early spring, when dripping noses and hacking coughs were so much a part of the background static of his classroom that Sam only noticed if one of the kids sounded as if they might cough up a significant body part. He dismissed his prize pupil's absence as another spring cold, and went about teaching the rug rat form of botany.

"Today," he informed the class, "we're going to plant sunflower seeds, and after they start to grow you can take them home and plant them in your yard."

The excitement that vibrated off his students grew when he told them, in a voice near a whisper, "They can grow over six feet tall!"

The parents would be less than thrilled.

They would get over it.

When Shane missed an entire week of school, Sam worried and asked the receptionist in the front office to call his home and see how he was doing.

She reported to him later in the day that Shane was better, and would be back in class in a day or two. Sam thought it was a long time to keep a kid home for a cold, but he respected his parents for not exposing the rest of the class to it; he wished more parents were as considerate.

Shane, pale and with dark circles under his eyes, was back in school two days later; he brought his guitar for Show and Tell again, mostly because he had learned two new chords and wanted to teach them to Sam.

"Someday," he said to Shane, "I'm going to get a guitar of my own and practice, so that I can show *you* a new chord."

Shane grinned and then snorted, "You'll never be that good."

Two weeks later Shane was again absent from class. Instead of asking the receptionist to call about him, Sam picked up the phone himself, waited through an abysmally long answering machine message, and left a quick one of his own.

Worried about Shane. Let me know if he needs anything. Call me at home, 555-4813.

He didn't expect anyone to call.

Perhaps Shane was just a sickly kind of kid.

Twenty minutes after Shane's father called, Sam was standing in the corridor outside a hospital room, listening as Shane's father spoke in hushed tones. He glanced frequently into the room where Shane was curled up on his side, eyes closed, tubes attached to his arms with wide stretches of white tape.

"He wanted to go to school," Mr. Hamilton explained. "After we got his prognosis we thought we'd keep him at home, but it was driving him crazy that other kids were going when he couldn't. We were afraid the loneliness would kill him even quicker."

"How long?" Sam managed to ask, swallowing down the huge lump that threatened to choke him.

"Tomorrow. Maybe the next day. But he wants to see you. We didn't want to bother you, but … "

Sam couldn't bear to see the tears that suddenly flooded Mr. Hamilton's eyes, so he looked back at Shane, whose own eyes were now open and fixed on him.

"It's all about perfect practice," Shane whispered when Sam sat next to him. "Maybe you really will be good enough someday."

Tim Anderson read through Sam's curriculum guide, taking notes as he went along. When he reached the end he flipped back through the pages and commented, "You don't teach music at all?"

"They have enough to learn without adding music to the load, Tim. They'll get that next year, with the music teacher."

Tim thought that odd, but didn't feel he should press any further, especially when Sam suddenly got up and left the teachers' lounge, door banging behind him.

"We have enough to live on for a year or so," Sam told his wife, after the kids were in bed and the house was quiet. "I can't do it anymore. I have to quit."

Sam's wife had heard him voice a quiet desire to do something else before, but this was the first time she heard fear when he said it.

"Be sure," was all she could say to him.

"Unless I have a good reason not to, I'll hand in my resignation at the end of the semester."

~

Normally, when seeing his student teachers bombarded by a dozen big red rubber balls, Sam would have laughed. At the very least he would have grinned.

He couldn't make himself care very much that Tim Anderson was on the wrong end of the dodge ball line. If Tim wound up with a split lip from a well placed throw, he would react, of course, but he wasn't sure he would really care.

He stood by the classroom door, leaning against the brick wall with his arms crossed in front of himself, and watched the game, trying to ignore the ear-splitting laughter.

Tim Anderson could handle them.

In fact, he decided, Tim would be a good replacement for him. Still young and full of fresh ideas, he would do just fine.

Sam watched the game with a surge of renewed interest, mentally running through a list of things he needed to be sure to tell his successor. He watched so intently that he didn't see the woman who walked up to him, nor the small child whose fingers she gripped with one hand, nor the package she held tightly in the other.

Sam only realized she was there when the small boy sniffed hard. Surprised, Sam pushed off the wall.

"That kind of concentration and devotion is why Shane liked you so much," she said, releasing the boy's hand so she could extend hers to Sam.

"Well, hello," was all he could muster as he shook her hand. The boy was looking up at him expectantly, so Sam offered his hand to him and asked, "And what is your name?"

"Rider," he replied firmly. "I'm four and a half."

Mrs. Hamilton laughed and said, "Rider is just his

nickname. But he is four and a half, and looking forward to being in your class next year."

Sam didn't think it was the right time to mention that he didn't intend to be there next year.

"You knew my big brother," Rider stated, impressed by that little bit of trivia.

"Yes, I did. And I liked him very much."

Mrs. Hamilton pulled away the paper from the package she'd been holding tightly. "One of the last things Shane asked us," she said as she ripped away the last shred of paper, "was that we make sure you got this. He wanted you to have it."

Without thinking, Sam reached for it. "But his father gave this to him."

"We have dozens of videotapes of Shane playing it. This is what he wanted, Mr. Moore."

"Yeah," Rider added, "so you hafta have it!"

Sam wrapped his hand around the neck of the guitar, feeling the strings bite into his palm.

There were dozens of things he wanted to say to he, but all he could do was whisper, "Thank you."

"I know five chords," Sam told his students, who were sitting on the floor in front of them. "I learned them just last year—someone your age taught them to me."

He fumbled with the guitar, strumming awkwardly at first, until he felt comfortable with his fingers on the strings.

"I'll play, but you have to sing. *Row Your Boat*, okay?"

Tim was sure the racket could be heard down the hall and into the office, and he couldn't believe that something so unbelievably bad could sound so good.

Sam sang as well as he played the guitar.

He played for only fifteen minutes, until his fingers hurt and the kids were laughing too hard to sing along.

He refused to smile.

Because he hated it.

Really.

Vignettes From The Life of a Young English Gentleman

Alistair Coleman

1974: PiSS

I was eight years old and shared a bedroom with my brother. My bed was a huge wooden thing, the headboard fashioned out of an entire tree resting on a frame made out of spare parts from the Titanic. It was pretty huge for a small kid. And it spelt my doom.

I blame television entirely for my downfall. I saw a TV programme about the work of engravers and the intricate work they do. Carving metal, wood, anything. I can do that, I thought. So I did.

I found the first relatively sharp instrument I could lay my hands on - a metal cogwheel from my Meccano set, and got to work. With a deft and unshaking hand, and knowing not exactly what I was letting myself in for, I neatly engraved the word "PiSS" onto the headboard of my bed in eighteen inch high letters. I sat back and admired my handiwork. Lovely job.

It was about ten seconds after this particular point-of-no-return that I realised something. I had written the foulest word known to my eight-year-old mind on the wooden headboard of my bed. And it wouldn't come off.

I rubbed it. I soaked it in a mixture of water, soap and spit. It came off. Ten minutes later, it had dried, and there was the word PiSS, back again, taunting me. I was mortified, and mum was coming upstairs. I draped the curtains over my headboard and announced "From now on, I want to sleep like this".

"You'll get a draught down your neck" was her wisdom-filled reply.

"I don't mind, I get hot in bed"

She was right. For three dread-filled months, I slept with a stiff neck, with the curtains covering the word PiSS on my headboard. For three months I did anything to cover it up. I diligently made my bed each morning so mum wouldn't have to. I slapped stickers over the PiSS, but was told to peel them off as they would "spoil the wood". I cut out pictures of airplanes, pets and family photos and stuck them over the dreaded PiSS, only for them to fall off in the night, exposing my Nemesis for the world to see.

Every night was a struggle against discovery. PiSS was taking over my world. I was tired, stiff and my school work was suffering. I was pilloried by Mrs Jones at school for absent-mindedly doodling "PiSS" on the cover of a school book. It was getting too much. I was turning into a pre-teen crack-up.

PiSS.

PiSS. PiSS. PiSS.

PiSS. PiSS. PiSS. PiSS. PiSS.

Then came the glorious day. I came home from school

one afternoon, and ran upstairs to make sure that I hadn't been discovered. Instead of the two beds side by side - my brother's World War II relic and the PiSS bed - was my saviour, a lovely brand spanking new bunkbed in gloriously white-painted wood. I danced with joy.

It gleamed. It sparkled. And best of all, the PiSS bed was already on its way to the dump. Gleefully, as older brother, I bagsied the top bunk and revelled in my new found freedom. And I got a good night's sleep for the first time in months.

It was not long after that I noticed that my brother was becoming a little particular about covering up the end of his lower bunk. He hung spare clothes, pyjamas, dressing gown over it in a frankly suspicious manner. I took a peek. "BoLLockS".

BoLLockS. BoLLockS. BoLLockS.

1981: Firestarter

In America it's July the fourth. In England, we celebrate November the fifth, where the people of Britain commemorate some Guy from York who had horrible things done to him in return for his part in trying to blow up the King and his Parliament. A fair exchange all round, I suppose, giving us the chance to set fire to stuff, totally legally, for several weeks a year.

The Twyford Guy Fawke's carnival is a torchlight procession of decorated floats from the station to the recreation ground, where there's a fairground, the mother of all bonfires and what is reputed to be the largest display of fireworks in the South of England. The bonfire is what can only be described as a towering inferno, built over several days from railway sleepers, wooden palettes and all the trees within a five mile radius. You can feel the heat of this conflagration over one hundred yards away and it burns all night to the sound of local teens puking up over the side of fairground rides.

The following day was always very different. Where there were several thousand people the night before, the Sunday saw several dozen kids meandering round the rec looking for dropped change while the fairground folk slowly took their machines to pieces. The largest crowd was always around the embers of the fire; which the night before had been the size of a house, now reduced to a smouldering pile of ash and still pumping out a tremendous heat.

There were dares. On pain of being called a poof, you had to walk across the flames, hoping beyond hope that your flares wouldn't catch fire. On reaching the other side, you were formally inducted into the hard lads' club, while the trembling pooves on the other side still had to face their ordeal. Those who had made it were easily identified. They were the ones with smouldering trouser hems, smoke still rising from the soles of their melting shoes.

My brand new trainers were completely wrecked with the imprints of red hot nails, and it took me hours that afternoon to pare off all the blackened rubber with a knife to keep my parents from finding out.

But the real fun was to be had with the stuff you could throw onto the fire. There were heaps of torches which had made up the torchlight procession the night before, long candle things, as big as your arm, dipped in wax, that stoked up the fire nicely. We would also threw on great piles of rubbish, which the Great British public had thoughtfully left behind; and when the flames were really licking up round our ears, melting the nylon fluff on our parka coats, on would go the first of the fireworks.

Yes, dear reader, we really were that stupid. Gaz, one of the tougher kids in school had brought his own supply, which he ladled on liberally. Within seconds, it was like a war zone, as we dived for the cover of our bikes, hedges, other kids, anything. A rocket fizzed past my head and exploded halfway up the only tree for miles around. I still swear to this day that it actually parted my hair, leaving a frazzled streak across my scalp. An inch lower and I would have grown a third eye socket.

Fireworks, we all agreed, were stupid. Anyone could throw a firework on a bonfire for an easy laugh, and besides, we were rather attached to our facial features rather than risk having them blown off by a passing airbomb. We would, in the words of Barney the Dinosaur, use our imagination.

"Meet you back here in twenty minutes."

And what an arsenal we collected. Every single bin, shed and garage was raided for every last aerosol can, paint tin, and anything marked with those wonderful words of wisdom "Keep out of direct sunlight, do not burn or puncture." Wise words indeed, for there would be no puncturing. Plenty of burning, though.

An experimental can of underarm deodorant was cast onto the flames. Minutes later, there was a satisfying explosion, and the Great Smell of Brut wafted round the park. This was good. It was immediately followed by a shower of cans as everybody flung their booty onto the fire. The resulting cacophony was something to behold, and I'm pleased to report that there were only minor shrapnel injuries and very few burst eardrums.

Then Gaz came back. He had just one item for the fire.

It was a one gallon Castrol GTX oil can. You should understand that is wasn't one of those plastic things you get these days. We didn't do plastic back then, this was cold steel. About to get very hot steel. Straight onto the flames it went.

"Errr, Gaz mate?"

"Yuh."

"Was there anything in that oil can?"

"Yuh. A bit."

"How much?"

"About half."

"Oh shit."

We watched as the can developed an ominous bulge. We backed away slowly. The bulge got bigger, until the can was almost twice its original size.

"Lads," suggested a mature yet rather frightened voice, "I think it's time we legged it."

We legged it.

BA-LAAAAAAANG-NG-NG-NG-NG-NG-NG!!!!!!!!!!!!

The fireball was a good thirty feet across, and the heatwave knocked us off our feet. A rather pleasing mushroom cloud hung over the recreation ground. Several of the fairground people could be seen running around in wide-eyed panic, still clutching their oversized spanners. As a matter of fact, several of us kids were running around in wide-eyed panic too, as an explosion like that could only mean one thing: trouble. At the very least, a visit from the local police; at the very worst - parents.

No pack-drill, no questions asked. We scarpered.

When the coast had cleared, and the bomb disposal people had gone away, we went back to survey the wreckage. The fire still burned, and would do for at least another two days. Of the oil can there was nothing except a small crater in the ashes.

"Hey lads," said Gaz.

"What?"

"My dad's got another one in his garage..."

1997: Lucky Bag

I'd come a long way by 1997, and surprised myself by not only being alive, but also married with two wonderful children. My wife and I sat down at that point and decided that we had both reached the point in our lives where it would be unwise to breed further, and that I should go and have The Snip. I would present myself at the hospital and allow a perfect stranger to cut a hole in my ballbag and do strange things with my plums until they didn't work anymore. It seemed totally fair at the time, after all my wife had gone through the pain of child birth twice **and** endured a lifetime of marriage to me.

I put my name on the list, and waited, knowing full well that such was the state of the National Health Service, it would be upwards of two years before they got round to me. Six weeks later, I got a cunningly worded letter asking me to present myself at Battle Hospital in Reading, and don't forget your gonads. Arses.

Despite a morbid fear of blood (my own) and incredible pain, I bravely faced up to my ordeal. I am, after all, the son of a doctor and a nurse, so what possibly did I have to worry about? An entire lifetime of regular supplies of "The Lancet", the journal of the medical profession, for starters. Every month it would flop through our letter box, and every month I was introduced to a new skin condition, hideous disease or bizarre injury, all in glorious technicolor on the front cover. Even the postman complained. It put me right off following in my father's footsteps, and I have steadfastly pursued a career path that has taken me as far away from these knife-wielding goons as possible. And now I was going to let one of them loose on my bollocks.

Bright and early I awoke on that Monday morning. I showered and shaved. And shaved again, a process done with the utmost care so as not to cut any more holes in the scrote than was absolutely necessary. All this was done in a bathroom resembling Piccadilly Circus, with people from a five mile radius bursting in to use the lav, and to check out how I was getting on with the 'nads, which by now resembled the last turkey in the shop on Christmas Eve.

With the kids packed off to relatives, I took the short journey down the road to the Battle Hospital. It was deserted. Not a soul to be seen. Like the Marie Celeste, there were signs of habitation, a half drunk cup of coffee, a coat on a hook, but no-one was there. Eventually, after a search of the hospital's empty corridors, I collared a passing nurse and asked where everybody was. She told us.

It was Monday morning. Princess Diana had forgotten to do up her seatbelt the previous Saturday evening, metamorphosing from "Sex-Crazed Royal Tart flounces round Paris with Egyptian Boyfriend" in the early editions of Sunday's papers to "We'll Never Forget You, Princess of all our Hearts" by the following lunchtime. The entire hospital staff was allowed the day off to go and have a good cry over it.

"Even Dr Norris?" I asked.

"Especially Dr Norris", she replied, "Though I suspect he'll be remembering Diana with eighteen holes of golf."

I took to my heels and ran, my wife struggling to keep up. I got out of the hospital building, and kept running until I reached the car. My gonads were safe, although slightly chafed from an unwise application of aftershave. Dr Norris was hacking about with his seven iron on the golf course instead of hacking away at my crown jewels, a situation I could easily accept. I jumped into the car and sped away, never to return. Except to go back and pick up my wife.

After all the national grieving, the crying, the media hyperbole and the bloody awful Elton John song, I feel the time has come to finally pay my respects to Her Royal Highness Princess Diana of Wales, who died saving orphans, poor people, kittens and my plums. A fitting tribute to a great, great woman. It's what she would have wanted.

About The Authors

ALISTAIR COLEMAN (ScaryDuck) is a journalist and freelance writer based in the United Kingdom. He has an award-winning website at http://www.scaryduck.com, which he would happily swap for an island in the Caribbean, if there are any takers.

DONNA EYER (Daclaren) is an aspiring author who lives in south central Pennsylvania with her husband, stepsons, and a spoiled dog and cat. Her short story *A Picture Of Death* was published in *'Boxer Shorts*.

ANGIE MANSFIELD (writergirl) hold what her mother calls a "real" job to support her writing habit. She is currently going bald due largely to her third rewrite of his first novel.

TONY LEE HEALEY (StarQuestarian) is and English and Photography student at Varndean College, Brighton. He aims to write a book (of some sort…*) by the time he reaches 21. *That, or fulfill his plans for world domination…

MARK CARPENTER (VeganDude) is a programmer, auto-mechanic, published photographer, and budding writer, though not usually all at the same time. His website is located at www.bay13.com.

ELISA REDMOND lives in Dublin, Ireland, attempting to keep the Celtic tiger alive. She is working on her first book.

CHRISTINE TRAINELLO (Nayir)—this marks Christine's debut into the publishing world outside college and the Internet, She maintains a weblog at www.hact.net/blog where she tackles the difficult issues of life such as, "Where exactly do my cat's toys go?"

JOELLEN DRAZAN (Jade Dragon)

STARGAZER (stargazer) Stargazer is the Otter Princess, and enjoys all things soft and fuzzy . She enjoys her Furry Blankey as well as a Tummy Katy Kat who may or may not be controlling the minds of all humans. If you wish to learn more about Otters, her true joy in life please visit http://www.seaotters.org/. Learn a little, Love a little and give something back.

RICHARD GAZLEY (dreaming_in_rlyeh) is a some-time role playing game writer and tinkerer. He tries writing fiction and poetry as time and his sloth permit.

RUSS UNGER (Roughy) lives with his wife Nicole and their daughter in the suburbs of Chicago. Russ bides his time with work (www.bluechromedesign/com) and play (www.blinktag.org) and keeps a weblog at www.unrealisticexpectations.com. In his spare time, he happily responds to customers at Monolith Press (www.monolithpress.com).

CAROLYN COLLINS PETERSEN is a science writer specializing in books and documentary scripts in astronomy and space science topics. This is her first published work of fiction.

JONATHAN CROSS (starcross)

J. GRADY is a lazy nogoodnick. He currently has a million ideas for stories, but only one published. And that one wasn't even very good. He hardly posts on his website a-regular-joe.com because he'd rather waste his time watching television.

ROB MONTANARO (SushiRob) is a contract software developer living in Reno, Nevada. Hobbies include Role Playing Games, particularly Call of Cthulhu, video games, RTS games, Babylon 5, and ferrets! He also has every cooking gadget known to man. http://www.doombunny.com

K.A. THOMPSON (Thumper) is a freelance writer ant the author of three novels: *Charybdis, As Simple As That*, and *Finding Father Rabbit*. She is currently living in Ohio with her husband of 22 years (affectionately known as the Spouse Thingy) where she complains often (read: whines) of winter cold and summer humidity. They have an adult son and a psychotic cat named Max. Peek inside her head at http://kathompson.blogspot.com.

MICHAEL MATTESON, editor, is middle aged, overweight, and very, very tired. He is currently engaged in researching cures for serious diseases, attempting to bring about World Peace, writing the next Greatest American Novel, and sings daily at a roadhouse in Branson, Missouri. He also lies quite a bit, and spends most of his time looking for the "Boobies" tag at www.fark.com.